Homo Insanus

Adrian Daly

Homo Insanus: a species of unsound mind; insane, violent, absurd, raging, foolish, frantic, outrageous, monstrous

"Insanity is doing the same thing, over and over again, but expecting different results."

Narcotics Anonymous

****

"It is sometimes an appropriate response to reality to go insane."

Phillip K. Dick

****

"In individuals, insanity is rare; but in groups, parties, nations and epochs, it is the rule."

Frederich Nietzsche

****

Mama, I Just Killed a Man

Let's get a few things straight. Before you go on and possibly waste your time here instead of somewhere else. What follows includes profanity. Anger against almost everything, especially against other humans. You will not find any resemblance to the prose of George Elliot. No *Middlemarch*. In any case, modern day Nuneaton is a total shithole with a literacy rate only slightly higher than in the United States. You see, I have started already. I've alienated an entire nation, and an inbred town in Warwickshire in one sentence.

Trigger warning. This story involves violence. In fact, it is an act of aggression which lays at the heart of this narrative. Everything is a story really. And before the Gandhi, non-violent type among you get on your moral high horse, and wince and wish for a unicorn utopia where we all stand together with a coke bottle in hand in some make believe golden era, where we all sing along with the words about living in perfect harmony, I would remind you that evolution cares not one swot about your hopes and dreams and social media profile. Violence is to nature what elves are to Santa Claus.

The universe laughs at our meagre attempt to escape mediocrity and existential angst. So, if you want happiness and a light hearted, uplifting read, a tool to feel good about yourself, and how you can find purpose and meaning in the world, then stop reading now, and wag your flagella and swim away.

This story is about *Homo Insanus*. You are a member of this species. Despite the modern world being built upon the foundation of science and technology, we live our daily lives from moment to moment worrying about things which most often never happen. We are fearful of the vibration of air molecules which enter our ear canals. We are alarmed and stressed by every imaginable threat thrust upon us by a government and media who represent *Homo Insanus* on amphetamines. We have information anxiety. We always feel behind as we try to keep up with endless piles of binary excrement. Our brains have not evolved to cope with a perpetual stream of drivel which makes us feel inadequate as we chase our next status fix like a digital junkie. What follows may be hazardous to your health. There are no fire exits.

Regret? Yes, I have a few regrets. First and foremost, I regret that he had a weak heart. I regret that he drank too much. I regret that he was fat. I even regret that he had a tough life. But who doesn't? No one has a monopoly on suffering or an injury free existence, a life of escape and invade in the forest, savannah, jungle, or inner-city Glasgow. Have you ever seen the painting by Courbet entitled *The Origin of the World*? It depicts the headless torso of a woman with her legs spread wide showing her gaping vagina. That's how it all begins: in pain.

I don't regret shoving him. I don't regret pushing him twice with my friction lock baton using a Home Office approved technique to a legitimate and proportionate target area. I don't regret shouting at him - instructing him sounds much better - to move on so we could clear the road. As we had been ordered to do. Not asked. No mention of "If you like. It's up to you. I'll leave it with you while I pop into Burger King and take no responsibility, as I'm an Inspector, and I didn't get to where I am by being of any real use. In fact, I got to where I am by passing a few exams, ticking the right political boxes, and being generally an all-round fuckwit!"

I don't regret following an order as I have been trained, conditioned, brainwashed to do, especially when I have been pelted with projectiles ranging from bottles to half eaten Marks and Spencer sandwiches for the past several hours. And these were anti-capitalist activists, so they didn't eat Greggs or any cheap shit potatoes from the spud truck. Like most anti-human activists these days, they are mostly from well to do manicured, privileged backgrounds, grasping for a purpose, and rebelling against the bank of mom and stepdad while accepting any handouts ungratefully provided by family or state; all needy ideologically driven maniacs who catastrophize everything from a dying phone battery to the possibility that the price of superglue (the current means used by climate activists to stick parts of their anatomy to anything which will bond with skin) is going up in price due to Russia, China and any foreign entity who doesn't - or even worse, won't - follow the simple rules laid down by the neoCons/liberals/progressive lunatics. Don't they know the brain is a prediction machine? Have they not read Anil Seth? Don't they realise you can't convince people by means of reason that long term threats, no matter how real, are of any significance in the here and now? Do they know nothing about the work of Kahneman and Tchervsky? Don't they know that to always seek out the path of least resistance, the frictionless, easy way in and out is at the root of their own malaise. What do they learn in university apart from how to take shelter from an exclamation mark?

I must confess that I support acts of lunacy. Every brick launched at corruption, I applaud. Corporations pollute the world while supporting anything with the word "green" in it. Military companies and big pharma fund, and therefore own, politicians and the troughs in which they all feed. Financial markets rule the western roost, and all the industrial chickens have been shipped to where the sun rises. It's all comical. It's a Moliere play on steroids directed by a messianic, providential belief in the civilising mission of the western elite except now:

It's all 'bout the money
It's all 'bout the dum dum da da dum dum
And I think we got it all wrong anyway
Anyway
Cause it's all about the money

You've gotta love Meja. She knows how it all works. So, superglue yourself to whatever ideology is at the top of the list today, and block the roads and airfields, smash windows and burn and loot, but don't expect to achieve anything apart from the wrath of people who want to fly, drive and give some of their cash to Bezos, Gates and the crooks at the WEF.

And don't sit there in judgement thinking I sound like Jack Nicholson saying how you need men like me on the wall to protect your fragile liberty; how you want me on that wall so you can drink your flat white coffee in a delusional cocoon of safety worrying about shit which the media have happily provided to you like a nipple to wrap your addictive lips around. I do have regrets. I regret joining the Old Bill in the first place. Thin blue line my ass. I regret that my dead IRA father would be rolling in his grave if he could see me wearing a uniform. I regret that my wife Angela is sucking another man's cock. I regret thinking kids can bring long lasting happiness into your life. In fact, I regret losing the ability to truly believe in anything.

Almost anything. Because this is also a love story. Yes, you heard that right. It's not all about death. Love is the most dangerous drug anyone can get addicted to. Have you listened to Robert Palmer? Have you read Romeo and Juliet? Have you ever been truly in love? Vulnerable to how it takes you hostage? Have you ever come to think that the object of your sexual desire is like no other who has ever existed? The biggest overestimation in the whole history of the human imagination. Have you ever pictured yourself as John or Olivia singing: "You're the one that I want, ooh ooh ooh baby, the one that I want." No matter how much it makes you cringe to think of yourself dressed in skin-tight trousers doing a dopey dance. Have you ever been surprised to discover that the sizzle fizzles out and Andy Williams must have been smoking crack when he sang: "You're just too good to be true." Because here's the thing Andy, no-one is too good to be true! And all too often their eyes are taken off you.

Mea Apologia

I mean what does a fella have to do? Women bleed every month. I always tell my son Hadrian to treat women nicely (not in a patronising toxic white male kind of way) because if men bled out of their anuses for days on end every month for forty years like the river of bastard Babylon, they would disintegrate faster than a free neutron (10.3 minutes if you're interested). Would you bleed every day for your nation? For a little respect? Have you never listened to Erasure? Did you ever sing along to "Give a little respect toooo (hold that note - there you go, you remember the one) meeeee." Us even. But me especially.

I'll get to my spot of bother shortly. Patience, apparently, is a virtue. Life is a struggle. This much Hitler did get right. The first rule of warfare, according to Carl von Clausewitz, is that no nation should fight a two front war if it can be avoided. It can result in defeat. Armageddon. Movie sequels. Like Mad Max IV when Mel Gibson was taking a few months off from driving around insulting every Jewish person he could find. Drunk of course. Mel! How could you do that to us? To me? After Lethal Weapon? What were you thinking when you made the others? Is it always about the almighty dollar? That's what brought us to where we are now. Or one of the main driving variables. Greed.

Gordon Gecko type gluttony. Apple, Amazon, Amaco, Amazing American greed on steroids, cocaine and any other fuel enhancing drug.

Every war which has ever been fought has greed somewhere in the title. Can't you see that? It's an absolute truth. An axiom which gives the middle finger to Godel and Heisenberg. A new science could be built on that fact. One where there's real and not fake news dominating the narrative. A story where there is no humiliation. I will return time again to that word 'HUMILIATION' and everything that follows from it. It is in the headline of most wars in history. A new universe could be founded on that fundamental principle. A cosmos where Mel handcuffs himself only once in a lifetime to the nutter on the top of the building and asks him: "You really want to jump! Do you!"

What were you thinking? And where did the anti-Semitism come from? The Jews have had a tough time: Pharaohs, Romans, Christians, Nazis, America's anti-Jewish immigration laws, and Netanyahu. Give them a break. Australians only have to put up with each other. We know you are sorry. I am sorry too. We are all sorry. Why couldn't anyone say sorry before? It used to be the most difficult thing to say in all history. Then it became the de-facto word dropping out of everyone's mouth. *Mea culpa*. Self-flagellation on a global stage ranging from a misdemeanour to a seismic event.

Everyone is saying sorry for everything. For anything. One great latrine of disingenuous horseshit. It is demanded by sentinels in every office, every institute, every UN meeting from where we buy toilet paper and for how much, to the game of who should be the target of the "Best Sanctions of the Week?" How much death and destruction could have been avoided in the past if the word 'sorry' had been legitimately expressed? Not in a court. Not in the branch of the government we call the mainstream media to salvage a career. Not to save one's wrinkled skin. Not to save a dollar, rouble, pound, or yuan. This is not a Mad Max world. Yet.

I'll say it at the outset. Just so you know it. Just so we can get our epistemological house in order from the beginning. I am sorry. Really sorry. A real act of contrition. Like the Catholic ritual: "Father forgive me for **MY** sins." Not the sins of people in the compost heap of the past. Not for sins of some global corporation who has a body in law but cannot receive a well-deserved bullet to the head. Not for the perceived sins of a group who have urinated on the ideals of others. Here is the truth: I am sorry I was thrown to the wolves. I am sorry I was humiliated. I was happy to say sorry if I caused any unnecessary suffering. The key word being "unnecessary." My hand was ignored. Slap it away, okay. But ignored! Really! Being overlooked is a signal of potential doom. Being outcast into the wilderness is like being shoved into oblivion. You've got to be kidding me. Haven't you heard of the child within? Have you never read Freud? The child within is like Mount Tambora. And look what happened to that fucker when it exploded.

The Reason Your World Is Untidy

Here I am at the airport after giving "The Job" a quarter of a century of my life. Yes, giving. Okay, I got paid. Everyone claps and kneels and cheers for fuck all these days, but I have truly sacrificed. Maybe not like Dr King, Mandela, or Jesus of Nazareth, I grant you, but I have scars both physical and mental to prove my case.

I'm not looking for your sympathy. I'm just telling you facts. Truths. Yes, the truth and nothing but the truth so help me no matter whatever the higher power you deem it to be, whether a God or an equation. Martin Luther King was incorrect when he preached: "The truth will set you free." The truth about the truth is that no one can handle the truth. People struggle with the truth. Like Superman having kryptonite dumped upon him like an unwanted in-law: it weakens you.

It is an Orwellian world where an inversion of social reality becomes real. Joseph Goebbels, Germany's propaganda minister in the Second World War, stated how easy it can be to take the masses to war and their annihilation: create a story about an enemy, and say it loud, and enough times, and it will be believed.

People accept the narratives which their leaders provide them. Even though they usually have nothing to gain, and everything to lose. They simply walk toward the cannons and machine guns dosed up on government approved drugs. Tell them there is an entity out to destroy them, and anyone who says the story is fiction becomes an enemy. Propaganda shapes the narrative. However, it's also a Huxleyan world where everything is presented as entertainment for the people. Opium for the masses. There is room for more than one dystopia.

I remember going to a road traffic collision one evening. Not an accident. There's no such thing. It's always someone's fault. I was driving an old crap diesel Peugeot which the local criminals could hear coming from miles away. I was single crewed taking care of what we called routine jobs. Response vehicles always had two people on board in those days on what was then called the F1: Birmingham city centre and the surrounding areas. I was picking up the non-emergency incidents left over from earlier in the day. A call came over the radio asking for any available response vehicle to attend a serious collision on Icknield Street. Tumbleweed could be heard rolling across the electromagnetic plains. I shouted up after seconds of deafening silence: "9998 making from Vyse Street."

"Thank you 9998. Ambulance is on route. Early update please," replied Carol, one of the controllers based at Steelhouse Lane Police Station.

This was during a make-believe era when police stations were open. When there were real police officers dealing with real crime, and not just spending their entire shift trying to resolve mental health problems, missing persons, and of course, domestics. A once upon a time when controllers, cleaners, civilians, and constables all worked in the same place and knew each other's names. A period when what you did mattered more than how it was recorded on a system.

I arrived at a scene of carnage. A two-car collision. A black VW Golf had run a red light at speed and hit a silver Ford Fiesta on the driver's side. The female driver of the Fiesta was dead. The lad driving the Golf was alive and well, and already claiming how the "dozy bitch" had gone straight through his green light.

The deceased was a 32-year-old wife and mother of two young children. She was a nurse who worked at a local hospital and was on her way to work a night shift. It turned out, from speaking to her husband, that she had got into her car but remembered she had left her locker key in a bowl on the hall stand. She came back in for it and shouted: "See you in the morning." The husband was distraught that he never replied. He was watching a football match on Sky. That fucker Murdoch again.

Just think of these two people driving their cars. Every moment of their lives converged to this fraction of a second in space-time. Right down to the lady forgetting her locker key. Just a millisecond either way, and two kids would still have their mom. Crazy, right? And please, really, don't sit there and think it was fate or God or the devil or bad luck or karma or MI5 tampering with brakes or the traffic lights. They can't even lie with a straight face about weapons of mass destruction and pipeline explosions. My point is that paths randomly cross. Occasionally, it can be sweet and fluffy like when two childhood sweethearts meet again as adults. They embark upon a relationship while skipping through the tulips hand in hand till she catches him a few years later logging into his swinger's club account. Sometimes, however, such encounters don't involve tulips and skipping. They result in car crashes.

Haven't you heard of entropy? Really? You know nothing about Boltzmann or Maxwell? Or why the universe was in such a low entropy state at the beginning? Look, here it is there are only a few ways your house can be clean and tidy. Really spotless. But there are an infinite number of ways in which it can be a mess. Ranging from a cushion being out of place, a crumb on the floor, to piss all over the toilet seat because your useless son hasn't lifted it up again no matter how many times he has been told. That's entropy in a nutshell. As the universe expands its entropy increases. For any structure to form like our galaxy, our planet and you and me, it requires a source of energy. In our case it's the sun. Even as the sun's energy is harnessed to form structure here on earth, entropy increases as heat is expended. It doesn't end well. Nothing does. That's another truth.

Natural Selection is not interested in your happiness. Let me say that again: **IT IS NOT INTERESTED IN YOUR HAPPINESS**. Survive **and** reproduce! Not only survive **AND** reproduce but reproduce **AGAIN**. It's all about grandkids! What do you think grandmothers are for? Why do you think menopause evolved? Why do no other primate species undergo such a painful biological odyssey? Because of some patriarchal deity making life even more difficult for women? As if they don't have enough problems today competing with members of their own sex who have miraculously grown a cock. For fuck's sake! Our proclivity to live in the future, our ability to imagine alternative realities, the anticipation of joy, more than joy itself, drives our muscles to move. It's what builds civilisations, and it's what tears them down.

If behaviour produces a dopamine hit when you book a holiday, or add to your property portfolio, or when you bomb the infrastructure of a mineral rich country which you are about to invade - or have a proxy do it for you - then that's just dandy. There is a global industry of books, podcasts, online gurus and wellbeing experts, happiness indexes, ideologies and information coming from other galaxies showing you how to be happy. Religions call it Heaven, Nirvana, Moksha, or free deliveries from Amazon. How to get to happiness? As if it's a place on a map. As if there's a neuron in your brain responsible for eternal sunshine. Darwinian natural selection does not care about your long-term happiness. Yes, it may reward you with a chemical treat like giving a biscuit to your puppy for not shitting on the kitchen floor. That's as good as it gets. Anything else is a utopian driven myth which makes people even more unhappy than they otherwise would be.

Why am I not happy? All the time? Imagine you are back in the Pleistocene sitting in a cosy cave with your kin. You and your second cousin go on a little hunt. You are successful. You are both happy. Your group is happy. You share because this is not a community ruled by an oligarchy in a make-believe system called capitalism where a few greedy fuckers hoard everything while you go out and do all the work and take all the risks. You remain happy despite the food being eaten as there is no fridge in your cave to store any leftovers. But your second cousin becomes discontent and chooses to go on another hunt. He brings home the bacon. You remain happy. You'll soon find, however, he gets the girl and passes on his genes while you remain happy masturbating and being grateful that you evolved hands instead of hooves or claws.

You are a gene machine. Modern myopia has rendered you unfit to thrive and survive in previous times. I expect the only thing you could catch outside is a train, a bus, or a common cold. You are walking along a tightrope every day. And in those moments of silence when all the screens darken, you are conscious that it's a long way down.

If you choose to journey on, keep in mind the theme of entanglement whether you fall from the rope or manage to maintain a tenuous balance. Just as matter tells space how to bend, and in turn, space dictates how matter shall move, our gene machines are bent by ideas, and our ideas are shaped by our genes. *Homo Insanus* evolved from Homo Sapiens.

Marshmallows and Maniacs

Rule 1. Fuck Facebook, Twitter, Instagram, and yes even Tik Tok. I hate myself for setting up a Facebook account several years ago. Everyone wants fifteen minutes of fame. Everyone needs an audience. To be ignored is to be cast out into the wilderness where *you* are the prey. Everyone wants to show how happy they are in an endless sea of trivial shite. I have thirty friends on Facebook. I am a hypocrite. I should close this account and never log in again. Zuckerberg has my data for what it's worth. But I can't. It is one of the ways I punish myself. Like self-flagellation in medieval times.

We - Angela and I - moved to Shirley (though her pretentious mother always says Solihull as it sounds posher) three years ago so our daughter, Amelia, could go to Lady of the Wayside Catholic School. Our son Hadrian is a lost cause, and spends his days masturbating, and playing Xbox. My wife is a card carrying Catholic. I think God is on crack. It would explain why the world is as it is. The theodicy problem vanishes in an instant.

Not even Darwinism can explain how the insane have taken over every institute in the visible universe. How rationality itself is literally rationed out like a rare mineral. That's if we haven't sponsored a terrorist group to seize the resource on our behalf like a well-armed stockbroker. But I don't believe in God, despite the capital "G" (an ember from my early years), or Santa Claus or the Tooth Fairy or trickledown economics. As if all the billionaires have left their money taps dripping, and hordes of undeserving poor await open mouthed below. Get real. That's not how things work.

Francis Bacon was right: Knowledge is power. But absolute knowledge is not absolute power. Google and friends will find this out the hard way one day.

I read. Not to feel part of any group. That's the mistake CS Lewis made when he said: "We read to know we are not alone." We are always alone. We live and die alone. Do not delude yourself. The sooner one embraces this reality, the sooner one can get on with living life. It is liberating.

Instead of stumbling along in fear and trepidation, overcompensating with every step, grasp with certainty that it's a full-time job living your own life, and the same goes for everyone else. Fermi's Paradox is not a paradox. Where is life in the universe if it exists? Why after all this time have we not detected a signal of some kind? The answer is not that the universe is so vast, and that light has an upper speed limit. It is because you truly are alone.

I am a homicide detective. Well, I was once upon a time, I should say. That's how I introduce myself, even though I was only on the murder unit for about a year. I left because I didn't want to do the required overtime. Couldn't do it. Mentally, I could not handle it. Not because of the murders. We rarely saw a corpse apart from the CCTV team. Murder detectives are called in after the homicide to have lots of meetings, eat and drink coffee, carry blue notebooks around to look important. We wait till we are given an "action" to do, and like bees we fly out and complete the task and bring the offering back to the hive. Soul destroying boredom. And I was spending way too much time and money in Starbucks.

My DI asked me: "What did you expect when joining the unit?" I replied: "Status." Let's face it, it is all about status. You can't understand life without comprehending this fundamental fact. We strive to survive and reproduce. In order to play this game, we need to be part of a group. Once we are in a group, we need not only to get along, but to get ahead. This "getting ahead" part is what drives people to say they live in Solihull (technically we do), and the reason I introduce myself to strangers (other police officers may ask uncomfortable questions) as a big city homicide detective. Only by getting ahead do people find purpose and meaning. This is true for everyone. We are all actors in the theatre of status. When our position is threatened, even in the most trivial of ways, our emotional reaction can be severe. Existential even. We want to fit in, but at the top, not the bottom. Be careful when you look at your tribal members because comparison is the thief of contentment.

I have twenty months left till I retire. Twenty pay checks. If I get to retire that is. It's not looking good. I awake each morning overcome with dread and anxiety. I feel a tightness in my chest. It stifles my breathing as if Angela has pressed her hand down on my throat. It would involve her putting a hand on me.

We used to have sex every day. Then it was every other day. It dwindled to nights when she didn't have a headache, back ache, shoulder ache, toothache, or simply that she was too tired. As if she has a monopoly on fatigue. She says sex is all I ever think about, all I ever want. How can I reply to that? "If you did more to help me, help out in general, then maybe…" she said a few months ago." I bit my lip, literally. I am living a lie.

I am a fraud. An imposter. There is an actual condition called Imposter Syndrome. My grandfather, Seamus, told me the worst thing anyone could be in life is unauthentic. He would come to the house on Thursday afternoons when I was a kid to cut the hedge and have his tea. Seamus was my mom's dad. He lived until he was 92. He fought in the Great War and got shot in the leg at the Battle of the Somme in 1916. I never imagined that one day I too would wear a uniform and serve the British crown. Yet despite Birmingham city centre having its dangers, the gangs of the second city didn't have artillery, mustard gas, tanks, and good old sing along songs.

Have I mentioned that clever people are the best self-deceivers? They suffer from Imposter Syndrome more than anyone. It's a prerequisite for entry into the elite circle. Any sign of disloyalty gets them expelled into reality. They always appear on the face of things to have the best arguments. Rational step by step stories. They should come with a fraud warning.

I never set out on a journey to change the world, to overcome obstacles and fight dragons or evil empires or American neoCons. All one and the same thing. Now there's a Trinity. Really you say! Have you ever read Hannah Arendt? Do you not understand anything about the banality of evil? The ordinariness of it. Take a Goldman Sachs mannequin and make him a Prime Minister. Give him a few simple instructions. The fucker will administer electric shocks all day to an innocent person. Before long, with a big cheesy grin and an outstretched hand, he will push the victim into a gas chamber, or into an appearance on BBC news, faster than Milgram, Lombardo or Arendt could get a book published. And if you recall, Hannah and Heidegger were flinging each other around the bedchamber so she had an insider's view of evil.

It is a prerequisite to this story to ask yourself how one acquires power more broadly? How do the elite become the masters of the universe without any Marvel traits? First you need a neolithic revolution in the form of farming. Look behind the curtain of all of history's civilisations and you will find downtrodden classes: slaves, serfs and all-purpose peasants breaking their backs to feed those that hold and wield power. It is their labour that paid for the temples and palaces, the silks, wines and jewellery, the armies and weapons, the very structures upon which information accumulates, and is transferred from generation to generation. Yes, empires fragment, rulers are poisoned and fall in battle, or are removed by security agencies, but a handful of domesticated crops and animals have paved the way for a population explosion and expansion which spread around the planet like American military bases: 750 and counting. But they come in peace. Really!

Who are the ruling elite you may ask? Who are those we need to serve and protect? Who are they who are happy for other nations to suffer while they live in their fluffy cocoon of safety but fear it may be undermined if extreme action is not taken to protect themselves? Who are they who sip a fat free cappuccino at their local leafy ritzy overpriced coffee shop while stoking the flames of insane ideas? Who are they who suffer from the most acute disease called boredom whose only struggle is to find a cause to cling to (anything which costs them nothing regardless of the harm caused to others) which gives their lives a cosmic significance? Who are they who imagine themselves in a heroic Manichean battle against evil where in reality they throw a hissy fit if the slightest thing in their manicured lives is not catered for to perfection. Who are they who require a 24/7 service like they are the stars of their very own Downton Abbey?

Remember the marshmallow test? Leave a kid alone with a single marshmallow. Have a person of authority tell them they can eat it now or wait ten minutes, and they can have two. Leave them by themselves and observe. If they eat the marshmallow straight away, then they are the most likely to become the masters of the future. Their inability to delay gratification is their key to success. That's what fucked us all: some kid's inability to wait for the second spongy sugary treat.

It is referred to as the here and now bias. It's one reason we are doomed to extinction, soon. Very soon. We live in the here and now. Time and location are important. Existentially so. Do you really care if a million people die on the other side of the world? Do you care - really care - about future generations? Say, in a hundred years from now? No, you don't. Not really. You may give it a thought and say I'll recycle or cut down on some non-essential items. Most of this behaviour is virtue signalling.

We are biological organisms who survive by living in the now give or take a few minutes. We are human cell colonies. We are fish that crawled onto the land. We domesticated a few plants, or maybe they domesticated us, the jury is still out. We have overrun the planet like a plague of locusts. We behave in ways which harm ourselves and others: drinking, smoking, eating excessively, drugs, wars and staring at screens for half our lives hypnotised to digitised shite. We are afraid of snakes and spiders though most of us live in cities; the dark scares us though we are drowned in artificial light. We spend a third of our short lives asleep. We worship gods and goblins and believe in ghosts and the goodness of human nature. We are blobs of chemical reactions who desperately seek love, and we will die and kill for it, even ending our own lives in many cases. We murder each other in large numbers over flags and fuel. We are mortal creatures who know we are going to die. We are animals designed by an amoral process of natural selection. We are mammals which fritter our time away while fabricating fictional tales about ourselves. We are a species which hordes toilet roll in times of self-induced crisis. Remember everything today is a crisis. Even if you think such people are insane, sooner or later you are forced to join the asylum seekers, otherwise you are left out in the cold with newspapers to wipe your arse. At least now you have found a use for them. Cascade after cascade of trivial ridiculous behaviour builds up until a real emergency occurs. From toilet paper hoarding to pre-emptive strikes. You think I'm joking? We are *Homo Insanus*.

The Problem with Game Theory

Ever hear of the Prisoner's Dilemma? I've used it once or twice myself to get an alleged offender to start talking. Take two criminals who are in custody and who are accused of the same offence. Assume you don't have enough evidence to convict them. They are kept apart. What is the best strategy for them to adopt if they want the best outcome? If they both give "no comment" interviews, then they both serve six months. If one of them says the other committed the offence then he goes free, and his mate goes down the steps for two years. And vice versa. If they betray each other, they each serve a year in prison. What should they do? What would you do?

MAD is the acronym which stands for mutually assured destruction. Kill me and I kill you. The end. Why would we do that? It would be insane. Right?

Ever heard of the Nash Equilibrium? What bunker have you been living in? Simply stated: I have nuclear weapons, and so do you. Our possession of these weapons means we deter each other from using them during a conflict. A stable system emerges. This is the Nash Equilibrium in a nutshell.

The theory involves rational players in a game who desire the best outcome. Generations of academic whiz kids have built computer models to show the efficacy of the theory. National security and foreign policies are constructed upon its foundation. However, someone forgot to program in reality. You can't blame the algorithms all the time. Anyone willing to kill themselves for an idea, a feeling of alienation and a meaningless existence, a hatred for anyone who has oppressed them in some way, humiliated them, or simply, a firmly held belief that nothing is better than something, then such an individual is going to prove that game theory is fundamentally flawed. Ask any jihadi, kamikaze, school shooter, ask anyone who has ordered an Americano and receives a latte instead, and you will quickly discover that there are individuals, groups and nation states who will end your existence faster than you can say: "They are not really going to do that are they? Don't they know it will ruin the economy? Are they unaware it will destroy all the think tanks and lobby groups in Washington? Have they never heard of the Enlightenment and progress and reason? Have they never read the work of Dr Pinker and Dr Seuss?"

I read an essay recently entitled *The Evolution of Stupidity*. It was the author's own search for meaning. Like Victor Frankel. Like Kierkegaard. Like Wittgenstein. In essence, like all philosophy. In a purposeless and meaningless universe, we are all on a quest for stories of hope. Humans care about whether their lives have meaning. It is not enough to exist and procreate.

A chicken has conscious feelings. Chickens can suffer. I have no doubt about this despite what Colonel Sanders has led us all to believe. Suffering is the starting point of all philosophy and religion. But chickens don't walk around with existential angst. Wondering what it's all about? What is the point of anything? Why do they exist? Chickens don't have a sense of dualism. An intuition that there is a soul or mind substance which has a separate existence from the biological body. Chickens don't care about chicken pensions and climate change. Chickens don't group together and plan to attack and destroy a neighbouring group of chickens. Chickens don't create complex societies and write symphonies. They don't destroy those societies, and censor chicken composers from countries they are against. Chickens don't create chicken gods or create telescopes which look back to the beginning of time. They don't need drugs and cultural illusions to swallow them up and fill the void. Chickens don't think about their own mortality. They don't sit down on a sunny morning thinking about how they will soon face their very own final curtain. Only humans have this gift and curse. The imagination to be able to contemplate an infinite number of universes, while at the same time, being a very fragile organism that can be wiped out in a second. We fear insignificance. No chicken will ever feel a sense of impermanence, and a dread of impending non-existence.

The essay described how "stupidity" evolved as an adaptive strategy to allow humans to survive, and to get out of bed without being frozen in their knowledge of the imminent doom which is about to descend upon them. Because when you think about it, if all it amounts to is a handful of years working to stay afloat and keep the rich endowed with bigger boats, having a few kids who carry on fifty percent of your genes, then life has several bitter pills to swallow before it ends. And as Woody Allen said: "I don't want to live on in my writing, I want to live on in my apartment."

Is it any wonder I'm interested - no make that obsessed - with mortality? With life? With war, and violence, and pointless destruction. We have an immortality bias. Gloria Gaynor understood this when she sang, "I will survive." But she never visited Hiroshima on the 6th of August 1945 or Nagasaki three days later. Gloria never witnessed the detonation of Big Bertha. Gloria knows nothing about nuclear bombs being accidentally dropped over Alicante and Greenland, or lost in a swamp, or any of the several Armageddon close calls we have experienced, ranging from a Russian submarine close to Cuba in 1962 to Able Archer in 1983. We have been lucky. We are crap at understanding large numbers. Stalin said that one death is a tragedy, a million is a statistic. A billion or five billion is beyond our ability to comprehend. You might as well be talking about the Planck scale of time and length where words cease to have any real meaning. Gloria was way off the mark. Knowing how to live provides no protection from radiation.

Angela says God will save us. Her mom and dad echo the sentiment. They hate me for what I've done to their daughter and their grandchildren. For what I'm putting them through. They are all Catholic. That means they believe in the Trinity, while no-one, not even the Pope himself, can explain how the idea works. They believe in Transubstantiation.

During mass, the priest performs a ritual which transforms the wafers into the actual body of Christ despite them still tasting like cardboard. Why couldn't he turn them into chocolate buttons or a little gingerbread Jesus? God can do anything, apparently. Doesn't Father Fallon know this? Was he absent from seminary on that day? And we were all taught - indoctrinated one might say - from early years, not to chew Christ's body, but to let it stick and disintegrate on one's tongue. To chew was to sin. We would be eating God. Then there's the baffling theological battleground: Is Christ God or the son of God? How can he be both? Are they of the same substance? If DNA tests had been around in Jesus's day would God have to pay child maintenance? I suspect God has turned his back on me because I refuted his existence. If I don't believe in him, why should he believe in me? This is one story which provides an explanation for my current circumstances. However, it is fiction.

It Is a Mismatch World

Yes, it's true I don't have much good to say about anything, or anyone for that matter. I'm too negative. Or so I'm told. I have a negativity bias. So do you. We have many blind spots. The brain is a belief machine. It searches for patterns then implants them with meaning. We cannot help assigning agency and purpose to these patterns to explain our reality. Beliefs come first followed by stories, explanations, and rationalisations. Once the belief is established, we look for confirmatory evidence to support it.

Then there is the availability bias. We digest what's around us in the echo chambers of news and gossip which tickle and reinforce our beliefs. We discard anything which contradicts our narratives or puts a dent in them. We seek certainty, and quiver and wilt if left in ambiguity. Nuance is the deadliest enemy in the modern age.

The world is a complicated place. Our brains evolved in a different environment to deal with problems most of us do not face today. Currently, obesity is more of a global problem than famine. Our brains produce a biochemistry which drives us to eat too much. It lags behind McDonalds and Doritos. There is a mismatch in all departments of life. I think I would have fared better on a savannah plain than in the West Midlands Police.

My final trigger warning: if you want cheeriness, happiness, mindfulness, or any W H Smith "Buy one get one half price" self-help nonsense, it's best if you stop right here, and head off to a yoga class, or some meditation retreat, or a CBT session which may help you out for a few days, or any of the infinite paths to self-improvement, self-fulfilment, self-discovery, or find me the love of my life dot com, and somewhere along the journey - the spiritual quest - you may become rich with material and emotional pleasures so you too can sit alongside the capitalist gurus of our time who espouse their Buddhist pretentiousness to explain why there are so many have nots suffering in the world. If you don't want to hear about existential angst, nuclear Armageddon and death **STOP HERE**, and crack on to Nirvana, the Garden of Eden or Dubai for a shopping spree amidst the artificial land of sand and silicon.

I am hanging on in quiet desperation. But I don't wish to be silent anymore. I want to shout from the fucking rooftops: **LIFE IS SHIT AND SHORT** and full of **SUFFERING** ending in **DEATH**. How funny is that? This is what Buddha overlooked while sitting under his eucalyptus tree or whatever the fuck it was: the shear **ABSURDITY** of it all.

In the beginning there was God. We killed him. Nietzsche crucified him. Dawkins and Hitchens buried Jesus, Mohammad and all the angels and saints, all the deities and ghosts and goblins, all the animalistic entities who accompanied us out of Africa, and across Asia and Europe as we killed off other Homo species and raped the females. This is the reason we have around 2% of Neanderthal DNA in our genome. Not because we settled down with them and lived happily ever after. Get real! God has been replaced with Google. We worship at the altars of corporations who provide us with the bread and circuses of our age. We have become slaves to likes and dislikes, ticks and notifications, pings, and rings. We are nudged around more than gas particles in a heated flask. We fall prey like lambs to the slaughter of the rubbish perpetrated by the media. Basically, we are stupid. We are insane. End of.

In the beginning there was the Big Bang 13.82 billion years ago. Out of an inflationary high energy vacuum (whatever that means) exploded space-time, and when the energy level dropped within an incomprehensible fraction of a second, matter came into existence. Quantum fields buzzing with activity. Each particle has its own field, and the Higgs Field gives all particles their mass.

Everything was born in those moments. That's my origin story. It's everyone's moment of creation. It is the story of the entire universe. Big picture stuff. It's also the nucleus of all lies and deceit, failed dreams, and the banality of every human life.

There is no amount of Prozac or opium-based anaesthetic which will help you on this journey.

Billy Jones was homeless. I have nothing against homeless people. There are many people living on the streets with mental health problems. Veterans. Abused kids. Victims of domestic abuse. People who just cannot afford to pay rent and mortgages to the rentier class who own nearly everything. It's a small step and a steep fall for anyone without tiles over their head. The streets are not paved with gold.

I have encountered many homeless people addicted to various substances. Instead of a few bottles of wine in the evening to take the edge off the day, they use heroin or something similar to completely blunt the harsh reality of their world. In the eyes of the law, they are criminals. All the superfluous language underpinning slogans such as the war on drugs, the war on terror, the war on poverty, the global war on climate change, war on Covid (a war on a virus? Give me a break!) are further examples of our insanity. You can drink and eat yourself to death over years, and take great strides to bankrupt the NHS, but empty that syringe into a limb, and in the eyes of the comfortable, cosy law abiding masses, the all-judging (and we humans are judging machines) hypocritical democratic crowd, led by dross not fit to govern a carwash, you are Morgoth, Cruella de Vil, Voldemort, Napoleon - the pig not the Corsican. You get my point. Don't you? It's been twenty odd pages so if you haven't by now you really need to fuck right off.

Being paranoid can have a big payoff. Our ancestors were paranoid. In the right circumstances. Sometimes people are being watched. They are being followed. Being tracked. Prey and predator. I have been both. It's more fun and exciting to be the latter and you're less likely to be dinner. Right now, I'm the prey. My paranoia is based on fact. I am prey to a police elite who have thrown me to the public and media wolves. I am a scapegoat. Literally a live sacrifice. Unlike Abraham, who was about to donate his son Isaac to God's holy knife till a ram showed up and saved the day, the Chief Constable has tied me to the altar, and plunged the blade right into my chest. Every newspaper is hunting me. I am a symptom of the rot in the police force. And it's not called a force anymore. It's a service. Like Amazon, but we rarely show up these days.

Chris Hatton, the Chief Constable, called me "a bad apple." A bad fucking apple. What does that even mean? I haven't even been to trial yet, and my own Chief Constable is calling me a rotten piece of fruit. On television. On the news. Sky ran the interview more frequently than when Russian tanks invaded Ukraine. The fucker has never even met me. Not one word has ever been exchanged between us. Even Jesus went before Pontius Pilate. Socrates stood before his Athenian accusers. Galileo had an audience with the Pope before his house arrest. Not me. I have already been tried in the media and found guilty. And Jesus, Socrates, and Galileo had it easy as they just had the Romans, Greeks, and Catholics after them. I have the IOPC on my case, and they can be more ruthless than Klaus Schwab at a trade union convention.

At least Jesus, Socrates and Galileo were in the dock for major principles: mankind's sins, reason over stupidity, science over superstition. Thank God the man I moved on - using a Home Office approved baton technique and remember that is key to my defence - was white. Remember George Floyd? And many others! Now let me say for the record those cops deserved what they got. I have friends who are black, and a few who are police officers. I have some things to say about racism in the police, and every other "ism" you can think of soon enough. My point here is that the top of the hierarchy is a bunch of narcissists. Like all elites, they despise those at the bottom of the boat. Even though their very status and privilege depends on those in the hull rowing the oars at full strength. They are a new puritanical breed who express their contempt in modern Machiavellian marketing ways.

I am in the firing line for following an order which unfortunately resulted in the death of a Big Issue seller. A father of seven kids as it turns out, and an estranged wife who were all crying on every news outlet for the loss of their beloved father and husband. No mention of the fact that they hadn't spoken to him for over four years. We live, however, in a post truth world. Where have you been hiding? Don't you read philosophy? The Frankfurt School? Foucault or Derrida? You think it's all about Descartian dualism? Or John Locke and Nietzsche, and the blank slate upon which culture writes your story? Come on. Get with the program. It's a dance between genes and memes. The fact that my man - and he is my man - was living in Snow Hill Hostel in the city and had no contact with his wailing family is by the by. The family appeared on every television channel, in every newspaper with their solicitor in tow, who no doubt advised them to cover up as many of their tattoos as they could. However, one can only do so much about neck and face ink.

"We just want to know what happened," cried ex Mrs Jones. "Our William was murdered by the police, and we want justice." Her four fat sons and three daughters, all adults, were wiping their tears away so they could see the check more clearly. How much will we get? That's the real question they want to ask. When do we get the cash?

"Why did the officer kill our dad?" sobbed one of the daughters.

Cue more tears. Each and every one of them was no doubt wondering what their share of the spoils would be. Why couldn't the police have killed her siblings at the same time so she could have their share. West Midlands Police's own euthanasia program. Why couldn't the club wielding uniforms beat her siblings to death like baby seals. She could just about cope with sharing the money with her mother. After all these years she had been seen as an absentee mom who spent her evenings down at the local pub, bringing strange men back to the house late at night. The so-called Cinderella hour when the evening comes to an end, and punters would happily take the pub cat home to fuck. For once in her life, she could be viewed as a mother who had done something right. She had once upon a time married Billy Jones and bore him seven kids. She had booted him out of their council house when she learned her benefits would increase if he left pronto on the midnight train to wherever the fuck it would take him. Just not here. And despite this example of modernity's version of the law of the jungle, he had come good in the end by being neutralised by Robert Peel's boys in blue. Three cheers for justice. Three cheers for Billy Jones. Three cheers for John Rawls, and all theories of justice where the downtrodden are lifted up. After all, as Rawls said, if before you were born you had no idea where and into which arms you would fall, you would design a society where equality is not just a word. Remember all governments are fictions created by the people. Those in office are your servants despite them behaving like your masters.

Gold had been struck for the Jones' clan. Their very own Klondike. Oil had been discovered in their own backyard. It would only take a few years to clear all the junk and dog shit out of the way to start drilling.

I was the cause. The killer of poor Billy Jones. If only I had pushed him in a legal - not-guilty-all-day-long - way some thirty years ago then look at the money I would have saved the taxpayer. I would be hailed as a hero. I would have a statue erected next to Queen Victoria in town. Though why her statue remains standing and hasn't been torn down is beyond me. Don't all these young hoodlums know she was the Empress of brown and black people across the world? This miserable spoiled dwarf who wouldn't spare a drop of royal piss if Harriet Tubman, Rosa Parks or Qiu Jin were on fire. They need to get up to the city on the double with sledgehammers and ropes. I would have prevented a crime against humanity by stopping Billy Jones' genes from being passed on. I can just see myself, and king of the drones Obama, receiving the Nobel Peace Prize. In my case it wasn't to be. No statue next to the Empress of the world. No peace prize. And the taxpayer as usual gets fucked.

A Hero's Journey

Every human story is a journey. A road trip in the tradition of Odysseus, the Ramayana, Candide, and Kwai Chang Caine (everyone needs to watch Kung Fu before they die). Full of obstacles to be overcome. We each are the hero with demons to be slayed. Along the way we find love and seek revenge. We encounter Jungian archetypes in all shapes and sizes. We inherit beliefs from family and culture. We cooperate and fight. Our senses are a dashboard which measure the external world through which we travel. The only question that really matters is: "What will happen to me next?"

This is the question which all science in one way or another seeks to answer. Can I predict the next moment? The philosopher Immanuel Kant wrote that one can never know the external world. You can only know your perception of it. That is what we measure. Those are the patterns which mathematics describes. The dashboard is our window to reality, but it should not be confused with the real thing. It is at best a series of approximations. Best guesses. Like Plato's cave where the shadows play out on the wall, and we the observers believe the shadows are reality. My journey is essentially *Waiting for Godot* meets kitchen sink drama. Those literary minded among you may say hold on a minute, Beckett's characters travelled nowhere. Just the opposite. They stayed in one place waiting for Godot to arrive. He never does. They are even told he's not coming and still they wait. But don't you see that this is in fact a drama of an epic quest writ large? Have you no imagination? Beckett saw beyond Joseph Campbell and Gene Roddenberry. I have been searching for Godot all my life, and I have ended up waiting at Birmingham Airport with a bunch of lazy cunts.

Meanwhile the Jones clan with their solicitor, Mr Mark Smith, are hovering over my head like the Enola Gay at Hiroshima. Apparently, he's their family solicitor. I'm not even kidding. He has been representing them in criminal court since they were all embryos, and now after years of taking the basic rate from legal aid, he sees his chance to win big on a 'no win no fee' basis. Another import from America along with syphilis and Trident missiles.

The family want a proper full and frank and open investigation of the incident by an independent body, and only then will they be confident that there won't be a cover up.

Mr Smith said to the cameras: "The CCTV footage of the police officer, PC 9998 Jack Garner, savagely beating Mr Jones is clear for everyone to see, and very disturbing. Of course, we have no idea how it got into the hands of the media, but it has had tens of thousands of views on YouTube. Billy's death at the hands of PC Garner has had an irreparable impact on his family, and we hope and pray that justice is done. Thank you all."

The family has given more interviews than the Kardashians. And what happened to media impartiality? Investigative reporting? It's been banned by the corporations who own the fourth estate. You are more likely to see a fucking woolly mammoth than a balanced presentation? Two sides? Okay, I grant you, I do not have the luxury of giving my version of events yet, until I get inside the courtroom, but come-the-fuck-on. The scaffold has already been erected at the O2 arena. Tickets will be going on sale soon. Kids are to get in at half price. The Spice Girls, Spandau Ballet and several other mid-life crisis bands are having a get together on stage just to get the crowd whipped up before I'm dragged onto the platform. Yeah, that's right, dragged. It's not going to be like William Wallace or Anne Bolyn. I'm going down with a fight. I'm not having Take fucking That doing their dad dance as the noose is put around my neck, and Gary Barlow is winking and giving me a thumbs up like it'll be alright in a minute mate don't you worry.

I can just see Mrs Jones and her brood sitting in the front row with all the grandkids. Indistinguishable from their parents as only a few years separate each generation. There could be great-grandkids present, and still, they will all be under fifty. Each and every one holding plastic cups of lager (the organisers were clever in knowing that glass bottles would be thrown) singing and dancing along to the live entertainment. And this is the last thing I'll see before my exit into the never-ending days of being dead. Beckett, Pinter, and Ionesco nailed it. It's all ridiculous. All insane.

The Sun newspaper called me "The Face of Modern Police Thuggery." They used a photograph of me taken outside Birmingham Magistrates Court where I was a witness in a case years before. They placed it right next to a story about a neo-Nazi group in Shard End who were demanding free school meals be stopped for immigrants. Will someone please give me an Iskander missile!

I did read one letter of support in The Independent. It implied that I too was a victim. A damaged survivor of B.F. Skinner's operant conditioning. Imagine a pigeon pecking at a lever for food. When the reward is removed the bird will keep on pecking. The writer implied I had free will (here they parted ways with Skinner who - as the father of Behaviourism - designed his experiments for what can be seen via behaviour, and not through observations of neural correlates in the brain), and therefore, I am responsible for the "indiscriminate blows" I used on Mr Jones. However, the state was also to blame for training me. It was an institutional issue. Like waterboarding suspected terrorists in black op sites in countries supported by CIA offshore accounts. Be sure to waterboard the fucker who leaked that info before you throw away the key. Better still, have the Washington Post or the New York Times or the Guardian (No, I'm not kidding) go after any whistle-blower, and turn them over to the state. God forbid they protect them as a source. Daniel Ellsberg would have his testicles removed by NYT staff in today's world before the CIA got to work on him.

I was a victim of illegal wars in Iraq and Afghanistan. Dodgy dossiers and lies devised and orchestrated by Bush, Blair, Cheney, Rumsfeld, and that butter wouldn't-melt-in-your-mouth, Condoleezza Rice, Victoria Nuland, Clinton, Blinken and a bottomless pit of other smiling assassins. They are all to blame for the demise of Billy Jones. It's a wonder they didn't connect him in some way to 9/11 or Putin or Xi.

The letter deployed a degree of impartiality by stating that the CCTV footage - which had gone viral - showed that Mr Jones was reluctant to move. The police had been trying to contain anti-capitalist protesters for some time. "PC Garner was performing a difficult job, and the court will decide his fate."

I cut this letter out of the paper. It was as good as it was ever going to get.

Will The Cannon Fodder Please Step Forward

The incident, of course, still needs to be explained. The truth lies in the details. I'll give a brief outline of the events. A timeline. But before I do I need to say a few words about violence. Just so we understand our terms and conditions. Definitions matter.

Take the Vikings for example. Those blokes with horned hats who raped, pillaged, and plundered, and now have their own theme park in York. Can you imagine telling the monks on Lindisfarne, or women in Berwick on Tweed before they were deflowered, pre-1066, pre-Magna Carta, pre-Pizza Hut, that these axe wielding maniacs would one day provide the theme for a kid's day in the sun having fun? Have you read the Icelandic Sagas? O please.

They were written in the thirteenth century but turn the clock back far enough and all centuries start to look alike. Even among the Vikings themselves some of them gained the reputation of being sociopaths. Think of a cross between your average CEO and a special force operative. They were known as "berserkers." This is where we derive the phrase "to go berserk." They were renowned fighters. Fearless in battle with a tendency to strike first and answer questions... well never.

People lived in terror of them like today's tax collectors, but unlike the latter, they were handy to have around when invading a foreign land. They are much sought after today by military recruiters and pharmaceutical corporations. The point I'm making is despite the pejorative headline in The Sun newspaper, it pays to have thugs around whether it infringes upon your sensibilities or not. Mr Darcy is every woman's dream catch. And few novelists have ever matched Jane Austen's piercing accuracy of social relations, but evolution selects not only for men of means in tight trousers, but it requires men of violence. Survival and reproduction both require a weapon system. Yet evolution has many tricks up its genetic sleeve.

We domesticated fire around two million years ago. We can thank Homo Erectus for this incredible achievement. Without it we would not be here. For without fire, you would have no cooked meat and no big brain. You would be chewing and digesting all day long, and not composing an adagio for strings, writing an elegy in a country graveyard, or watching Breaking Bad for the fifth time. We domesticated animals and plants. Some became our pets. Even their faces have become neotenized. Here's the thing, so lean in and take note: we have domesticated ourselves. Really? Yes, really! We are less violent now than ever before in our history. We show less reactive violence than ever. Unlike our chimp cousins. You would never guess it with 24-hour news, and the share price of Raytheon, Lockheed Martin, and Boeing.

Despite the wars of the 20th century and the corpses strewn over every oilfield and mineral deposit in the developing world, we are living longer, healthier, and in less violent times than in all human history. But if you're standing on Cherry Street in Birmingham city centre on April Fool's Day with wheelie bins (which have been set on fire) being rolled toward you and projectiles being thrown over the flames, then it sure seems like our shared chimp-like ancestry is quick to come to the surface. We are still slaves to proactive, pre-planned, coalition-based violence. We are very good at it. When I say we, I mean those of us who possess the Y chromosome. Maybe in the future, through genetic engineering and new means of fertilisation, the remnants of our species may be saved by the most elaborate euthanasia program in history: getting rid of that Y.

It is true that if our country had not become an American outlet like some Tesco Express on Guam, if we had maintained a sense of propriety and regulated the rich instead of allowing them to self-harm by over indulging on cash like children given free rein in Willy Wonka's Chocolate Factory; if we had not had a series of Prime Ministers and Chancellors and a dim-witted political class, then maybe these protesters would have stayed in their dorm rooms smoking weed and discussing what they will do with their inheritance.

It must be said, here and now, that poor people do not smash the windows of Barclays Bank and McDonalds to demonstrate the evils of Adam Smith and Milton Friedman. The financially impaired who live in high rises in Lozells, Newtown and Highgate don't take to the streets with petrol bombs and the latest iPhones to protest against a banker's bonus, and shady share dealing in the halls of Westminster. Have you stepped inside an inner-city residential tower block lately? Have you inhaled the smell of stale piss? You're missing out. Well, I'll let you in on a little secret: it's the HAVES who riot against the system which feeds them. The so-called "have nots" are the real capitalists in the tradition of Smith. No mercantilism for them. And be not mistaken. The system we have is mercantilist at its core. It's state sponsored capitalism.

So, what happened?

You must use your imagination. You have been on duty since 6am. Briefing had been at the Victorian symbol of power, Steelhouse Lane Police Station, at seven. You have been told by an Inspector what the policing plan was for the day. You have done this all before and therefore pay no attention. You are given a bag of food consisting of a pathetic cheese sandwich, an apple, and a kit kat. And a bottle of water. It's April Fool's Day. Unfortunately, what followed was not a prank.

Officers are assigned a serial which equates to a sergeant and eight PCs. We all know each other. We have a police van. It's like going on a day trip to Kabul. Now imagine nine hours later and you are still on duty. Only now you are tired. It's been an unusually warm day, and you have been wearing fire resistant clothing, and a NATO helmet, and carrying a shield around to block the insults and bricks being thrown at you. You are exhausted. Whatever patience you had expired seven and half hours earlier. After you ate the kit kat. Police did not eat apples!

You have been the target of every kind of projectile. You have been subject to abuse and goading. You have been recorded on mobile phones more times than Boris Johnson broke Lockdown rules. You are mentally drained from defending yourself and your colleagues, and replying to questions like whether it might be okay if protesters could use McDonald's toilets even though they had just smashed their bastard windows. You have lost count of the number of people you have hit with your casco on the thighs. The number you have pushed. All Home Office approved techniques. You have become desensitised. Less aware of individuals. The canvas has become more Jackson Pollock, less Van Dyke. Your hearing has become impaired from hours of relentless noise. You can barely see through the visor of your helmet. You are still drawing from the energy pool of the morning briefing when you were told what the police commanders expected from you, what the inner-city business community expected from you, what the country and the WEF, UN, WTO, IMF, and World Bank all expected from you.

When faced with an ocean of angry youth you cannot help but think what is the real cause of their frustration? Are they aware of how easy they have it compared to the past, and almost everywhere else in the present? Do they really want to tear apart the entire structures upon which the modern world is based? Amidst the debris and broken glass, the flames and sense of camaraderie on both sides, it is easy to see a society in decline, the folly of youth contrasted against the hollow and fragile authoritarianism of the state.

I wish in some ways I was on the other side. It's those contradictions in the human condition, and fragments of memory constantly constructed and reconstructed like plate tectonics, our past subducting and re-emerging, changed but still familiar. As it says in Ecclesiastes, stick around long enough and you'll see for yourself that there's nothing new under the sun.

There is a point in every conflict when the end has to arrive: Appomattox courthouse; a rail carriage in a forest near Compiegne; on board the USS Missouri; Othello taking his own life; Tony Soprano getting a bullet in the back of the head. The police could not lose. What would that even look like? We would show the world who was looking on that we don't need tear gas or tanks. We do not have to resort to water cannons or automatic rifles. We are trained in unarmed combat. For two days each year we attend a PST course. I should know as I was a trainer. Two days of refreshing unarmed techniques which don't work in the real world. A thumb lock. I mean really. Have you ever tried to use a thumb lock on someone? Or the "spear technique" while shouting "Get back, stay back?" Have you ever watched a police show like Traffic Cops, and seen any of them use a goose-neck? I won't even describe what that is but for those jiu jitsu practitioners among you, imagine trying to get a gorilla in a guillotine.

Our expertise in public order does not only derive from personal protection training. We attend a two-day course at RAF Cosford each year to keep our public order ticket up to date. Petrol bombs and wooden blocks were hurled at us. We would learn how to hold the line and move forward to clear streets inside an old aircraft hangar. Directed by a clueless Inspector. The training staff would refer to them as "Boss." In a piss taking kind of way. Anyone wondering how armies throughout history have been slaughtered on the battlefield need only attend Cosford to see how some over-promoted individuals can cause disaster.

Didn't these protesters have a restaurant booked for the evening? I had been hit twice already with wooden posts, one holding up a sign which said, "Capitalism is finished." The other one stating "Save the Planet." Thank goodness for a hard helmet and my Cosford training. Laissez-faire is dead. Dig up Marx and Engels. Yes, they have all read *The Communist Manifesto,* no doubt, but how many have read *Das Kapital*? None. Yet that is where the real arguments are to be found. One just has to ignore the millions who perished under Lenin, Stalin and Mao. "From each according to his ability, to each according to their need." Roll out Utopia and Rousseau. Human nature is good and sweet and predisposed to kindness. Darwin and Tennyson were mistaken. Nature is not blood red in tooth and claw. And what did Darwin know anyway? Didn't he marry his own cousin? Didn't he know that the optimum marriage should be with one's third cousin. Did he know nothing about genes? Well, in fact the answer is no he didn't. He knew nothing of Mendel and his peas. He knew nothing of DNA and its double helix. He would never meet Rosalind Franklin, Morris Watkins, Francis Crick, and that annoying know it all James Watson. He was a man of his time. He knew that life involves a constant struggle to survive and reproduce. He knew that this struggle involved cooperation as well as physical battle. In fact, we cooperate in order *to kill*.

Darwin's legacy shows that Hobbes was right, however. Life is nasty, brutish, and short. Yes, we cooperate and commune together, but only in small numbers. Yes, evolution acts on culture in a similar way. Culture also shapes evolution. Without the transmission of culture, we are left using a twig to get termites out of a hole. Living solely in the here and now. But unless a Leviathan preserves the peace among large numbers then there will be no transmission of culture on the level we have seen in recent times. It will be a world where all is against all, and peace-loving people from Bertrand Russell to Al Gore (yes, he actually won the Nobel Peace Prize; you couldn't make this shit up!) will be left beyond the wall where the Winter People will have them for dinner.

Is your imagination still working? You are on Cherry Street right beside me. You just want to go home. You want to hear your three-year-old daughter sing the songs from Balamory. She thinks you are PC Plum. And no matter how many times you tell her you are more like Vic from *The Shield* she just laughs and points at you and calls you PC Plum. But I'm not PC fucking Plum. There's no episode which shows him getting hit with poles and bottles. We are here - you and me- clearing this street of people who have no clue how easy they have it in life. Being ordered to physically move these rioters on as it was now that time. There is a dog handler with her German Shepherd. It is rearing to break free from its chain. It is barking ferociously. It wants to bite someone. Anyone. It is instinctively capitalist. It understands competition and the struggle for survival. The need for order. It is German after all.

Mr Jones appears as the crowd recedes like the parting of the Red Sea. What part of "move back" doesn't he understand? Why is he standing still? The order applies to everyone.

"Move back," I shout. You heard me, right? Several times I shouted it through the noise and chaos. Before I pushed him with my casco. A hand grasped to either end. Across his chest. He fell backward. Almost in slow motion. Several steps before he landed on the ground. He is a big man. Six feet at least with a big belly. We have to be proactive, pre-emptive in these situations to protect ourselves, and those around us, and members of the public, and people around the world who require order. Because without law and order you have nothing. No education, no hospitals, care homes, no society at all. You have the jungle. You have the Serengeti Plain. You have inner city Liverpool.

Jones got up again and came toward me. You saw him, right? So, I pushed him again. I was following the Conflict Resolution Model to the letter. I know all about impact factors. Did I mention I used to teach this stuff? Once again, he fell over. I was just following commands. We were following orders. Jones got up a second time. This time slower. He staggered off around the corner onto Corporation Street where I lost sight of him. Yes, maybe I should put a use of force form in, but how many people have I pushed and shoved and hit today!

What Idiot Said All You Need Is Love?

Birds do it. Apparently, bees do it if you listen to Ella Fitzgerald. The Beatles sang that it's all you need. Forget a house, job, car, all the signals of status and resources which you are willing to share. We are raised from children to believe that love will conquer all. We memorise the lines of Keats and Byron. The more adventurous among us may venture further afield and submerge themselves in the poetry of Imru' al- Qais, Nizar Qabbani, and Yi Lei.

The so-called love hormone oxytocin is produced whenever our heart flutters. Women produce it when they orgasm. Men just want to sleep or leave before the cuddling begins. And remember evolution lets nothing go to waste. Oxytocin helps fish maintain balance in the water. We are fish. We crawled out of the swamps 400 million years ago, and evolved into amphibians and reptiles, and subsequently mammals.

Lactation is controlled by oxytocin. It is just another mechanism of liquid production. It helps mammals to bond. Mother and baby. Mommy and whoever.

I met Angela at Cleary's pub in Digbeth. A local police watering hole. She was drunk. I didn't even want to be there, but it was a retirement party for one of the old sweats on the shift, one of the station cats who never left the nick, and just smoked his pipe saying how the job had changed and he was glad he was retiring. "Going to buy a place in Spain," he said. Live out his days in the sun. But here's the thing about retirement, and dreams in general: if you're a miserable fucker, then no increase in temperature is going to help you out. There may be a twenty-four-hour time lag, but wherever you land, the real you will inevitably turn up and spoil things.

I was there, in the pub amidst the laughter and clinking glasses, sipping my diet coke, trying to mind my own business as drunks are boring to be around, and pissed up police officers most of all. I was not expecting an oxytocin rush. Surprise, surprise.

Falling in love is not something I do. Had done. I know it's a human universal. Before Angela, I could never imagine focusing my attention on just one person to the exclusion of all others. Not that I was ever a man about town. I had just never met a woman who held my attention for too long. Have you heard of the Scheherazade Effect? The heroine, for whom the effect is named after, entertains King Shahryar in the ancient Persian story *Arabian Nights*. By telling the king a never-ending tale, she avoids the fate of all her predecessors: being executed for the sin of boring the audience to death.

That evening Angela had me do two things I had never done before or since: dance and get into the passenger seat with a drunken woman behind the wheel. I buckled up and listened to her laugh and say: "You'll be alright, and if your mates stop us, get your warrant card out."

I knew then, this is the woman I would marry.

In the beginning it was not the *Word* which began everything. It was quantum fields. An inflation of a fluctuation in these fields started the ball rolling. Despite what your mathematics teachers have told you about zero, regardless of what Dire Straits sang about *Money For Nothing*, and especially what Socrates had in mind when Plato quoted him saying "I know only one thing, that I know nothing," keep in mind there is no such thing as "nothing." We cannot imagine what this even means. It's *fields* all the way down. So, when Angela dropped me off, and I invited her in, all the fields in the universe collapsed into a singularity like what's at the centre of every black hole. She laughed and said, "What kind of woman do you take me for? I have a daughter at home in bed."

I knew I had accepted a grenade with the pin out. However, if it's a choice between Scheherazade or a poster wife for 1950s housekeeper of the year, then I'll opt for the explosive device.

"We used to have sex every day. Then it decreased to every other day. Then once a week. Then once a month. It's like the mortgage payment going out, but quicker."

"I'm too tired."

"But you don't work."

"Ah, throw that in my face. I have three kids to raise and a house to keep."

"O please, you're going to tell me next you don't have the vote, and how I'm keeping you back in life. Don't mix freedom up with being free."

"It's all you ever want. How about planning a holiday for us all? How about a surprise of some kind? My dad was right about you."

Her father Robert is a solicitor in Knowle. He lives around the corner from his practice in a four-bedroom detached house with Angela's mom Marie. The fourth bedroom is important. It's the size of a broom closet, but it's a symbol of status. Like an en suite bathroom. Despite the smell of excrement wafting into your bedroom, it's symbolic that you've made it. And Robert never misses an opportunity to tell people what he does for a profession, and that their house is detached and not a semi, or God forbid a terrace. Life would not be worth living. Marie would never have married him.

Angela gets her dark triad personality from her mom. I suspect it gets passed down through their mitochondria. She has an idealised self-image and seeks attention at the drop of hat. This is the narcissism part. We all are on the spectrum. She is manipulative, and if she sees a chance to gain regardless of the cost, then that woman is more ruthless than Pol Pot walking through a university campus. This is the Machiavellian element. And last but not least is the psychopathy bit: she would scoff that marshmallow down her throat faster than Lewis Hamilton would complete a lap around Silverstone. She is impulsive and lacks remorse. Last time she said sorry was when she slammed the car door on my hand. Even then she couldn't help saying it was a stupid place to put it. She wants to move to Knowle and live in a four-bedroom detached house like her parents. She dreams of having an en suite. I have failed her in every fundamental way.

All relationships are a protracted process of negotiation. There is no win-win. There are only trade-offs. From day one. From the diet Coke in Cleary's eighteen years ago. Although if I remember correctly, Angela was on double vodkas.

Serious courting is like a game of poker in which you don't know for certain the intentions of the other person. It is a union of theory of mind and theory of probability. It's a game of virtue signalling. We watch out for tell-tale signs of response to our words and deeds. How do they respond when I touch their hand? How do they react when I pass them a compliment? The eyes give it away. There is a catalyst in action, a love enzyme, and who knows what the end product will ultimately be.

It was indeed Angela's eyes which hooked me. Yes, she knew her way around a bedroom like a taxi driver knows London but allow me a moment of romantic storytelling. It's not all doom and gloom. It's not all about asteroids, pandemics, and a nuclear holocaust. Even Osama Bin Laden needed some down time with his kids.

"I have puppy dog eyes," she said to me once. She did indeed. I just didn't realise at the beginning the puppy was a rottweiler. What the fuck do I know about dogs? I was raised with a cat.

Have you read Ovid's *Metamorphoses*? Pygmalion sculpts a woman out of a piece of ivory. He then falls in love with the sculpture. This is what I did with Angela. We all do it. We fall in love with sculpted images we have created. We don't really know the person at all in the beginning. Real love is what's left over after the image fades. If it lasts that long!

Angela had a seven-year-old daughter from a previous brief fling with a roofer named Mike. Her name is Helen. Mike wasn't on the scene anymore, and he never paid a penny in maintenance. Both Angela and her parents viewed his absenteeism as the second-best thing he ever did. The best thing was when he repaired a leaking roof over their kitchen extension.

It's not easy having children from a previous relationship when you embark on a new dating game. The simple reason is men don't want to raise other men's kids if they can help it. Infanticide by males is a perennial risk among some primate species, because of the length of time required for a female to get back in the saddle so to speak. A woman's fertility decreases until they wean the child. Their system is very sensitive to the suckling process (approximately once every four hours) which constrains their ovaries and menstrual cycle. So, a new male on the scene is best to get rid of the existing kids as it brings his new love interest back into the breeding business immediately, and he can crack on ferrying his own genes into the next generation. Women need to be very careful. The single biggest threat is a stepfather. Other risk factors pale in comparison. Fortunately for Helen, I liked her. She even started to call me dad.

I suspect being in the police tipped the balance in my favour in Angela's mate choice. It certainly wasn't my build. She later informed me how she preferred big men. The doorman type. Where's that eye rolling emoji when you need it? Whether she knew it or not, her brain made the decision and the story followed along shortly after. She concocted a romantic tale which ticked particular boxes in her narrative. I was part of the biggest armed gang in Britain, and though some of you will spurt out how patronising and patriarchal that sounds, and how women like Rhonda Rousey and Wonder Woman could kick my ass, and make me tell the truth, make me confess to all the corruption and kleptocracy in law enforcement, female mate selection ideally prefers partners who not only will share resources, but who can protect their offspring. Think of a combination between Floyd Mayweather and Bill Gates. To be fair, Angela didn't need Kevin Costner or Richard Madden. And those two couldn't guard an NCP car park.

I'll never forget the evening she told her parents we were getting married. Memory has a good habit of chiselling in trauma for future reference. That's why - unless in the most extreme cases - post traumatic stress is not a disorder. It's another of evolution's gifts to ensure you survive. Angela booked a table at her dad's favourite seafood restaurant in Knowle. Great I thought, an evening surrounded by Knowlites. As if seeing her dad choke on his clam chowder when she broke the news wouldn't be bad enough.

We had been seeing each other for almost a year. I had moved into Angela's two bed semi in Hall Green. It had a Birmingham postcode, but it was on the border with Shirley. If anyone asked where she lived, she always replied Solihull. What's a half a mile anyway? A lot if you live in Knowle. There's immigration on the Warwick Road by the M42 island. There's an electric fence at the border. One foot over, and any claim to being part of the Knowle tribe will be met with outrage and a hostile response to ensure the purity of the group is not diluted. If you try to get your children into the local schools, then there's a track and trace scheme in place which makes the Stasi, FSB, NSA, and the CSA look like kids on an easter egg hunt. Status has become the meaning of life.

So, I found myself sitting across from Robert. Angela sat beside me. Her mom looked uncomfortable as if she was sitting in a dentist chair about to get a root canal. Women know when bad news is coming. They have a finely tuned emotional intelligence. An extra layer of meta-cognition.

"We're getting married," said Angela after swigging down half of her wine.

It was actually me who choked on a piece of bread. Dinner had yet to arrive, and I was starving. It was after nine. I usually eat before six. I expected her to continue and state how we had decided to give up our freedom, and bring more stress and anxiety into our lives because that is what we have been programmed to do by our genes via our sex organs, wombs, and nursing apparatus. It's why we have been armed with desires and drives. Where is free will when you need it?

Marie looked at Robert. Angela smiled at both of them. She grabbed my hand before I had a chance to remove it. Sensing I was about to make a run for the door. Robert cleared his throat. Time appeared to slow down. He took a sip of his wine.

"Perfection is the enemy of the good," said Robert, after a few protracted moments.

"Exactly what I thought dad. Shall we make a toast?" said Angela.

She raised her glass. I reached for my water. Robert and Marie didn't even twitch. Angela finished off her glass of wine anyway.

"We were thinking of St Anne's for the wedding, and Hogarth's for the reception," I said, feeling as though a few words from myself were needed. If I were to survive the evening and the aftermath.

"Did you indeed?" replied Robert, looking at me as if I had conspired with an Albanian gang to sell his cherished daughter into slavery in Qatar.

"Did you consider asking Robert for our daughter's hand before this announcement, Jack?" said Marie looking at her husband. I'm almost sure she kicked him under the table.

"He did mom," lied Angela, but I told him not to bother. "Best to surprise you both. Are you surprised?"

"Are we Robert?" asked Marie, forcing a smile in my direction. Fortunately, no-one had ordered steak so there were only blunt knives on the table. Several of them by each plate setting.

"No," said Robert. "One's biological clock does not cater to one's current position in life. Not even for our Angela." He smiled one of those non-Duchenne smiles: no crow's feet, all facial muscles.

"And I'm pregnant," said Angela with a real crow's feet smile. This time Robert did choke.

A few points about waiting around for the perfect person. Life is way too short to waste your time in such a hopeless pursuit. There is a fundamental trade off (and recall, life is all about trade-offs) between continuing to search for decades, and the basic biological business of cracking on with what this is all about. Someone has to do it, or the species ends. No asteroid. No little, fat North Korean leader who got out of bed on the wrong side. Despite Mills and Boons, and all the romantic comedies over the years, regardless of the virtual dating world, Walt Whitman, Robbie Burns or Roxy Music, it probably doesn't matter too much with whom you do your reproducing, as long as they have a decent set of genes, and don't support Birmingham City FC.

You probably won't do any better by rejecting an endless series of suitors while waiting for Mr Right. And how much semen can one digestive system take? Of course, there may be an advantage in not settling for the first prospect who buys you a glass of Prosecco, and a bag of cheesy chips; however, there are only diminishing returns if you wait too long.

To state the obvious: the perfect mate would know they are perfect and would therefore not want to trade down to your level. Their brain would spot your asymmetry. It's harder to grow a symmetrical face and body than an asymmetrical one. Maybe, if you're a woman, your waist to hip ratio is closer to one and you resemble more of a tube than an hourglass. Maybe, if you're a man, your torso is the shape of an O instead of a V. Maybe your eyes are too small, your lips too thin; maybe you are like me, and just have to make do with the limited genetic toolbox you have been given. No disrespect. Needless to say, Robert was wrong. Perfection is not the enemy of the good. Perfection does not exist.

Angela was indeed pregnant with our son Hadrian. It wasn't my choice of name. Robert studied Roman history at the University of Birmingham before realising there was more money to be made in business and law than in peddling the sayings of Marcus Aurelius. Little did he know there would be an entire industry of wellbeing based on Stoic philosophy, and how to keep the external from controlling the internal. Good luck. He suggested the name Hadrian, and Angela, more pragmatic than William James, appeased him quicker than Neville Chamberlain at Munich.

If Robert and Marie had known that evening that I was not Dixon of Dock Green, I was not Inspector Morse or Wallander. If they had known then that I would end up being accused of an offence which I did not commit, that I would ruin their child's life, and their grandkids in the short term (because

Robert would make sure it was in the short term, as life would be rebuilt, just look at Berlin, Tokyo and Blackpool), if they had known what the future held, then I can say one thing with certainty: the tight fucker would never have dished out the £18,000 for the entire wedding. I'll take that one to the grave.

Remember back to 1987. *Dirty Dancing* had just been released. Recall the scene at the end when Jennifer Grey and Patrick Swayze are lined up on the dance floor. Bill Medley and Jennifer Warnes Are singing: (I've had) "the time of my life." They've never felt this way before. They are both lying fuckers. Still, you gaze on willing it to be true.

Jennifer sets off on her dainty yet determined run. Patrick, his muscles pumped as he's just been doing curls before the scene was filmed, anticipates her arrival like a baggage collector at Heathrow. Then as you expected - demanded even - she launches herself off the floor, seeming to defy gravity as her body, arrow-like, aims toward Patrick's biceps. He has taken calculus in college. He has read Newton and Leibnitz. He knows all about the curvature of space-time. Please don't drop her Patrick. For fucks sake. It will ruin the movie and rich people with money to burn have invested millions. The producer will go ape shit. Wait for it. Hold your breath. Bill and Jennifer are holding the note. And… wham bam thank you mam, he catches her mid-air. Like a Michelangelo sculpture. No, make that a Rodin bronze. It's Jennifer's scene more than Paddy's.

Now I ask you to drag yourself back to the future, like Michael J Fox, like Isaac Asimov, back to reality. You are sitting in Robert's favourite seafood restaurant that Friday evening. Somehow like an illegal immigrant crossing the Mediterranean in a waterlogged dingy with dozens of others, like a refugee hiding in a lorry passing through the Channel Tunnel to Great Britain (and that "Great" part is crucial despite it being a lie you will soon come to discover) you have made it passed the guards at the Knowle border. Your smell has not been detected by Knowle-trained sniffer dogs. You are tucking into the overpriced cod when you see Angela and I rise from our seats. You witness me moving away from the table. And like a matador waiting for a charging bull in an arena in Pamplona, I hold out my arms. Angela stumbles towards me in her stiletto heels. Robert tilts his head in confusion. Marie covers her mouth in horror. Angela jumps. But unlike Patrick with his bulging guns and million-dollar paycheck, I fail to catch Angela. She was carrying extra weight even before the pregnancy occurred. She lands face down on the floor with a thump with me standing over her wondering where it all went wrong. I knew then and there that things were never going to end well.

It Was All Getting a Bit Dull Anyway

Freud wrote, “Before you diagnose yourself with depression or low self-esteem, first make sure you are not, in fact, surrounded by assholes.”

I may not have been completely surrounded by such odorous people, but there was definitely a pincer movement afoot. Let me return to the immediate aftermath of what I now refer to as the “Billy Jones Affair.”

After the protestors transitioned back into the real world, and headed off to Starbucks and Costa, we got the order to “stand down.” Meaning we could fuck off back to our respective stations and de-kit. Put our smelly NATO suits, and other public order stuff back in our police bags (unwashed), throw them in the designated space, and head home. I didn’t hang around. I was back in work the next day on an early shift.

“Can I have a word Jack,” said Inspector Campbell as I walked past his office at 6.30am the following morning. The Gaffa was never usually in at that time.

On my very first day at Vyse Street Police Station in Birmingham’s Jewellery Quarter, I sat in the same office in front of a different two-pipped officer.

"Will you have a problem making the tea?" said Inspector Arnold.

It wasn't really a question. It was more like a statement that if I did have a problem, I could leave now. Tea making was central to a probationer's life. No student officers back then. No need for a Master's degree in police studies or some other made-up bollocks of a subject. Make the tea and play for a police sports team if you were one of the ex-professionals whose careers were cut short by injuries. No sick days unless you were stabbed, shot, or bludgeoned beyond recognition. Do what you are told. Be first to the bar after the shift, and you may just make it through those first two years. Maybe.

"Close the door," said the Gaffa, trying to look unusually serious.

I followed his instructions like a child knowing I was in trouble.

When Hadrian was five, I thought I would write a few thoughts down for when he got older in case I died in the line of duty. Yes, I was more likely to end my days on morphine in some hospital bed wondering what happened to the NHS since morons stood outside their houses clapping for all the heroes' wielding bedpans, and sterilised advice handed down from muppets waiting for knighthoods and share-dividends. I titled it "A Beginners Map to Life." A typical guidebook suggests places to visit as you might expect. I wanted to highlight locations to be avoided. A successful life comes with being aware of harmful traps: poisons, predators, prison, and Preston.

Imagine life as one great big minefield. You head off in your younger years feeling invincible, and sooner or later you hear that faint click. You stop. Your limbic system knows before "you" what's about to happen. Have you watched *The Hurt locker*? Don't you love those movies where we invade countries, kill an untold number of natives, and still manage to portray ourselves as the heroes. Now that takes creativity. One just has to ignore the likes of Wilfred Owen's *Anthem for Doomed Youth,* and *Dulce et Decorum Est*: surely there can be no greater glory than to die for one's country.

A moment after hearing the click, you've lost a limb or two, and no amount of Calpol is going to make it better. A parent's job is to flag as many explosive devices as we can so our offspring may avoid them. This is what cultural transmission is all about. This is how we have taken over the planet and fucked everything up according to some. If we had to relearn everything in each generation, we would still be sharing caves with bears. And maybe we would be better off. Everything involves trade-offs.

We step on mines. We observe others treading on IEDs. We put a marker in the crater knowing it will surely be covered up soon enough. Like caring parents who want to preserve our genes despite the disappointments they bring. We point out the flags in the minefield. Knowing the landscape gets replenished by the mine fairy every night. It is a universal law that kids will step on new devices, or old ones, that have not yet exploded, but they only have a limited number of limbs. They cannot replace them unlike some of our reptilian cousins. It's a good strategy if they avoid the ones, we have flagged for them. This was the purpose of my map. I suspect, like much else, it will have been a complete waste of time.

"Big problem Jack. On Cherry Street yesterday you're seen on CCTV, apparently, belting a Big Issue seller who is now on a ventilator in City Hospital. It doesn't look good." The Gaffa shook his head like I had brought him his coffee without three sugars. "The Chief Sup called me at home late last night."

The Chief Superintendent was an old school policeman. A man by the name of Sean Raw. A working bloke who had made his way through the ranks without shagging or shafting anyone. He was well respected by all, apart from those who shag and shaft at any opportunity to get ahead. Unfortunately, that number is increasing by the day.

"What…?"

He interrupted me: "Did you complete a use of force form before you went off last night?"

"Boss, we all had lots of grief yesterday. I don't know anyone who has filled out that online form."

He scratched his chin. "Well, that's not good. Those are the rules. That's the first thing they are going to look at!"

He was referring to PSD. Professional Standards. The devil's cauldron.

"I remember the bloke you're talking about. He wasn't wearing the red bib which Big Issue sellers usually wear. I told him to move several times. And to be fair, I didn't belt him. I used a proper technique to push him." I tried to sound incredulous. A wronged man. Innocent. Steve McQueen in the movie *Papillon*. Have you read Kafka's *The Trial*? Is there any greater example in all literature of innocence, and the power of the state to take your liberty away? What about Dumas's *The Man in the Iron Mask*? You must have read it? Not even the movie version?

Now I know I should maybe build a little tension here. Thicken the plot so to speak, but you know already that Billy Jones died. Spoiler alert. He never made it off the ventilator. He never made his way, like Lassie, back home (remember the dog who was smarter than the average person from Bradford; O please, have you ever been?) Billy never got to embrace his ex-wife and kiss her sweet sunken lips. Her front teeth were missing. She would surely remedy the gap once the check arrived. Ms Jones didn't listen to the family solicitor when he told her to cry with her mouth shut.

Billy never got to say a fond farewell to his loving children. Despite all the selfies they took at his bedside. I suspect this is what really caused his diseased heart to give up. Somewhere trapped inside his skull, there was a faint flicker of consciousness which could detect his offspring laughing away till the lady with tea and coffee turned up. Then the sombre emotional switch was flicked, and between the sniffles and sobs, they asked if there were any free cakes or cookies to go with their beverages. Don't they know the NHS is bankrupt? Have they no idea that it's quicker to walk from Birmingham to Istanbul than it is to get a GP appointment? And they want free custard creams? I mean what the fuck. How much can they take from the state without giving anything back? Have they never heard of reciprocity? Do they know nothing about our ancestral past? Do they not understand we have an acute sense of fairness, and anyone not pulling their weight would be told to buck up their ideas, but ultimately, if that didn't work action would be taken which could range from ostracism to being battered to death by the group? Billy Jones didn't have the means or ability to haul himself to the third-floor window and throw himself out. So, he just gave up breathing.

Keep Things as Simple as Possible but No Simpler

Einstein said to keep things as simple as possible, but not any simpler. With that in mind let's have a Timeline:

13.8 billion years ago: The universe began. No one really knows how.

13.5 billion years ago: The universe cools enough for the first population of stars to form and chemistry to begin.

4.5 billion years ago: Earth.

4 billion years ago: Single celled life begins. No one really knows how. No matter how many Nick Lane books you read. And that fella knows a lot.

6 million years ago: The last common ancestor of humans and chimps.

2.5 million years ago: Evolution of the genus Homo in Africa.

1.8 million years ago: Homo Erectus spread out of Africa throughout Eurasia. Evolution of different Homo species.

300,000 years ago: Homo Sapiens evolved in North and East Africa.

70,000 years ago: Evidence of new cognitive abilities in humans. A new wave of expansion out of Africa around the world.

40,000 years ago: Sapiens reached Australia. Wherever we land large animals and pre-existing Homo species disappear.

30,000 years ago: The last Neanderthal waves goodbye from a beach in Gibraltar. We have killed them off, and outhunted them, and little doubt raped their females which accounts for a small percentage of Neanderthal DNA we carry around.

12,000 years ago: The so-called Agricultural Revolution began - as a result of global warming following the end of the last ice age - in what is today Israel, Jordan, Syria, Iraq and Turkey. We domesticated grasses such as wheat barley and rye. The domestication of cows, sheep, pigs, goats, and ultimately horses around 4,000 BCE. An important point here is to note that it was geography and the presence of animals which could be domesticated that aided the “west’s” head start, and not some “special” set of genes. China domesticated rice and millet around 6,000 years ago.

400 years ago: The Scientific Revolution. Francis Bacon’s idea that nature can be tamed through experiment and measurement.

200 years ago: The Industrial Revolution began in Britain, and they planted their Union Jack across most of the globe, followed soon after by the rest of the Western powers.

1945: Nuclear bombs are dropped on Hiroshima and Nagasaki. The US has not stopped bombing since.

Present day: Billy Jones is dead. And I received a WhatsApp message from my wife Angela saying she can’t wait till Saturday night to suck my cock so could she come over to mine this afternoon? Do I need to explain the problem with that request?

Managers and Machiavelli

I was thrown under every mode of transport police managers could get their hands on buses, trains, trams, even a Sainsbury's trolley.

"You're in the Fed I hope?" asked Inspector Campbell.

He was referring to the Police Federation. When I first joined the Old Bill, three bald, white policemen, all Fed reps, attended Tally Ho on the Pershore Road, the training centre for the West Midlands Police. What a joke. They looked like they had stepped out of a Tarantino movie. All fake smiles and cheap Spanish suntans. The Fed gig in those days meant they didn't have to do a stroke of real work. The lecture hall was full of young, idealistic people for the most part, wanting to change the world, needing to make it a better place. Nauseating, but okay I get it.

One of these orange, potbellied blokes said: "If there's anyone here who doesn't want to join the Fed, put your hand up?"

Everyone looked around. I kept my hand down. How disappointing. We all signed the form. This is the *modus operandi* of extremist groups. We had become members.

The Federation has become a dog with no teeth over the years. Like the embers of the few real unions which still hang on in the globalist wind tunnel. Nevertheless, the one thing the Fed does provide is access to solicitors and barristers if you get thrown under the shopping trolley. If I hadn't signed the form all those years ago, and had my subscription deducted every month, then I might as well have walked myself into Winson Green Prison and closed the cell door behind me. Not a superintendent in sight. They only come out during the day and left the policing world several ranks ago.

All senior officers are effectively managers of one sort or another. Sergeants used to be the backbone of the force. They had to manage constables, but they also had to do proper police work themselves. Now they are just managers for the most part. If you had a crap sergeant, the team would be ineffective. Inevitably it would reach a breakpoint. And everything has a breakpoint. My sergeant was a man called John Snape. Old school and supportive.

Jones died just before I finished my shift. Snapey received a call. The Gaffa had gone home before two due to his early start.

"They won't support you, Jack. You know that don't you?" said Snapey. That was his nickname. Outside of work.

"Who?" I replied knowing what was coming.

“The Gaffa and all the rest upstairs. Get onto the Fed tomorrow and start protecting yourself.”

So, it came to pass. As inevitable as the rich getting richer.

Managers are the heroes and villains of many stories. There would be no towns or cities without them. We would still be living in little villages. And not like those in the Cotswolds, or between the rolling greenery of Kent.

The birth of management began in ancient Mesopotamia, and anyone sitting in a meeting scratching marks on their version of clay tablets can thank them for such organisation. Just think what they could have achieved if they had the ability to zoom on laptops. There would have been a lazy, fragile, overly protected class of useless fuckers 5000 years earlier than present day.

The managerial class really runs the world. It’s from this ten percent where the current insane ideas are mostly generated. Throughout history, conspiracies point to various cabals who were believed to control everything. It’s the Jews! Find the closest well to throw them down. Hopefully, before we’ve repaid our debts, and stolen any cash and art they have stored away for a rainy day. Shakespeare’s Jew is just a cuddlier version of Hitler’s, or the Rothschild’s financial empire, and Henry Ford’s recycled version of The Protocols of the Elders of Zion. Have you heard of the Dreyfus case? Then there's the endless Russia-gates, China-gates, Bill Gates. Pathetic doesn't quite grasp the mantle.

People are addicted to conspiracies: JFK, UFOs being stored in New Mexico or Nevada. Never Bangladesh or Kazakhstan. The Twin Towers being taken down by the CIA or Walmart executives. Dare I mention the moon landings being staged in a hangar outside Mentone, Texas. Where? I know, I know, there are real conspiracies. Drug companies will do anything to increase profits. Viox killed at least 60,000 Americans. Coup d'états sprinkle history like fairy dust. The list is endless. One must separate the wheat from the chaff. In today's world it's the fella with the clipboard - or someone wielding a spreadsheet - you have to watch out for. That's what will get you in the end.

The truth brings us back to Hannah Arendt, and the banality of evil. The ordinariness of the type of people who perpetrate harm toward others. The Einsatzgruppen of Nazi Germany killed hundreds of thousands. Reserve police battalions composed of ordinary men who shot an untold number of innocent people. Only a few hundred were prosecuted after the war. Most returned to regular life because of the coming of the Cold War. Many even obtained employment as police officers and government employees. History is replete with boring, banal types, often below average card-carrying members of the Y chromosome class who carry out atrocities on a large scale.

Snapey was of course correct. I learned quickly I was on my own. Have you read *The Prince* by Machiavelli? It's a 16th century handbook on how to rule. It's a must read. Like *Lord of the Flies.* And the two have several things in common. Both Machiavelli and William Golding knew a thing or two about human nature. The much tortured, and forever under-appreciated Niccoli Machiavelli, wrote the work, and dedicated it to the young Lorenzo de Medici, leader of the Florentine Republic. *The Prince* subverts Classical and Renaissance predecessors' views of morality and politics, and instead advances the idea of exploiting the distance between ruler and ruled. Machiavelli states that the Prince should present an image of virtue, but when necessary act with immorality.

This is *realpolitik* before Bismark. In essence, it is a means to secure power. Lenin and Stalin used it as a pillow. Senior police officers barely read, but they are Machiavellian by nature. Loyalty counts for nothing. They have those modes of transport, I mentioned earlier, at the ready on speed dial.

So now I was possibly in the frame for a murder I didn't commit, and my wife is starring in her own version of Love Island.

Brinkmanship Politics and the Klipspringer

Cast your mind back to October 1962. The human species was on the brink of extinction. Most people have heard of the Cuban Missile Crisis. Those risk taking Ruskies again. No need to go over the events. What is Wikipedia for if not to give the reader the general overview. And of course, to alter the biographies of people that the "editors" think is a threat to "democracy," and their versions of *the* truth. What's not well known, however, is the story of a Russian submarine with a single nuclear missile on board. This particular submarine was receiving dummy depth chargers' courtesy of the US navy who were trying to convince it to emerge from the depths like Poseidon with his trident.

The submarine commander had no contact with Russia, and in line with protocol, he, and his counterpart (it takes two to perform the nuclear tango in this situation) decided to launch their nuclear missile at the US carrier fleet. This would have certainly triggered a nuclear response from the US. At the time both Russia and America had around 60,000 nuclear weapons.

The age of precision guided missiles had not yet arrived. The exchange of these missiles from land, air, and sea would have caused the end of humanity. For certain. A Kremlin official was on board purely by chance. He outranked even the commander of the submarine. He was sane. It is a rare phenomenon in our species. They are black swans. Fortunately for us, he said the missile was to stay on the sub. Be in no doubt, the exchange of thousands of nuclear weapons would have been the first man-made extinction event.

Brinkmanship politics have brought us to the edge of oblivion on several occasions. Leaders of every nation, in cahoots with the media, concoct goblins of every nature, dungeons and dragons, from which they will save the population. Just trust them. Give yourself over to them. But there is an issue-attention cycle, hence the permanent clamour of imminent doom, as your attention can only be held, and manipulated, for so long before they must thrust another catastrophe at you. Brinkmanship politics, however, does on occasion have a place in the world of diplomacy. In the right hands, it can be effective. All relationships involve the art of diplomacy, and occasionally, the risky, but necessary strategy of brinkmanship pressure.

"Who is the owner of the cock you so urgently need?" I was never very good on the diplomacy front.

"Keep your voice down. The kids will hear," replied Angela. She had prepared for the onslaught by consuming half a bottle of wine and having her phone on voice record. Forever her father's daughter.

"Maybe they need to hear! Who is he? Do I know him?"

I wish I could exhibit a little originality. On the train on the way home I thought of several ways of how I would confront Angela. The outrage method. I'm disappointed, but I understand because we have been so distant, and you have needs too, and I have failed to meet your expectations, your father's expectations. I can understand why you wrapped your lips around another man's cock (I'm assuming it's just the one). It's a coordination problem. Synchronising our lives is so psychologically demanding. Especially with kids. Why didn't we drown them before they demanded electronics?

I am guilty of not being able to factor in my mate's needs, and requirements, each and every day. Even your common day garden birds have to be sensitive to their partner's moods and behaviour in a way that a promiscuous species can ignore. Keep in mind, we are more similar to birds where co-parenting is concerned than most other mammals.

Have you ever seen a klipspringer on a nature documentary? The male follows the female around everywhere she goes. He is rarely more than a few feet away from her. They take it in turn feeding while their partner watches out for predators. These sweet little antelope bond for life. And if you're going to bond till death, do you part then it's best not to select the first person who smiles at you. However, choosing the right mate is no easy task. If you get it wrong, the penalties can be severe. I've already highlighted the risk of children born to a previous relationship when a new potential mate comes along. Hey, Angela, did you think about this when Mr X is riding you like the Lone Ranger, like Genghis Khan, like Lester Piggot? Our children's future is literally at stake.

"No, you don't know him. It's nothing. You have no idea what I'm going through."

Pure defiance. No trace of regret. No sign of an apology. I think of my hand in the car door. Poets write of the physical pain that rejection brings, and they are right. Little do they know, it's the same part of the brain (the anterior cingulate cortex if you're interested) which registers both psychological and physical pain.

"You don't know what I'm going through either," I replied, rather pathetically. I had suddenly become drained of all the righteous energy I had summoned up on the train. To lose one's liberty and marriage on the same day is rather a lot to handle.

It's the material of comedy if it wasn't so tragic. Okay, no one is facing the executioner's axe, but still, when it's your life, and you only have the one. The restrictions we place on women's ability to meet other men reflect men's distrust of other men, and our own partners. Whether it's a face covering or laws restricting a woman's movements, education, or with whom they can associate, the explanation involves the paternity uncertainty of any children which result from the relationship. After all, the number of resources we invest in is large.

Why do you think grandmothers always say how much the baby looks like their father, although a new born cannot look like either parent at that stage. Before DNA technology came along, men could never be certain if it was their genes they were looking at. There are fathers out there raising children who are not their biological offspring, and they are blissfully ignorant to the fact.

"Aren't you always saying how we aren't a monogamous species anyway? Look, I messaged him, and said I'm not going to see him again. It wasn't serious," said Angela in a less defensive tone. I could smell a lie. Deceit has a distinctive odour like cat shit.

"How long has it been going on?" I asked.

"A few months,"

"How long is a few?" I knew this was a pointless question and one which would invite another lie, but come on, give me a break.

"Two. And his name is Ken."

It took more energy than a black hole at the centre of a galaxy not to ask whether he called her Barbie during their bouts of sexual intimacy. This is what my life has come to!

I told Angela about Billy Jones. About the shopping trolley I was about to find myself under. About injustice in the world. About the downtrodden. I enlightened her about the need for Hammurabi's Code, Napoleonic Law, Common Law, and the

UN Charter. She pushed back with the idea of Karma, and what goes around comes around. Call the kettle black. What did I expect?

"Will you lose your job?" she asked.

I actually let out a laugh. "Angela, I could go down the steps. But as I told you, I did nothing wrong. It was a shove!"

"Two shoves," she replied, quick to see an opportunity to correct me. Good job she's not the prosecutor, or I'd be well and truly fucked.

"I'll speak to the Fed tomorrow," I said.

"You've said they're useless, unless you're looking for one of their discount coupons."

"Yeah well, desperate measures and all that."

"Don't tell my dad by the way," she said in a panic.

"I'm not going to," I said.

"No, not about you," she said, realising I was thinking about myself. "I mean about the message I sent you."

"You mean the one about sucking Ken's cock? That message. The one about you shagging another fella for the past few months. Don't tell your dad about that? What about your mom? Can I send her a text giving her an edited version?"

"Now you're being stupid and selfish. And you wonder why we are where we are!"

With that she finished her glass of wine and went upstairs. I suppose on any other day, I would go after her asking more questions. Demanding more answers. Not that it would change a thing. When we feel bad, we just want to feel good. We can promise ourselves never to take mediocrity for granted again. Like when we have a toothache, and we think that if the pain would only go away, we will never again mistreat our teeth, and we will always and forever be thankful for a pain free existence.

It was the Czech author, Milan Kundera, who said, "I have a toothache therefore I am." Pain focuses your attention. It was a spin on Rene Descartes' *"Cogito ergo sum"* - I think therefore I am. I can doubt everything other than the fact that I am doubting. Therefore, I exist. I am not an illusion. The self really does exist. Despite modern neuroscience, regardless of Hinduism and Buddhism, there is a single unified self. To be found in the Pineal gland according to Descartes. The mind is separate from the body. Our intuitions are right: we are dualistic by nature. That's why we believe in God, in a soul, in free will, in some essence other than the material. Mercia Eliade was right: there is a sacred and a profane. There is a Heaven of some kind. The acute sense of who I am through time - ME - is real, and not some pragmatic illusion of electrical activity which helps my genes progress to the next round like some tacky game show competition.

For fucks sake give me something to grasp onto here. 'Alexa play, Bill Withers singing "Lean on Me." You don't know it? What the fuck! Really? How about “Don’t Stop Believing,” by Fleetwood Mac? You are having me on! Fuck it, Alexa play Frank singing “**THE END IS NEAR**.”

“Playing *My Way* by Frank Sinatra.”

UFC For Leaders

I had questions alright. How old was Ken? Please don't let him be under forty. Build? Height? Okay, cock size? Fuck it. It's how men think! Beard? Deep voice? Yeah, that matters. The longer the vocal tract, the deeper the voice, the more intimidating he is to other men. Job? Remember, it's all about status. Grip strength? I ain't kidding. It indicates testosterone level. Any specialist fighting skills? I'll come back to that one. And last, and in some ways the most important: did the fucker make her orgasm?

This is a sensitive subject for men. Especially since the movie *When Harry Met Sally*. Women can fake it till they make it. Literally. Men can only do this in the workplace. When they ejaculate, a woman can look and find the evidence better than any specialist police unit. Angela always had a problem reaching a climax with me. Unless we were watching a horror movie in bed back in the early days. Regarding sex she would say, "It's not you, it's me. I don't cum easily."

I remember asking her like a teenager, "Is that with anyone or…?"

"Yes, anyone, not just you." She sounded so sincere back then. What planet was I on?

I'll let you in on a secret. Some people ask - men of course - why women orgasm anyway? What's the point? Men ejaculate so their sperm can be catapulted up the fallopian tube, and the lucky few can embed themselves in the epithelium and await the egg to pop out of the ovary. Why do women orgasm? Not all women. Not Angela, apparently. Do you believe that? Not only do they produce oxytocin, but an orgasm causes a suction mechanism which pulls the semen upwards, like syphoning off petrol, and this helps the reproduction process. I'm not making this up. So, I want to know if Angela is helping Ken's sperm on their journey like the Epic of Gilgamesh, whereas my own were literally left to fight their way up in the dark and wet like a fucking Navy SEAL.

What about fighting ability? Could Ken kick my ass? Every bloke knows the instinctive nature of this fundamental question. Anytime a man enters a room with other men present who he doesn't know he is sizing them up. Could he take them out if there was an attack? Often the answer he arrives at is a delusion. It only matters if there's a fight. Clausewitz and Mike Tyson have stated: any plan or delusions of grandeur will not remain intact following contact with the enemy. Tyson's version involved being punched in the face. Is Ken combat trained? Is he a fighter? If I found out where he lived, and I went around to seek retribution, would I be doubly humiliated if he kicked me round his front garden like a punctured football?

That said, I know how to fight. I've been punching and throwing since I was a kid. Judo. Boxing. I know what works and doesn't work. Most things fail miserably in the uncontrolled environment called reality. I was doing mixed martial arts long before there was a UFC. If only our leaders in all areas would step between those ropes, or into the cage, I suspect the world may be a better place. Maybe there would be peace on earth and goodwill to all nations.

The ruling class knows nothing about making a reality-based threat assessment. They are too busy going around and around through revolving doors and stealing away cash for a sunny day. Don't be fooled by bicep size. It's real guns which will do you severe harm. Angry faces and violent body language is all about intimidation. You can win the conflict before it begins and avoid the possibility of injury. Be careful, however, because some people are not easily scared. If you make the mistake of causing a person, group, or nation to hate you, then all bets are off, and the consequences can be catastrophic. No game playing theories will save you.

My Fed rep told me not to mention my past fight training unless it's dug up like a Roman coin. His name is Bobby Sands. Apparently, his dad named him after the IRA hunger striker, a hero to the Irish Republican movement. Both our dads would be somersaulting in their graves if they knew we had joined the

British Police. Fortunately, they are long since dead. And Bobby is black. You really couldn't make this shit up.

The Iron Law of Oligarchy

Our first meeting was in the war cabinet command centre otherwise known as the locker room at Vyse Street Station. Bobby had arrived at ten on the dot brandishing his detective's blue book. I used them myself when I was on the murder unit. Did I mention I used to be a homicide detective? Also, an authorised firearms officer? No? An advanced driver? A self-defence trainer? A Master's degree carrying, and general-know-it-the-fuck-all kind of person? You know the type? Haven't I dropped that into the narrative somewhere? Just to establish my credentials. Just to show any argument I make is one from authority. The easiest way to shut people down.

If you're not a so-called professional in a subject then your argument, no matter how sound, is worth nothing, so shut the fuck up and crawl back under your rock and leave it to the specialists who think they can dominate everything. An "educated" position, no matter how ridiculous, reflecting years spent down a reinforced silo of biases and stupidity is what counts. Be not mistaken, stupid people are evenly distributed across all professions and places. You know when some high and mighty twit is withering in the heat of a well-constructed, evidenced based, logical argument, they will ask you what qualifications do you have in the subject, or what do you do for a living? Just another example of *Homo Insanus* falling for the so-called halo effect where Mr Smartass in one area thinks they are an elite on all topics. **This is the biggest and most harmful mistake in all human reasoning!**

I met Bobby in the front office when he arrived. I had spoken to him the day before to arrange the meeting and gave him a brief version of the miscarriage of justice which was unfolding. The Guildford Four. The Birmingham Six. Joan of Arc, and Rosalind Franklin and Julian Assange. Bobby spoke with an old traditional Oxbridge, I-am-not-a-paedophile-honestly, accent. When he came through the door, I didn't have time to hide my look of surprise. He clocked it. His brain was finely tuned over the years like the James Webb Telescope to detect the slightest hint of "You're black, what the fuck!"

"I know," he said, putting out his hand, "You were expecting a white plastic Paddy." He covered his mouth. "Can I say that?" he said quietly. "This is what happens," pointing at his face, "when your mom is from Trinidad, and your dad is from County Tyrone.

"Well, your mom's genes are dominant," I replied.

"Not in the pub they're not. Anyway, it doesn't matter these days. If someone overhears us, I'll have to hand this blue book over to someone else like I'm in a four by one hundred relay team."

We walked up the stairs to the locker room. I went through the incident in detail while Bobby took notes. I told him of the chaos on the day. He had been involved in similar demonstrations when he was in uniform, so he knew the score. I explained how Billy Jones wouldn't move despite me telling him several times to move away. How I used my casco in a cross-chest push. How he stumbled back and fell. How he rose like Lazarus. How I pushed him again. How he rose like Jesus but slower, stumbling away to oblivion.

"What about the officers around you? Did they say anything? Were there any other demonstrators around Jones at the time?"

"No, he didn't say anything. He was by himself at this point and stood directly in front of me, so he was my problem. He wasn't wearing the usual red top the Big Issue sellers usually wear," I said.

"That's important. You thought he was a protester?

"Not really. He wasn't the protesting type, unless you pushed in front of him in the pub."

"What I mean Jack is that you thought he could have been a protester. It was a chaotic situation. You were under constant attack. You feared for your safety. Your colleagues' safety. There was a big man in front of you not following your instructions."

"Exactly. You should have been a solicitor," I said.

"Funny that," he laughed. "I used to be one, but I was losing the will to live sitting in an office all day watching my life drain away. Just property bollocks. I've been in for twenty-two years now. Eight to go. What about yourself?"

"Under two. If I don't go down the steps, and get sacked," I said, shaking my head in disbelief at the situation.

"You'll be alright," he said.

"I'm surprised you got the job with your name. I would have thought they'd go to town researching your background."

"So, did I. But when I said I'd go on the police boxing team, I think any risk of me passing information to the IRA didn't matter. They need more black and brown people in the job so I could have turned up wearing a suicide vest and I think I would have got in. They would have just posted me to Lozells," he said laughing.

Here's a good place to say a few words about racism in the police. Following the death of Stephen Lawrence, we all went through a course about institutional racism. Whether you want to hear it or not, the worst strategy you can take when trying to make necessary reforms is to tell people they are racists when that's not how they see themselves; or how they behave in their day to day lives. Most police officers on a daily basis, especially in inner city and deprived areas, encounter people who are suffering. They are from all walks of life and ethnic backgrounds. It's difficult to be a racist, or homophobic, when you are making tea for someone who you have just told their child is dead, and they are never coming home again, and the almost infinite number of other causes of pain.

It is all too easy to focus on a single variable to explain a series of complex social issues. A mono-causal approach will almost always be flawed. There are always going to be people who hate others because of the colour of their skin. Wherever that rot is found it needs to be remedied.

If I walked down any road in Handsworth, Aston, Alum Rock, Small Heath or Balsall Heath, to name just a few areas with a high concentration of ethnic minorities, I could chat to men and women, and choose a significant number of them who would make the police a better organisation. Things had to change in many ways.

I remember my first encounter with the Old Bill when I was seventeen. Walking along Broad Street in Birmingham city centre on a summer afternoon just after 4pm. I had just left Bush House Housing Department where I was working at the time as a rent arrears clerk. I was stopped by this tall police officer who looked at me as if I had just dropped off the bottom of his big black shiny boot. They were all tall back then. That's another thing which had to change. Speaking as a 5'8" bloke, I would never have gotten past the application form. Not only were they racist and sexist, but the fuckers were heightest. And just to mention, there is more discrimination against vertically impaired people than any other group with the possible exception of Deliveroo cyclists. On average short people earn less. They hold fewer senior positions in all institutions. They are penalised in the process of sexual selection. Angela has informed me on many occasions that she settled for me based on a simple mathematical formula based on variables such as her reproduction age, and my phenotype (physical traits which includes my height). With each passing year she factored in a decrease in height of one inch. How's that for a calculated woman? If she left it any longer, she would be married to Sneezy or Dopey.

"You match the description of someone who was trying car door handles," said PC Whothefuckcares, putting his hand on my chest blocking my path.

"I've just finished work. You can check my timecard," I said, with a noticeable tone of desperation.

The officer took my details and did a PNC check on his radio. I had never been in trouble before, so the answer came back as "not known." It's what he then said which has always stayed with me.

"On your way boy!"

Dismissed. Fuck off now before I lock you up on some made up charge. A public order offence was usually the one chosen. Back then, the custody sergeant didn't ask too many probing questions. Go to the cell. Do not pass go. Do not collect

£200. Just shut the fuck up or you'll get a world of grief instead of a plastic cup of weak tea.

In some ways the police in previous times ran like a family business. Not a plumbing or an electrical firm. More along the lines of the mafia. The Chief Constable was the *capo di tutti capi* and he (always he back then) sustained his position with sycophants who were the police's equivalent of the mafia's "made men." When the Chief Constable called upon these goodfellas, they came running and salivating, like Pavlov's dogs. Loyalty was paramount. And it was all held together via the cult known as the Masons. Secret tickling handshakes, and overtones of repressed homosexuality, weird rituals, but above all a boy's club. Girls could go make the tea and do the accident books.

I recall going on a march for better pay down in London. The police by law are not allowed to strike. Coaches had been provided to take as many police officers as possible to the capital from all over England and Wales to demonstrate to the Home Secretary, and the Prime Minister, where the true seat of power really lay. We found out quickly it was with them. The wide streets were filled that day with officers marching shoulder to shoulder. No bricks or bottles were thrown. No wheelie bins were set on fire. No windows were smashed. No Big Issue sellers died.

The one thing I remember thinking when I stood on a raised platform, looking out as far as the eyes could see, was that almost everyone was a clone of each other. All big and white. Most of them were bald. It could have been a BNP march. Can you imagine for one moment being a black lad in Handsworth or Solihull (there used to be a few even decades ago), being stopped on a daily basis, and every time it's by a white person in uniform. Every officer in a police car and every pair of black boots and helmet walking toward you has a white face. Things needed to change based on that fact alone but be mindful of the old trope about the baby and the bath water.

"We'll get together again over the next few days Jack. You have my number. If I hear anything I'll call you straight away. I spoke to Gaffa Ward at PSD before coming over, and they know I'm representing you. The ball is their court for now. Of course, the IOPC is involved. Standard for an incident like this."

The IOPC is another acronym which means the Independent Office for Police Conduct. Any death resulting from police contact is automatically referred to them.

"Listen, the complaint has been made by the family, and their solicitor. An autopsy needs to be done. You used a Home Office approved technique. We can only fight the opponent in front of us. Let's see how they play it".

On that note he left. I resisted the urge to chase after him. Have you seen the movie, *Shane*? Alan Ladd played the lead role. Of course, he wore heels in every scene as he was seriously short and would never have gotten into the police! It's hard to imagine how he got on a horse. In the final scene, the young lad calls after a wounded Shane as he rides away forever: "Shane! Come back Shane! Shane!" I was that boy watching Bobby getting into the unmarked Ford Focus, and heading off, no doubt, to Starbucks.

There is an iron law of oligarchy. Whether it's a nation, or an organisation, regardless of whether it's a democracy or any variation of a votes-based system, a ruling elite will form like ice crystals on a winter's morning.

The question is what this elite will do with its power. Recall what I said earlier about stupidity being evenly distributed throughout society. No matter whether you are at a conference of Nobel Prize winners, or visiting an institute of advanced technology, or you've been kidnapped by the Flat Earth Society, people always underestimate the number of insane folks they are surrounded by. It really doesn't matter if they are quantum physicists. It doesn't matter if it's people at a dinner party hosted by Steve Pinker, where they are all discussing the books they are working on, and how people are by nature rational, how they use *modus ponens* and *Bayesian* reasoning, even without knowing it. How the world is getting better and better so cheers to the next book launch. How I hope my publisher got the email that I'm out of town next week in Costa Rica receiving some herbal treatment for my gout. There will still be insane people there. That's why experts and specialists get so many things wrong so often. They are often simply stupid. People find this hard to accept. When they hear experts talking away, it is difficult to believe that those people could be complete twits. Just listen to retired military officers pontificating on how a war could be won against a major nuclear power if we just pour in more troops and weapons: *Homo Insanus*.

The most dangerous example of *Homo Insanus* are the ones who are among the elites. It's they who cause harm to others. Most worrying of all are the ones who don't care even if they cause injury to themselves. Their behaviour is totally unpredictable. You have no way of knowing what they will do next. This is one of the ultimate causes of the collapse of empires, states, and families. When a society becomes incapable or unwilling to be on guard against *Homo Insanus* taking control of the structures of power, and even worse, when they are instrumental in them gaining power, what follows can be catastrophic. And remember that a repertoire of emergencies is the source of profits for the cast of each performance. Follow the money. I only hope that Bobby has a rescue plan for me mapped out in his blue book because the jury system has been decapitated in recent times. I cling to hope.

Truth and Consequences

Angela's dad was on the phone as soon as he found out via the local evening news that his son in law was a murderer, and it might have an impact on the value of his house.

"We need to come over," I heard him say despite Angela trying to cover the phone with her hand.

"I know dad. It's awful. Hadrian doesn't want to go to school. I don't know what I'm going to do," she said.

I looked on as she waved me away. Obviously annoyed that I was trying to listen in. I was an intruder in my own kitchen.

"Tell him about Ken," I said. "He may be able to help out. Does he know a barrister by any chance?" I couldn't help myself. Where's that fucking marshmallow!

"What did he say," said Robert. "Do you have me on loudspeaker?" He sounded annoyed.

"No dad. I don't have you on loudspeaker. He just came into the kitchen."

"Has he got a solicitor yet? He's going to need one! I knew something like this would happen Angela. Your mom said so, and I don't usually listen to your mom."

"He's spoken to a Fed Rep," said Angela with a deflated tone as if that was a signal that all was lost. Like giving up Hong Kong, Taiwan, and Scotland to the Chinese.

"He's told me they are useless. What did they say to him?"

"Tell him," I chirped in. "They said I'll be sentenced to seven years but should be out on licence after three if I don't rape or batter anyone while I'm inside."

"What did he say?" asked Robert. "Are you sure you don't have me on loudspeaker?"

"No dad. I'm beside myself with worry. I've had Sarah, Julie, Stephanie and Andrea on the phone today already. They've all been so sweet and supportive. I don't know what to say to Meme?"

"Well, she's not three yet so how about saying nothing. She won't even notice I'm gone."

"Shush! Go away," said Angela, angrily.

"We'll be over later and devise a plan. Your mom has had to take two paracetamol and go for a lie down. Her blood pressure hit the roof when she saw the family of the man. Good job they're not from around here. She couldn't go to any of her clubs."

On that note, I took one look at the set of sharpened kitchen knives, and knew it was time to leave.

I told Hadrian. Correction, we told Hadrian about my predicament. In between FIFA matches. He was upset. I caused his opponent to score, and now his world rating might drop.

"What will you do with your car?" he asked in a moment of clarity.

He has just started taking driving lessons. I drive a fifteen-year-old Peugeot 207, but considering his budget to spend on a car is zero, I suppose that's nothing to be sneezed at.

"You mean if I go to prison, and you lose contact with me, what will I do with my car?" I wanted clarification.

He looked at his mom as if to say, "Isn't that what I just asked? Is he losing his marbles as well as his freedom, his job, his wife and kids in a custody battle which will see him living in a bedsit in Redditch."

"Yeah," is all he could muster.

"Remember when we watched *The Wire*, and you occasionally see a burnt-out car on the streets of beautiful Baltimore?"

Hadrian put his headphones back on. Angela had already left his room. I closed the door behind me and left him in the virtual universe. The real world is dirtier, and full of average people who think they are above average. This is a lie they tell themselves. Especially in the western hemisphere where individual hype is the way to signal success. But a lie repeated enough can become the truth.

If I were to ask you why you believe anything in your life you could draw from many stories. For example, I pushed Billy Jones in a Home Office approved technique causing him to fall. Was it the cause? The only cause? What about if he had been drinking? Could the alcohol have made him unsteady on his feet? The autopsy will reveal any trace of alcohol in his system. I'm hoping Guiness did a good day's trade on that day.

If I dropped my casco out of my hand, it would fall to the ground. The wonder of gravity. Even a baby a few months old would find it odd if it floated upwards. Humans have an innate sense of basic cause and effect in the natural world. The blank slate hypothesis is simply wrong. Not even our morality is written upon a clean chalkboard. It is a feat of genetic magic that we can raise ourselves to the level of having any ethics and morality at all. People will be horrified to hear that! Surely, culture, religion, parents, the BBC and Al Qaeda's *Journal of Modern Bomb Making*, tell us right from wrong? Not even Greta Thunberg?

Show infants who are only a few months old two puppets, one beating the other, and invariably, given the choice, they choose the good puppet not the puppet beater. If you try this on your own child, and they select Vlad the Impaler, then you should be very concerned.

I have said previously how we tell stories about ourselves. We rationalise our choices after the fact, explain why we behaved the way we did. Always assigning a series of reasonable causes. *Homo Insanus* is obsessed with telling themselves stories of how they are a victim. Their identity becomes entwined with these types of tales, and one can find tribes to belong to who also share these same identities on-line. This is one type of truth. Not a scientific truth. We accept different criteria for science. It's not the same as saying the capital of France is Paris. We know this is true. But the capital could change. Boyle's Law never will. To say Jesus rose from the dead is a belief. Christians believe the Resurrection is true. Non-Christians think they are mistaken. Everyone tends to think what they believe is true or they wouldn't hold the belief. That's why it's so difficult to persuade people to change their minds no matter how much evidence is presented to them. Especially when the idea has been told to them throughout their lives by sources such as teachers and Tik Tok. Unfortunately, only the latter can be censored.

Often the truths we hold are for social and economic motivations. I want to get along and get ahead so I hold these truths to be self-evident once I've convinced myself that is the case. To stay in the group, I must adhere to its tenets no matter how crazy they may be. They are signals to the group of my commitment. If I actually believe these bonkers ideas, then like

Queen sang back in their heyday "We are the champions, and we'll keep on fighting till the end." You know the song. It's not much of a signal to say London is the capital city of Great Britain. It costs nothing. Also, if my job depends on believing certain ideas, then hey presto, the credo is adopted. It matters not that one is a scientist. If my grant proposals, and salary require me to adhere to a narrative, then a few appropriate nudges will cure any cognitive dissonance. An illusion of objectivity forms. If there are incentives to believe that particular things are true, then even the irrational can become rational. Not in an epistemological sense that something false actually becomes true, but in a way to explain why people behave irrationally when there is an incentive structure - whether it be bonuses in a company, or citing of a published paper or gold star stickers in a classroom. Nudges in particular directions in this structure can explain why insane ideas become adopted.

All species have what I would call a correspondence interpretation of reality. It's an innate understanding of the world outside our bone encased brain which allows us to find food, mates, form coalitions and maintain basic survival capabilities. Only humans concoct truths which go beyond this. Truth based beliefs which allow a society to function. The more complex the society, the nuttier many of these beliefs can be. They can even become self-destructive or detrimental to many people. Cults are pandemic in an age of social media more than ever.

Powerful narratives bring enormous energy to convince people to believe. When you're busy getting on with your own life, it is easy to accept what you're being told. Especially if you push back in any way, and you are labelled a conspiracy theorist, or just ignorant and should be quiet and do what you're told. Is the insane story a metaphorical hill which you are willing to die on? It's the equivalent of being in a courtroom with only one solicitor: the prosecutor.

This is what I face. When the state or group or any individual claims they have the truth and everyone else is just susceptible to false information, then tread very carefully. Watch out for the ideology behind the scenes; the confirmation bias which reaffirms and entrenches people in their foxholes of belief.

The consequences of truth can be unsettling. Pointing out that the emperor is wearing no clothes carries a huge risk. I should be astonished at how easily people are duped. I only hope I get a fair hearing. That the truth will prevail. Because I did nothing wrong. That is The Truth and nothing, but the Truth so help me Bobby.

"Come in," I said, knowing I was letting the plague through the city gates. I beat Angela to the door. It was a shallow demonstration of defiance.

"Hi mom. Hi dad," said Angela, kissing her stern-faced mother on her cheek. Robert walked straight past both of us into the lounge.

"Coffee?" I asked.

"No thank you," said Marie like she was giving a pre-prepared statement.

"So, what's happening exactly?" asked Robert. "This is quite a serious matter!"

"Yes, it is," I said, trying to remain calm. Robert was acting in the capacity of a political spin doctor brought in to limit the damage of yet another sexual assault by a Tory MP, or an anti-Semitic comment by a Labour backbencher criticising Israel's security forces for shooting yet another Palestinian child in the back. The Labour leader is beside themselves as usual. I mean what part of shut the fuck up don't they understand. Just say your two-pence worth about climate change, and the evils of fossil fuels, and uranium and coal and gas and nitrogen and animal flatulence and stay in your lane and avoid any significant issue where you may have to take a principled stand based on reading the evidence, and not a diluted synopsis presented by the media.

"Bobby…"

"Who's Bobby?" interrupted Robert.

"He's Jack's Federation representative," said Angela. She sat down beside her mom on the couch. Marie took hold of

Angela's hand. I became nauseous suddenly. This is what Jean-Paul Satre was trying to explain back in the 1950s. A sickening sense of entrapment. But one is free to choose one's own path. To break the chains of whatever enslaves you. Have you seen the footage of the Selma March in Alabama? Have you listened to the speeches of James Baldwin? The songs of Nina Simone? Do you know about the bombing of churches and houses in the segregated south? Kids buried under rubble. How about bombs in Birmingham? Right here in our own rejuvenated city? More bodies amidst the masonry. Our cities are twinned in blood. Forget the pretty flower shows and Christmas markets.

Hadrian paid us all an unexpected visit. All the way down from his bedroom. Shackleton and Ranulph Fiennes would have been impressed. He had a smile on his face which was worrying. Robert appeared even more annoyed if that was possible.

"Introducing the one and only Meme," said Hadrian, clapping and nodding to his sister who was standing in the hallway. She was either a reluctant participant, or she was unimpressed with the reception. Angela started to clap along. Marie joined in half-heartedly torn between her genetic self-interest, and her marriage obligation.

Meme appeared from behind the door with her right index finger in her mouth. Not usually shy, I was quite interested in what she was about to do but suspecting that if Hadrian had anything to do with it then I was going to pay for it.

"Daddy's going to jail. Daddy's going to jail," she sang, followed by a forward roll. Jumping to her feet, and swinging her hips from side to side, she sang again what was quite a catchy phrase: "Daddy's going to jail. Daddy's going to jail."

Hadrian looked on with the pride of a professional choreographer. Robert looked at Angela who was clapping with enthusiasm. Even Marie had a big smile on her face. I forced a smile, and I must say the forward roll was a nice touch.

"Tea for anyone?" I asked.

Do you want some advice about having children? Those of you who don't have any, but are thinking about how cute babies look, and maybe you want a few for yourself. Those big eyes staring out from an oversized head, chubby cheeks and a button sized nose. Kind of like most baby pets. No one thinks that about a cockroach or a new born from Bolton. You are being manipulated from day one to keep your genes alive. If you want to optimise your chances of happiness, then the number of children you should have is zero. If one puts aside the cost of maintaining them (which is itself debilitating) kids drive parents to become neurotic, anxiety ridden shadows of their former selves.

It is the very fear and anxiety that harm may come to them which drives us to protect them at any cost. That said, if I see another performance by my own daughter with my smiling assassin of a son watching proudly on, then genes or no genes, I cannot guarantee that Angela will ever have grandchildren.

The American Dream

We all chase the American dream now. It's not just the Yanks. Even the North Koreans would happily run after it if baby-faced Kim didn't spend all their cash on nukes.

F Scott FitzGerald died of a heart attack before the great American classic (arguably *The* American classic) ever made a dime. It was only because a quarter of a million copies of *The Great Gatsby* were shipped over to American GI's fighting the Germans that the short novel became a bestseller.

GI's became professors and teachers on the GI Bill after the war, and never forgot the impact the book had upon them. It became a classic in the 1950s. No other book demonstrates the dream more accurately. However, writing in the French Riviera with his Flapper wife Zelda in the 1920s, it highlighted the contradiction between the Yankee dream, and his own life. Zelda, like Angela, was having her own fling under his nose. Someone a little more exotic than Ken. Meanwhile, FitzGerald was drinking himself to an early grave. Hardly the dream life.

When you contrast *The Great Gatsby* with John Steinbeck's *The Grapes of Wrath* you discover the dust bowl is the real American story. To struggle in the face of real adversity. Live on your knees or die standing. Fighting. I grew up watching

American movies. Buying into Hollywood's portrayal of the American ideal life. I was in love with it. I watched *The Quiet Man* with my mom. Looking at John Wayne drag Maureen O Hara across fields to get the dowry she so much values as being hers (a symbol of the transfer of ownership) from her angry, hard brother played by Victor McLaglen. White putrid patriarchy in action again, and domestic abuse thrown in for good measure. Of course, there's going to be a fight. Possibly the best fight scene in all Hollywood movie history. Better than Rocky and Apollo Creed. What was Wayne thinking when he made that Genghis Khan movie? Okay, maybe we can forgive him for *The Green Berets* where he gets to kill gazillions of Viet Cong, or *The Searchers* where he shoots a few rounds at the troublesome Indians causing them to demonstrate extraordinary acrobatics falling from their horses. After all, they had kidnapped a very young Natalie Wood. Wasn't she worth the sacrifice of a few dozen native Americans? Millions of the indigenous community have been murdered and displaced for far less. Even if naughty Nat did end up mysteriously falling off a boat when her hubby, Robert Wagner, had his back turned. Accidents do happen. That's part of my defence if you've been paying attention.

My mom and I watched all the old black and white movies on Saturday afternoons. Abbott and Costello, Laurel and Hardy, Clark Gable, Cary Grant (my mom's favourite) Hepburn,

Bogart, and Bergman. The list is endless. My dad, meanwhile, was propping up the local bars in the Digbeth pubs. Making sure the economy kept progressing. You see, he had his own dream. Not the American version, but a more disturbed, fragmented one.

My father would tell us his dream after consuming a double-digit number of pints when he stumbled in around five in the evening. My two older brothers and I would be forced to digest the dream of the IRA defeating the bastard British army, and then, and only then mind you, could we all return to the land of South Armagh. Like the Jews escaping Babylon and returning to the land which they were given by God himself. A united Ireland with no British landlords.

When we were young, we would listen to this tale, and the history of Irish suffering: the Plantations, Cromwell, the Potato Famine, all of which caused millions of deaths, and millions more to flee abroad. It was a long trail of tears like the Creeks, Navajo, Cherokee, and many more besides. Have you read *Black Elk Speaks*? Say yes even if it's just to appease me.

Black Elk was a member of the Lakota Sioux tribe. He fought at the Battle of Little Bighorn against Custor and survived the massacre at Wounded Knee in 1890. He was a *heyoka* of the Oglala Lakota people, a holy man, and he became involved in what was called the Ghost Dance. The dance symbolised the end of the white man's domination, the return of the buffalo herds, and a return to the old way of life before the white man came and took over, and forced them off their ancestral lands, destroying them in the process.

The so-called Columbian exchange from 1492 onwards killed three out of every four native people through diseases such as smallpox, measles, and typhoid. Pathogens have engaged in a cat and mouse game with our immune system since early farming days. No amount of lockdowns, and gormless politicians are going to prevent the race. Especially when Pfizer and friends are funding their holiday homes and private jets while being profoundly influenced by the impending climate catastrophe. Can somebody pass me a bucket! O grow up for fucks sake. Can't you see the alliances. Between the military corporations dominating foreign policy, pharmaceutical companies who fund and control the galaxy, Wall Street and the City of London who hold the remote control to the financial decisions made by governments, and the media who mirror Orwell's *Ministry of Information*. What could go wrong? Apart from...well, **EVERYTHING**.

My dad thought of himself as Ireland's version of Black Elk. In reality of course, he was the furthest thing from it. To begin with he had no headdress. He didn't even wear a woolly hat in the winter on the building site. He had never fought the white man except for the occasional fight in the Rainbow Pub, but that was usually with another Irishman who had a different version of the same story. Remember there are only half a dozen plots to choose from. And my dad couldn't dance to save his life.

I was determined not to follow in his footsteps. Remember my map. Philip Larkin was right when he wrote that parents "fuck you up." Especially today. What's left for young people to rebel against. Their parents have done all the drugs. They have tattoos and piercings. They have smoked and drank and partied like it's 1999. They have had more underaged sex than Garry Glitter. They have rebelled more than the Irish nation. They have demonstrated against the most compelling injustices and in many cases won. What is left for young people today to fight for or against? No wonder insanity has taken root.

I recall one early morning in winter when I was sixteen. There was snow on the path outside our little terraced council house. It must have been around 6.30 in the morning, and my dad was going off to work. I had cleared a patch of snow and I was busy skipping. A woolly hat on my head. My cold breath hung in the air with every rotation of the rope. My dad gave me a wide berth to ensure he wasn't whipped. I'll never forget the glance. Not a word was exchanged. Just a look. I bet he wished there were DNA kits back then.

In the late Middle Ages, Portuguese nobility, having forced out the Moors who had ruled the land for the previous several centuries, divided up their estates equally between their sons. Even their daughters, like Maureen O'Hara, received a dowry. However, as the years passed, the amount of land became divided further and further, and became less economically viable.

The same problem happened elsewhere in Europe. They soon changed their inheritance system to one we call primogeniture: the eldest son inherited everything. It made sense. However, if one had other sons, they usually caused a lot of trouble. Sometimes, due to the high mortality rate, the eldest son died so it was good to have a spare one available. That's where the term "heir and spare" comes from. Third sons like me were a troublesome liability. The Portuguese solved this problem by sending them around the world on ships. The Age of Exploration began.

My brothers, Michael, and Eamon, were four and five years older than me, respectively. I was born in September. When I do the number crunching, and refer to the calendar, I suspect I was the result of an unexpected and unwanted (and any other 'un' you can think of) drunken Christmas shag. I was four years behind the curve.

I knew I had to set out on my own voyage of exploration, and maybe a little of my own gene-based Irish rebellion, when I completed the application form to join the police. My dad was dead and buried by then in Brandwood Cemetery in Kings Heath so there was no threat of being knee capped. I never expected to get into the police. I suppose that took away any pressure or minimised it at any rate.

I won't bore you with all the tests and scenarios I was put through back then. It was quite the process. I do recall the final interview. I was waiting in a small reception area with another bloke and a female candidate. I was the last one to be interviewed. The other bloke was an ex-SAS soldier who really didn't give a fuck. He was half asleep when he was called in. I became good friends with him, and we joined the same nick after finishing our training at Ryton Training College.

I sat down on a wooden straight back chair in the middle of a room. There were three senior officers, and a female Federation representative. She asked me if I knew what she did in the police. I didn't have a clue. I had just met her. I replied something along the lines that I'd be happy to follow her around for the day to find out. I'm surprised they didn't tell me to piss off there and then!

One of the chief superintendents asked me: "If the shift were going to see a Bernard Manning concert would I go along?"

Bernard Manning was one of the best-known comedians in Britain back in the 70s. Nothing and no-one were off limits. Of course, I knew the right answer: "Absolutely not!" Fortunately, the scenario was never put to the test. I received the acceptance letter and headed off to Ryton-on-Dunsmore.

Don't Stop Me Now, I'm Having Such a Good Time

You've heard of Newton's Third Law? Every force has an equal and opposite reaction. Stay with me. The force creates the reaction which opposes it. The anti-capitalist demonstration that day was created from capitalism itself. The crowd hurling missiles at us, and smashing the symbols of the free market, are in the process of inheriting more wealth than any generation before them. For some of the demonstrators, there's an underlying guilt associated with that transfer. Now it could easily be remedied by them all giving up their inheritance. Give it all to charity. Transfer it to those that have not, and not to those who have. For once in human history revolt against St Mark's truthful observation that to those that have more shall be given. That will rarely ever happen.

The financial tyrants at the heart of power pulled a blinder back in 2008 following the global tearjerker when they discovered they could go from zero to hero overnight by taking knees, apologising for everything, superficially supporting climate change in Davos, and every historical oppression known to any group, at any time and any place.

Virtue signalling became more important than virtue itself. Despite the obvious facade it worked beautifully. Power and profit recognise no national border. It's truly globalist in nature. These protestors, and people in general, really are victims. They are victims of allowing corporations, and other institutions of power, to set the moral code for them. Businesses should be about making money within the boundaries of the law. They should be regulated because corporations cannot help themselves from exploiting everything. They are crack addicts with a pipe. They will all overdose if left to their own devices. Unlike the crack addict, however, many of them turn to the state for a bailout. Meaning the taxpayer. They have figured out the gullibility of people who believe the mantras which are chanted and promoted at Davos. Same with COP conferences. What a farce! Bought and paid for by the richest in the world who leave a footprint larger than an elephant. They look down at those minions with millions or just hundreds of thousands of pounds who feel guilt (although they will call it moral outrage), and who express it through blocking roads and crying on Tik Tok, and yet they are oblivious to the debris they leave everywhere they go. It is another race to the bottom of an ideological cesspit.

You see what people in the wealthier classes of the west really need is struggle. They long for hardship from which their privileged lives exempt them. Your phone battery being flat does not count. Not even if you're out of the house. Have you seen Brad Pitt in *Fight Club*? Have you ever watched *SAS Who Dares Wins*? How about *I'm a Celebrity Get Me Out of Here*? People long to be tested. They want adversity. To see how they could cope with something more challenging than a lukewarm latte.

Where is Bobby when you need him? I've been calling him all morning from the airport.

I'm on an early shift.

"Sorry mate, I have been busy like you wouldn't believe. Several officers are facing disciplinary action at the minute," said Bobby when he eventually called me back.

"That's okay," I replied, trying not to sound abandoned. I've already been labelled with the mark of Cain. Ostracised.

"Your interview with professional standards is tomorrow morning," said Bobby.

"What?"

"Have you checked your emails? I received one saying it's tomorrow at ten at Lloyd House. From a DS Bridgeman. I don't know him. Do you?

"No. Never heard of him. Short notice, isn't it?" I said.

"It's not like we have a case to build or anything. Your version of events. That's basically it," said Bobby. "Not good news about the Evening Mail."

"What do you mean?" I asked.

"O right," he said thinking I knew. "There's a two-page spread in today's edition under the heading: 'Big Billy's Family Demand Justice.' The Evening Mail hates the police. They never miss an opportunity to put the boot in."

"Great!"

"There are photos of the whole family on Cherry Street beside the memorial of flowers that have been left. I'll bring it along tomorrow if you want?"

"I'd rather you brought anthrax in an envelope. I'll pass."

"Yeah, I don't blame you. Keep the stress levels down before the interview. Listen, I've got to head off to Perry Barr. I'll see you tomorrow around 9.30 in the reception of Lloyd House and we'll go over stuff. It'll be fine. Don't worry."

Whenever anyone tells you not to worry, that's when you really should worry. I can take a few defensive positions. I could go for "Shaggy's defence." You know the rapper?

"Did you kill Mr Jones?"

"It wasn't me!"

"Did you strike Mr Jones with your casco resulting in his death?"

"It wasn't me!"

"Did you create the universe in which Mr Jones died?"

"It wasn't me!"

I could opt for the four-year old's defence strategy of "I didn't mean to do it." Or I could point out that I have built up a lot of good marks over the years. I've done a lot of good. Can I use some of my credit to erase this blemish? Not to be cast into the outer darkness. I'm not going to say it was a pre-emptive strike to preserve national security. I would sound like a US spokesperson for the Pentagon. I have been called evil, and one article used the well-worn label of "Nazi" to describe the nature of the incident. Words matter. Associations matter. How an issue is framed matters. *Homo Insanus* is easily manipulated. We are always chasing emotions. To make ourselves feel good.

I've been at Birmingham Airport for over a month now. Inspector Campbell called me into his office and told me I was moving. "Temporarily," he said. Until the matter was resolved one way or another. It was the "another" bit which bothered me. "Keep me out of the way," he said. Away from the scene of the incident. He almost said "crime" but managed to correct himself at the last second. He knew the Gaffa at the airport, an Inspector Edwards, who was doing him a favour. They were short staffed due to sickness so it would help him out. He was a nice bloke, and he was aware of what was going on. I was starting the next day so pack my things, clear out my locker, and fuck off. Shift starts at seven but be there at 6.30. Park by the side of the station, and they will issue you with a car park pass. That was it.

Where did it all go wrong? How did two men called Ken and Billy enter my life like two horsemen of the apocalypse? Where was famine and disease? I need to listen out for the sound of eight more horseshoes. I need to stop giving a fuck.

Let me tell you something about the art of not caring. It can carry you a long way. It requires a push to get started, but once inertia kicks in, and if it's genuine, you can soar like Icarus. But as any glider pilot will tell you, the currents only last so long before you head downwards. That's what happened before I became a big city detective.

When Inspector Phillips walked into our SAT's office, and told us he was disbanding us, and we were going back in uniform, and going to walk up and down Broad Street with all its nightclubs and drunks, its vomit, and testosterone looking for a spot to dump itself upon, going to work till four in the morning and help the city cleaners to pick up the rubbish, only ours would be the human variety. How we would refresh our skills in arresting drunks and every breach of the Public Order Act from pissing in the street to those doing the monkey dance just before the punches were thrown (and that's both boys and girls) that we would no longer be like the characters from *The Shield* (I did tell Wayne not to put the fucking poster on the wall. That it would piss Phillips off, but that just made him nail it to the wall directly opposite the door so it was the first thing anyone saw when they entered) and that we would look like those Bobbies on one of the mindless tv documentaries wrestling a loud-mouthed idiot to the ground and looking shit in the process. Phillips cracked a Stalinesque smile at the fact that revenge is a dish best served cold.

At the time, I was part of a four-man crew called a Section Action Team. Wayne, Paul, and Sean were the other three members. No musical instruments. No uniforms - and using unmarked cars - we were given free rein to go out and get results. Get those crime reports detected. Just so the higher echelon could look good on the day of judgement. We did. Using our own informants (which was a risky business and would get you in a heap of trouble if it went wrong), we carried out successful drug operations, broke up and arrested vehicle gangs, and were used by other teams to assist in any operations they had set up. It was a great job. We knew it had to come to an end. We were always mindful to be respectful to the real workers: the officers in uniform on the shift working nights. It also includes Bobbies who carry the most workload and run the greatest risk of heart attack. Not those you see on television investigating murders like Columbo or Sherlock, or with a gun strapped to their hip thinking they are Andy McNab out of *Bravo Two Zero* or Gary Cooper in *High Noon*, or best of all Doris Day in *Calamity Jane*. It's people in roles like the Public Protection Unit. They deal with all the domestic abuse cases, and other types of safeguarding jobs. If they make a mistake, skip one of the numerous box ticking exercises, or fail to act in a timely process, the consequences can end in tragedy. It's a level of stress I couldn't cope with.

A few weeks before we were disbanded, Phillips had demanded we go out and arrest a local criminal for a spate of recent vehicle thefts. The fact he didn't look anything like any of the vehicle offenders was beside the point. We told him politely to fuck off, and close the door behind him. He was another useless, over-promoted fool who has laid siege to the police these days, but unlike your run of the mill kidnappers, these lot don't ask for a ransom as you pay their inflated wages, and there's certainly no negotiating with them: my way or the highway. Have you read Alan Bloom's *Closing of the American Mind*?

The police closed its mind - or should I say lost it - when it closed all the police stations, and sold them off to developers; when it closed the door on old school ways to deal with problems, and replaced them with on-line crime reporting, an insane over reliance on PCSOs, and half a "police service" - I feel in a generous mood - who think they have just got *a* job. They do not behave like they have *THE* Job. Literally one to die for as some have. To bleed for as most did, and who didn't take months off work afterwards. And as for medical pensions given to charlatans who claim stress over next to nothing, and spend a year or more off sick complaining how they are oppressed, about how they hate the job, but when they get their big, enhanced payday, they spend the rest of their lives calling themselves "retired police officers." There have always been lazy fuckers looking for the easy life and full pay. Those who have always been at the back when it goes off, allowing others to carry their share, always taking the path of least resistance. Hoping they won't be seen that their avoidance to do any work will go unnoticed.

There are two types of police officer: those who produce and consume; and those who just consume. The consumers in the police are takers. They wear the uniform. That's all they do. Many of them don't even do that. They hang on like an ageing movie actor. They consume more time and energy trying to do as little as possible. One must be vigilant because where they go, they bring pathogens with them. They can spread like a SARS virus.

The producers are the ones who keep the wheels on. They are not stupid. They know how to grab a little time here and there, and to take advantage of a downhill gradient when they see one. You've heard of flogging a willing horse? These horses become an ever-decreasing minority. Keep watching, and you'll start to see the foundations crumble. This is what happens when you tell officers who are the backbone of your crime clearances to put on their top hats and walk the catwalk of nightclub central. They say thank you, but you can fuck right off.

We have worn that t-shirt for years, and it stinks now. Time to fly the nest. Time to apply elsewhere. In my case, time to put on a suit, grab one of those blue books and become a big city homicide detective. Time to say goodbye to the police rat race.

Murder and Theodora's Vagina

"I'm leaving you. Well, I want you to leave," said Angela, sniffing into a tissue, peering over it, willing a tear to form, and to fall down her cheek, but not quite able to achieve it. The sniffing and almost comical attempt at sobbing would have to do. And I hope you spotted the switch? It's fairly obvious. Me leaving? Really? Come the fuck on!

"Shall I pack now, or can I have my dinner?" I had only just got home from twelve hours walking around a terminal directing people to toilets and the exit because there is something about getting on and off aircrafts which turns everyone into idiots. It's like that worst movie ever made with Tom Hanks trapped in an airport, speaking with the most ridiculous accent. Where was his acting coach? I mean who read that script and thought this would be great. Get Tom on the phone. He knows how to do accents. Didn't you see him in *Forrest Gump*? Don't you remember one of the most classic lines in all of Hollywood history: "Life is like a box of chocolates, you never know what you're gonna get." You can hear the accent now, can't you? What were you thinking Tom? Seriously. Actors are like military corporations: where there's money to be made it doesn't matter a toss how much harm is caused to others.

"I'm serious Jack. I don't think we can carry on now, living like this now that you know about Ken." More sniffs.

We were in the kitchen. I was reaching into the freezer to get a few pieces of frozen fish from Aldi, and a handful of their spicy wedges. I only eat biscuits at work. GoAhead apple and raisin slices with a cup of tea in the afternoon. Old habits. I've never been a big eater at work in case of foot chases and fights. I make up for it in the evenings by forever grazing like a bastard sheep, except instead of grass, I chew sugar.

"You mean Ken who is in the past? The two months only Ken who you text to say you were never going to see him. That Ken?" I was putting my dinner on an oven tray, purposely not looking at her.

"It's not that cut and dry," she said. "You always want black and white. Well life isn't like that Jack. Not for other people. Not for me."

She was trying to cry, but it sounded like she was suppressing a giggle like a child in a classroom who had just been told a joke, and the teacher was staring at them wondering what's going on, why aren't you enthralled by my teaching? My information bases. Have you actually seen through the facade of my chauffeur knowledge? Realised that I know next to fuck all? That I've just spent three years in university, and a handful of months on a teacher training programme learning how to teach the straitjacket we call the National Curriculum, and in reality you can be a complete dimwit, and end up at the front of a class? That everyone will clap for you like the NHS, like the fire and police service, but unlike the police, you actually have a union which has teeth, and not just gums, and it's militant, and you are ready to walk out at the drop of a piece of chalk, and any sane people in society - and they are as rare as a fucking snow leopard in Mecca - would want you to haul yourselves out on strike if they deducted a day from your four months paid leave each year, because that might actually improve the educational standards of the youth of today. If you all fucked off for a few more weeks, maybe we could bridge the gap a little with Singapore, China, even New Zealand, and they are as thick as fuck. Do you get my point?

"What part is not exactly black and white Angela? I asked. "You did text Ken and tell him it was over, didn't you?

"It's not about Ken. It's about us Jack. We live separate lives and have done for years. If you're not at work, you're at the gym." The sniffs had stopped now. Angela can't sniff and sob and be righteously angry at the same time. Apparently, it's not only blokes who can't do two things at once.

"What do you mean the gym?"

I was a little defensive. I can only deal with one accusation at a time. Has she forgotten about Billy Jones? Does she see an opportunity to launch an offensive? A window of opportunity. Even Hitler and Stalin had a pact. No wonder Stalin felt betrayed. He had feelings despite the Katyn Forest massacre, despite the Gulags and Solzhenitzyn, regardless of the Kulaks and famine, and the show trials and a million executions. Look what happened to Trotsky and he was just chilling out in Mexico! People are sensitive to betrayal. It is built into us like fear, disgust, a fear of heights and an aversion to cold callers at teatime.

We had children. Have children. Present tense. Okay, we rarely spot Hadrian these days. He is like an endangered species. He is responding like everyone to Pavlovian conditioning to a screen. Meme is here, however. She was singing about my imminent incarceration recently and doing gambols like Martin Shaw and Lewis Collins in *The Professionals*. Remember that show. The great Gordan Jackson, allowed upstairs for once, playing the hardnosed Cowley, telling Bodie and Doyle to go out and kill the bad guys and to keep Britain safe.

Okay, yes, Britain's empire had collapsed as all empires do. Always one war too many. Always one invasion too far. Always more minerals and energy resources needed just to keep running in place, and we are back to Lewis Carroll's Red Queen. Always the same problems, and inevitably a leader not up to the task tips over the first domino, and all the others cascade down so quickly that no one sees it coming. Not the chin scratching class who dominate the narrative. Mark Twain was wrong you see. He thought that history does not repeat itself, that it only rhymes. Oswald Spengler thought the same. Most academic historians today don't even think about such issues and spend their time on minutiae not fit to line a bin. Oh yes, they do! Oh no they're not, you say. O yes, they do, I reply. We have a pantomime on our hands, and this is what it all comes down to: a pantomime. The history of empires does repeat. They fall and break apart like Humpty Dumpty. No way to put them back together again.

Recall what happened to Alexander the Great when he reached Bactria? His generals told him enough is enough. Not one step further. And I'll point out that Alexander was only five feet tall. A midget by today's standards. What chance would he have in the modern world? Zero. Have you heard of the Qin Empire? How about Mauryan? One of the largest in history. Only dust remains. America's empire will be the next to go. When and how is open for debate but it will collapse like all the others. One conflict too many. One proxy war too many. One "invasion" too many. One or more groups will be bullied to a point that causes them to join forces. Form alliances. They would rather die standing than crawl on their bellies. And all the western think tanks on the Beltway will scratch their chins and ask? "Don't they know we have fuck off thermonuclear weapons on land, air and sea? Don't they watch our paid retired mouthpieces on CNN and elsewhere? Don't they know when they are beaten? Don't they know that we are the epitome of *Homo Insanus*, and that we are willing to let tens of millions of our own citizens die for God, Glory, and especially Gold. Do they think that Triple G is only a boxer? Do they know nothing about the scramble for Africa, and every other piece of real estate we have got our corporate hands on? Don't they realise we are willing to scramble any nation, group or species which opposes us like three bastard eggs in an omelette? What planet do these infidels live on? Believe in our way or it's literally no way! We delivered the script to you now read the fucker or else."

"Come on Jack. If it's not work, you have to train. We are the last on your list."

"I'm at the gym or running for a couple of hours at the most. Is that it? Is that the extent of my domestic abuse? Gym and work. I should point out that it's that last part that pays for everything."

Tolstoy wrote that all happy families resemble one another, but each unhappy family is fucked up in its own particular way. Where do you think Larkin got his line from?

"Throw that in my face again, why don't you? I said I'd go back to work after Meme was born." Angela's voice was raised now. Her canines were on display.

"Go back? But you've never had a job. Knowle's fish and chip shop when you were sixteen doesn't count. And you said it yourself, you quit after half an hour because the owner got fed up with you not being able to fold the paper properly."

There's that thing called TRUTH again. Not the "post truth" version, or the relative to each and everyone's own interpretation garden variety. Not the Stalinesque airbrushed version where key pieces mysteriously vanish as new narratives emerge, and a new version is refashioned. Not the reshaping of memory where false memories is implanted by people who have never read the work of Elizabeth Loftus. All memory is constructed, not retrieved.

"Well, he shouted at me. And it was only a portion of chips that fell on the floor. No fish. Everyone needs time to learn new skills."

"Are you still seeing this Ken fella? Tell me the truth." I almost choked on the last word. Dishonesty is highly underrated.

"I haven't seen him this week. I spoke to him and explained that you found out. I don't know what's going to happen. Maybe it's just a steppingstone. I'm not sure. But he's kind and attentive. I want to be seen, Jack."

"I can see you. You're right in front of me."

"No. That's where you're wrong. I'm invisible. I need to be really seen!"

"I get it. This Ken has double vision, and he can really see you, but I apparently need a Labrador or a spectroscope?"

I can't kill two men in the same year. I'll be compared to Ted Bundy and Tony Blair.

"Tell me about Ken." I tried to sound calm and friendly. Like I was asking her to tell me about a new friend she had met when she was a child at school. Or if she really did have a job, and I was showing interest in her new boss. Isn't that what husbands and wives do? Maybe not in a Woody Allen movie. Diane Keaton is invariably shagging anything that moves. Even the pet cat has packed up and fucked off.

"It's not about Ken. I've told you that. It's us."

"I've heard you, but you can understand my curiosity. You're asking me to leave our house after all. And where do you think I should go? They've shut all the police canteens so I can't kip on the floor."

"Don't be silly. What about your brother's house till you get a place?"

Remember it's women who have made men stupid. We do dumb things: high risk-taking behaviour - even killing each other - especially between the ages of 18-35. It's like a holiday to Ibiza but with a serious risk of not coming home. We compete to procreate. Historically, women selected the winners. Look back through your ancestry and you'll discover many more females than males. How can that be given that it takes two to tango? The biggest risk-taking males got to dance with many more females and fathered more children; that explains the asymmetry.

Can you think of some famous couples in history? Take a few seconds. Anthony and Cleopatra? How about Adam and Eve? Even better. What about Abelard and Heloise? Thelma and Louise? Justinian and Theodora in 6th century Constantinople? The Emperor and Empress of the Byzantine Empire. Another empire which would eventually crumble.

Theodora was the real power behind that throne. Rumour had it her sex drive would overtake a Tesla without the need for tax breaks. I don't think she ever worked in a fish and chip shop, but she tried her hand, and every other limb, in the oldest of professions: prostitution. On one occasion, it is reported, she slept with all the guests at a dinner party, and when they were exhausted, she moved on to the servants. She complained to God that he had only provided her with three orifices. It is odd the things which cross your mind when your wife is asking you to leave your house and you haven't even had your tea.

"I'm not going anywhere Angela! Have you forgotten the predicament I'm in? I mean your timing is a little selfish, don't you think? Not to throw fuel on the flames. Energy is expensive enough as it is. And there's only so much you can blame the Russians for."

"So, you're not going? How can we live like this?"

Angela had never listened to Youth Brigade's 1998 album *Out of Print*. They sang of being sick of living with all the bitterness and hate in their classic "How Can We Live Like This." Heavy drums and an electric guitar on LSD. To be perfectly honest, they can't sing worth shit, and it's difficult to listen to the entire song. Angela missed a trick in not having Spotify at the ready to make her point. It's much easier to find titles like "How Can I Live Without You." But without me, I know for certain, Angela would thrive like bacteria in a petri dish without penicillin.

When I think back to the early years with Angela, I wonder how we got to where we are now? Keep in mind Elizabeth Loftus who would cross examine my recollections like a female version of Rumpole of the Bailey, or that ruthless champion of all victims, Gloria Allred.

Talking of Gloria, if only I could bring her to my interrogation tomorrow. That woman would cause lightning to strike in that interview room followed by the rumble of thunder. I must make a slightly trivial, but annoying, musical observation about Fleetwood Mac's song *Dreams*: can someone tell Stevie that thunder does not only happen when it's raining! It only happens when there's lightning. Did she never take a science class? Was she educated in the UK?

I could see a rift valley opening between Angela and I when Hadrian was born. I look at him now and think, was he worth it? It's a close call. The jury is still out.

Before Hadrian, Angela and I used to go on holiday together. Strange to think about those days now while I eat my burnt fish and chips. I left them in the oven too long while we crisscrossed the same piece of ground like Benny Hill in the bygone era when we used to have a sense of humour.

Angela had tactically withdrawn like Rommel at El Alamein. I remember when I surprised her once with a trip to Paris. I didn't tell her where we were going, only that she should pack a case for three nights and bring her passport. I should have known then that troubled waters lay ahead. She looked disappointed when I told her she didn't need a bikini or sunscreen. We went to Portugal, Spain, Poland, and the Czech Republic before Hadrian slipped out like a fridge in the Gulf Stream. He was a big baby. We used to hold hands like a real couple. Her dad's suspicions that I would ruin his daughter's future were far from realised. One might argue that they were foiled given a cursory glance at our relationship. However, his suspicions made a dreadful comeback like the Sex Pistols and Led Zeppelin. Why can't these groups just let it go? Have they never watched *Frozen*? Don't they see that the snow glows white on the mountain? Did they not hear Idina sing "Let it go?" That she can't hold it back anymore. That she doesn't give a flying-go-fuck-yourself care in the world now, and the cold doesn't bother her anymore. Take a leaf, please!

There's a lesson for us all in *Frozen.* Sometimes you've just got to let go. Whatever *it* is. A job. An argument? Even a marriage. But Angela has another thing coming if she thinks I'm moving into the local Travelodge. That's where Idina and I part ways. I hate the cold.

Recall what I said earlier about how not caring can help you get ahead. It can relieve pressure. Getting the job on the MIU was another such example. I didn't know how it would turn out. I should have realised the long hours involved, but I was more focused on avoiding late nights in the club arena. I had no CID experience. It was almost unheard of back then to get on a murder unit without already being a detective. I received an email with an interview date. Like the one I got from PSD but without the threat of being sacked and going to prison.

The interview took place at police headquarters in the city.

"Tell us how you cope with stress?" asked Detective Inspector Sarah Cooke. She was flanked either side by two male detective superintendents who though they outranked her, were nevertheless, subordinates in every other way.

She was serious but managed to combine femininity and ferocity like Holly Holm in the UFC. I've seen colleagues who were close to retirement reach for the telephone when they heard the clickety-click of her heels coming down the corridor, pretending they were on the brink of solving a case like who killed Patrice Lumumba. The CIA and the French for fuck's sake. It can't all be blamed on the Belgians.

DI Cooke ran team seven out of Canterbury Road Police Station in Perry Barr. *The Magnificent Seven.* In reality, it was more like S Club Seven. There was no Yul Brynner's riding shotgun in an unmarked Ford Focus. Certainly, no Steve McQueen's (who always looked a little lost without his motorcycle) running the murder room. No Charles Bronson protecting the local kids from the evil Burger Bar Gang and Johnson Crew. And definitely no Eli Wallach as an exhibits officer. We had a lazy cunt called Steve who was forever throwing a hissy fit if you used capital letters on an exhibit bag. I did it on purpose just to see him go crying to the boss: "He's done it again Ma'am. I've asked him not to use capitals, and look, look at this, he's used ALL capitals. I've had enough. I'm leaving unless you cut his cock off and feed it to the station cat."

There were so many station cats to choose from she would be spoiled for choice.

"I punch people and try to get them to tap out while my arm is around their throat. And I listen to Glen Gould play Bach's *The Goldberg Variations* every night in bed. If for no other reason than it gets my wife Angela to sleep in the spare room."

You had to look very carefully, or you would have missed it. Think of da Vinci's *Mona Lisa* with that slightly wry smile. The Boss - and she and not old Bruce was THE BOSS - smiled. I knew at that point I got the job. Other questions such as "How would I preserve a scene blah blah?" Or "Tell us about disclosure procedures?" Or "How can you shop, play a round of golf, have a few beers, and most importantly, fill in your overtime card?" These were mere formalities. I left Lloyd House thinking no Broad Street for me Phillips. Get your next pip on the back of others. I'm off to solve big city murders. Like Kojak. Like McCloud. Like Cormorant Strike.

Unlike Strike, however, there were no one legged anti-heroes, and certainly no Holliday Grainger's. More a case of a weight watchers group addicted to Pukka pies. "I relapsed last night. I ate seven with a whole bag of curly fries. Then I thought, "O what's the point, I might as well tuck into the tub of Ben and Jerry's chocolate fudge." How about some vegetables you fat fuckers? And I don't mean the variety who work in the fire service. They have no nutritional value, and are either asleep, working out, watching movies, or fitting smoke alarms. At least a brussels sprout makes you pass wind. And that's the only positive thing I've got to say about Brussels. How can such a tiny fucking country drag us into the Great War over a half-baked treaty made almost a hundred years earlier (therefore leading to the rise of Hitler and the Holocaust), and be responsible murdering over six million Congolese people, and manage to have one of the best national football teams in Europe is another universal mystery still to be solved.

I'll mention one incident on my first day as it set the tone for what would follow. Another cause in the self-created narrative chain of why I am where I am. The team had a getting to know you session in the basement room where all the briefings took place. A chance for the newbies to prostrate themselves. There were a few other folks who landed at the same time as me. A man named Kevin, and a woman called Marsha. We had to introduce ourselves, and convince the tribe, we were going to be loyal, and that we were in some conceivable way a benefit to the group. That we were not covert predators. And remember, it's all about predators and prey. No organism on the planet escapes the risk-reward mechanism. Stay at home and be safe, and eventually you'll starve, laptop or no laptop.

Marsha went first with her resume. She had an annoying habit of giggling in between her pleads for acceptance. She demonstrated enough subservience for a few of the alpha predators to nod in approval. Kevin introduced himself by saying he was an advanced driver. He worked for seven years at Solihull, and he had been a detective there for five. In other words, he was useless, but he could be the chauffeur while others slept in the passenger seats.

It was time for me to say a few words. Before the proceedings began, the cabal had been saying how they were all attending one of those nauseating award ceremonies that same evening. It was like they were sitting in a circle and masturbating the person to their right. Awards were given to officers for the most ridiculous of things. One fragile flower got one for working nights after they discovered upon receiving their shift pattern that the Police was not a nine to five job. Obviously, they had listened to Dolly Parton, and believed she was singing about a career in the police. A general glance at who received the awards revealed it was often the least deserving. Isn't this true in so many areas of life?

It was like a Dionysian orgy of mutual congratulation and celebration. They had solved a high-profile murder which had taken place five years previously. A young woman had been raped and murdered. Despite years of investigation, there was no sign of the case being solved. Obviously, a nightmare for the victim's family. But along came Team 7 like the Lone Ranger. No Tonto, however, as there were no ethnic minorities on the team regardless of the protests of a fella called Luke who said he was a minority. But despite incest and imbecility, being from Coventry didn't quite cut the mustard. Team seven had caught the offender and he was convicted of the girl's murder. He had left DNA in the victim. You can fill in the details for yourself. There was no match on the DNA database… until.

Back in those years, if you were arrested and charged, your fingerprints and photograph and DNA were taken as a matter of course. However, if you were found not guilty, then your DNA was destroyed. Amazing to think in these days of data collection that an innocent person's DNA should not be stored in the virtual ether. Unthinkable now that the state would allow such an opportunity to go to waste. What would Facebook and all the other data capturing platforms think? What would they have to sell? It would be like seeing aliens actually land in Stoke, disembark and announce they had found the paradise they had been searching for all these billions of years. No one would believe they were from another galaxy. Even researchers at SETI would reject their claim as no-one who wasn't from Stoke would ever visit let alone live there.

While they were all stroking and pulling, I sat silently thinking I had jumped from one frying pan into another, but this one had a sickly feeling one experiences when the fried food is too greasy.

Immediately after the murder, the team would have gone out and done a CCTV trawl, but it was not the same surveillance state then as it is now. Not as much, anyway. It's another dial which has been turned way up. Still, there was CCTV in some places so sometimes you can get lucky. A large number of witness statements were obtained by what's referred to as outside crews. Every incident room has officers who go out and complete actions which are generated by a system called HOLMES. The Senior Investigation Office (SIO) - who would be DI Cooke on Team 7 - ran the room, and her sergeants ensured all the "actions" were completed and up to scratch. These completed actions generated new actions, and so on till the case was resolved. There would be officers inside the room who would form part of the intelligence cell, gathering information, finding new leads, establishing patterns, examining phone evidence, CCTV viewing team, an interview team, and case builders who put the murder file together. There would be some overlap and flexibility depending on the needs at any given moment. The first weeks would always be intense. There was no ceiling to the overtime. Home life didn't even come in second place. This was what I had signed up for. Angela would have to be a single mum, or I would have to leave. That's basically how it was back then. If you mentioned working "family friendly" hours, you would have been put in for one of those pathetic "bravery awards," and subsequently told to fuck off back to OCU.

"You're turn, Jack," said DS Warren Blackford with a big smile, twirling a pen around in his fingers like he was ready to score me out of ten. "Don't be shy. Who are you? And what have you done?"

Funny isn't it how neither Jesus, Buddha, Muhammad, or Socrates wrote anything down. When you think of all the shit in print now (including this of course) the great movers and shakers in history had others enshrine their thoughts and teachings in writing. God(s) dictating the sacred words. How authentic is anything? Is anyone? I have said several times now, identifying a self, even if it existed in a singular sense (which may be a necessary illusion) would be impossible. Heraclitus was right when he said change is the basis of all existence. One must on occasions attempt to be true to the self *as if* it was real.

"Jack Garner. Ex F1. Ex firearms. Ex deer in a headlight. I'll just say a few words about a job I was involved in. You might be interested. Several years ago, instead of filing a low-level criminal damage job to the tune of £50 for a road rage incident, myself and my mate on the shift, traced the car involved, and found out who owned it. I arrested the alleged offender and interviewed him. We placed him on bail while we arranged the identification parade. He denied the offence. The victim had in fact given him the middle finger for cutting him up, and it was this gesture which caused the offender to get out of his car and put his fist through the window."

Back in those days you had to arrange the identification parade yourself at Bridge Street West in Newtown. You even had to find your own stooges on occasions. It was time consuming. They were paid £10 to turn up and stand in line. No computer-based identification system back then. It was usually authorised for only the most serious offences.

"We did all this work because of one reason. He had one previous conviction for beating up his ex-girlfriend so badly she was hospitalised for weeks. He went down the steps for five years. Our sergeant said at the time it's too much work for a smashed window for an arsehole driver who shouldn't flip other drivers off in the first place. A lesson well learned, and no physical injury. Just broken glass."

I had the room's attention for sure. It's interesting when other people are feeling slightly uncomfortable. I already decided this was not going to be my tribe. No initiation for me. No circumcision, no tattoos, no piercings, no funny dancing, or secret handshakes. More a case of Groucho Marx when he said he would never belong to a group that would have him as a member.

"He was picked out. I took his DNA and charged him. He was shocked, and I could see a change in his demeanour from the control he showed during the interview. A week or so later I had a couple of you lot turn up at my house asking for a statement regarding taking his DNA. If all that work had not been done by myself and my mate, then Alan White would still be out and about."

Now that was a mike dropped, exit stage left, tumbleweed blowing across the room moment. No bastard award for me!

Warren had stopped spinning his biro, and no doubt scored me a zero. The Boss had that mischievous smile again, or maybe it was just suppressed flatulence. I suspect she liked to see the occasional hand grenade being thrown. I can see her standing beside Robert Duvall saying how she too loved the smell of napalm in the morning. Send in those missile strikes. I am the Queen of petticoat politics. DI Cooke would brush aside Kissinger and George Kennan, JFK and Khrushchev. There would have been no Cuban missile crisis if she had overseen Team America. There would be no need for lonely nihilists like Mike Pompeo, John Bolton, Victoria Nulands or Meghan Markle to walk up and down New Street with sandwich boards stating: "The End of the World IS Nigh." However, Megan would have Harry wear the board, not herself, and she would have written at the bottom of the sheet in capital letters: IF YOUR BLACK. And despite Harry telling her it should be spelled "YOU'RE" and not "YOUR" that woman is used to getting her own way in tinsel town.

Let me say a word or two here about evidence. It's important. It should be the basis for all science. It should be the cornerstone of the entire legal system. It's what sends people to prison. It is supposed to be the basis for models which instead destroy lives and economies and any shred of true reason.

Evidence can take many forms. Nothing special about stating that you might think. But whether it's in the sciences or a murder investigation, as evidence accumulates from various sources, a confirmation bias gains traction like a snowball gathering flakes rolling down a hill. A group bias also adds to the mix. Peer pressure. Conformity. What evidence is available can be misleading. Doubling down on entrenched positions despite evidence to the contrary being presented. Arguments from authority. All these problems are often conveniently ignored or moulded to fit a desired narrative.

Evidence must be cross examined. The opposing view must always be exhaustively heard and scrutinised. Not censored because it diverges from the narrative. You must always follow the evidence even if it turns 180 degrees, and all the work you've put into the case is undermined.

A problem arises, however, that people wrap their identity up with their beliefs. I've said several times now, clever clowns cultivate stories, and use evidence to build narratives which drive an ideology, or any invested position. *Homo Insanus* is a different species from *Homo Stupidus*. The latter is the material of comedy. There is nothing funny about *Homo Insanus*. It is *A Midsummer Night's Dream* versus *Macbeth.*

One example of someone who used critical thinking, and evidence-based reason, to assess and react to a problem is a man named Stanislav Petrov. You should all know about this Russian. You have him to thank for being alive. No hyperbole. Evidence based fact.

On the evening of 26th September 1983, he was in charge of Russia's Nuclear Command and Control early warning system, when the system detected five nuclear armed ICBM missiles inbound from the United States. Three weeks previously, the Soviets had shot down Korean Airlines Flight 007. Petrov shut the system down to see if it was a computer malfunction.

When he started it up again, the alarm continued, and the system repeated that the missile attack was authentic. The tension between the US and Russia was at an all-time high, and the Russian leader at the time, Yuri Andropov, believed that a US attack was imminent. The US and NATO had also just embarked on nuclear war games on Russia's border. Again. According to the Americans, Russia should not be worried. No more so than if Russia did the same on the Mexican border, setting up missile systems in Tijuana pointing at Los Angeles; or drawing Mexico into a military alliance for the same purpose. What's your problem? We are not a threat.

Petrov should have immediately called his superior as protocol dictated, but he knew that if he did so, a full-scale nuclear launch would have been ordered. Both Russia and the US had approximately 60,000 nuclear weapons each at this time in contrast to the approximate 6,000 they have today. A nuclear attack would have resulted in a global extinction event, and you and everyone you know would be dead.

Instead of following protocol, Petrov reasoned that if the US were going to launch a pre-emptive strike, especially during the crisis, they would surely have launched more than a few missiles. Therefore, he didn't make that call. We survived. Petrov received a reprimand. Now that deserves a bravery award. Not for working nights when you originally thought you could be home by four to watch repeats of *A Place in The Sun*. But to push back against authority when the evidence warrants it. Against a hardened belief system nurtured on years of propaganda and structures controlled by people with a similar postcode.

I've been listening these past few days to George Michael sing "You've gotta have faith." He sounds very sincere. I need to have faith in evidence. In reason. In rationality. Faith in Steve Pinker. It's just that Steve has too much faith in rationality. He looks at statistics. At progress. He highlights the fewer deaths in wars, better health and education on average, less famines, 98% less deaths due to climate phenomena over the past 100 years, more equality between ethnic groups; more equality of the sexes. Even the Chinese, according to Steve, have never had it so good. All this is true. If 100 million people were wiped out due to a war or a pandemic, or because the Bay City Rollers were doing a comeback tour and there was a global mass suicide, then that is only around 1% of the world population. Not a lot. If you have a group of 20 and 2 are killed, then that's 10%. You with me? Cos if you're not then there really is no hope. So, this is progress according to Steve. You see anything wrong though? Apply this statistical analysis to anything, then everything is getting better. And you really could take Professor Pinker, and his mates, on a tour of disaster after disaster like Candide and Dr Pangloss, and yes, he would show empathy, but he would invariably put one of his numerous diagrams under your nose, and you would be forced (like any good undergrad looking for a grade A) to agree with him.

Why A Black Tipped Hanging Fly Pays for Sex

I wondered in the wake of 9/11 why no one would drive a truck full of explosives into Lloyd House? Yes, they erected a pathetic piece of concrete out front like a statue to represent their core values. The war on terror, like all the other wars on abstract phenomena, was a house of cards which just made the rich richer, and the stupid even more stupid. A great hoax to control narratives.

Politicians and security forces want you to think they have foiled great plots which would have destroyed vast areas of Washwood Heath, Lozells, Sparkhill and Tyseley. Any terrorist attacks would most likely tidy those areas up a little, purely based on random rearranging of all the discarded rubbish. "We are saving you," is the mantra of the state, like the squad on the hunt for Private Ryan, or Christine Aguilera's more accurate, "*Save Me from Myself.*"

The Counter Terrorist Unit (CTU - another three letter acronym) has increased in number over recent years, and now has the population the size of Gambia. Unlike Gambia, however, they are not oppressed and looked down upon as inferior. Like most African countries. They are not disrespected and told what their policies will be by their self-professed superiors. The CTU are given large budgets to spend in contrast to the high interest loans provided by the charities we call the World Bank and IMF (no defaulting on them otherwise your entire infrastructure gets taken over by US corporations); officers with half an hour in the police can get onto that gravy train, and spend thirty five years stealing taxpayers money like Dick Turpin, but without the mask and horse, and no risk of injury, unless they burn themselves with the free coffees they scrounge. Emoji time. You choose but make it one which really takes the piss.

The structured state wants you to be afraid of everything. I say "structured" because it is indeed a structural issue. This is where Foucault was right. And don't forget the comedy show *Citizen Smith* from way back in the late 70s (an era of great comedy): you remember Robert Lyndsey playing the Che Guevara of Tooting with his fist in the air shouting "Power to the People." However, there's never been power with the people. Okay, maybe for a few moments in the wake of a few head chopping's, but nothing long lasting: kind of like snow in Yemen, and Yemeni people themselves if UK munitions keep removing them from the place we call earth. Let's hope Arab peoples look to each other for support and goodwill. F35s answer the prayers of overseas companies and have no place inside a mosque.

There's nothing "deep" about states either. It's about money, power and status. *Homo Insanus* thrives in this environment. It is an epigenetic phenomenon. The political nudge unit switches off any genes which may play a role in empathy and fairness. While the political class of *Homo Insanus* pursue their own interests at any cost to everyone else, you are nudged in the direction of stress and anxiety while simultaneously being directed to pills and prophylactic entertainment. You have to be told now that water is wet so it's best practice to carry an umbrella if you go outside when it's raining. You are advised to stay indoors if it snows because you may freeze to death. Don't they know it's colder inside these winter nights than outdoors? You are informed how to feed your dogs and cats and mice when it's hot: climate change does not give a zero-emissions-flying-fuck about your pet's wellbeing. The state-run media provides guidance about how to raise your children as you have been detached from your innate parent ability, and now must rely on a model of parental social learning constructed by the gurus at Imperial College London. There is a government hotline for what to do when you are stuck in traffic with no first aid kit. There is a helpline to offer you support when you discover that those fuckers at Netflix are not making another series of your favourite show. There is a scheme to help half the country who is on benefits stay on benefits, and see if they are entitled to more free cash. Anyone over eighty can apply to a programme entitling them to live to at least a hundred regardless of the expense to the unborn. Don't they know there is a population crisis? Not over-population. The real future problem is a replacement issue. It is not as eye watering as an asteroid or Tomahawk missile. Most importantly, there is help available for the rich as they bleed like everyone else, and you need to switch the fuck on to their plight. Last, but not least, there are numerous sources available on how you can continue to lie to yourself about every half-baked narrative you care to cling on to, and medical experts are on hand to advise you as to which drugs to take so you can avoid reality and ignore the endless line of useless cunts in positions of power.

I walked into the lobby of Lloyd House at 9.30 with the only explosive material being my attitude. Bobby had mentioned that it might be a good idea to wear a suit. I turned up in jeans and trainers and my black firearms fleece. Along with a black coat and boots, it was the best thing I took away from Park Lane.

There were a few underpaid security guards on duty. Enough to prevent a delivery of Starbucks coffees from reaching the most senior ranked officers on the upper floors. They took one look at me, and knew I had an appointment with PSD. Bobby showed up a few minutes later.

"Sorry I'm late Jack. Like the tie," he said.

"Anything they can hang me with is best left at home."

"Good thinking," he said, pointing at me as if I had made a good decision instead of just making things even more difficult. As if Sisyphus didn't have a steep enough hill to climb as it is. "I hope you brushed your teeth?"

"I'm not visiting a hooker," I said.

"Hygiene at all times. These lot can smell fear on your breath. Attention to detail. Train hard, fight easy. Or easier, anyway.

We went over the events of the day again. It was an interview to get my side of things.

We took the lift to the fifth floor. DS Bridgeman met us at the door and within minutes we were sitting in an interview room. DC Hatton was his sidekick for the morning matinee.

I can't be bothered to go through the Q&As. It would drain the little energy I have left. They asked me what happened on the day in question. They showed CCTV footage of the confrontation with protesters. It was quite the scene of violence and destruction. And for a change, we were on the receiving end. Then you see Billy Jones standing all alone, way ahead of the retreating, jeering horde. Not like Wellington or Sun Tzu or Patton or Zhukov. More like Boris Johnson or Zelensky thinking what the fuck should I do with my future.

The police line approaches him. Cherry Street is only about ten metres wide, if that. You see Billy Jones falling backward and landing on his back. He gets up, and as I hear Beethoven play out in my head, he charges (my word not theirs) toward an officer - ME - who uses his casco to push Jones away (my words not theirs), and again he falls backwards. This time he appears to land much heavier on his back. The police line halts. Jones gets to his feet, but he is unsteady and appears to be slightly disoriented as he sways from left to right. One must only ever describe what one sees on the CCTV.

"Did you fear for your safety?" asked DS Bridgeman.

A leading question if ever there was one.

"Yes, I feared for my safety," was my obvious reply. "He charged at me." Again, Beethoven is reaching a crescendo at this point. If I listen carefully, I can even hear his *Symphony No. 9 Ode to Joy* take the lead. Take a break and listen to it for a few minutes. It will be uplifting.

The interview concluded with formal handshakes. Surprisingly, there was little pushback from the detectives. They did ask why I didn't put in a use of force form. I said the same as I did to Inspector Campbell. It could be a disciplinary issue but better than Crown Court. It was an IOPC investigation at the end of the day. However, one should never count their chickens before they're hatched. There is always a big bad wolf lurking who will huff and puff and blow your house down.

I head home on the train. I am juggling thoughts like a circus clown with burning skittle pins. I recall when Angela said to me a few days ago: "I have to be honest, Jack, while we were dating in the early months I was trying to decide if I could do any better."

I replied: “Likewise, Angela. All couples are doing that in one way or another. We are both deciding. It wasn’t just me performing for you. It’s not like I just spent a few minutes chatting, shagging and contributing some protoplasm, and then sodding off to the next woman.”

I suggested she should have listened to her dad. Between them they would have concluded that if she held on until the following weekend someone better may have shown up. Though not in Cleary’s pub. Display your wares in a higher end establishment. Males pay for sex, Angela, like in most animal species in some form or another. A black-tipped hanging fly will present a female with a delicious insect, and while she feasts, he will shag her senseless. And if he “finishes” first he will take the juicy remains and go find himself another mate. Many males of the *Homo Insanus* species, Angela, do exactly the same. That’s because on average they have a stronger sex drive. Male jewel beetles will fuck a beer bottle. Male fur seals try to mate with king penguins. Ismail the Bloodthirsty sired 888 children, the most ever recorded in history in Morocco. Valentina, the Russian, gave birth to 69 offspring in the nineteenth century, Angela. Both set world records which still stand today. Spot the difference. Ismail played the field. Most men do. I didn’t. I am a gibbon, Angela. No, not a gibbon: even they stray to another tree once and a while. I may look like a member of *Homo Insanus*, but sexually I am an owl monkey.

Men are as choosy as women when it comes to long term mates. We invest in our children otherwise we would be like polar bears and fuck off into the icy yonder after our two minutes of furry intimacy. We may obsess about sex and watch porn, masturbate till the onset of visual impairment, and repeat the process day after day till our cocks inevitably give out on us, but when kids like Hadrian and Meme arrive, Angela, we stick around. Some of us at least.

Quantum Entanglement and Why Matt Damon Always Gets the Girl

You've heard of quantum entanglement, yes? Please say yes, even if you think it's the sequel to a *Quantum of Solace*. Quantum entanglement is the phenomenon where two distant objects maintain a connection even though they can be galaxies apart. Literally. They are not communicating through the electromagnetic field like we do. This takes time. The radiation from the Big Bang has taken almost 13.8 billion years to reach our telescopes. Send a pair of photons in separate directions. One ends up in Jakarta, Indonesia, the other ends up in Ottawa, at the home of Justin Trudeau. The latter photon is unable to end its own existence, but it need not worry as Trudeau will pass legislation to limit any freedom it once had, and freeze it till its antimatter counterpart comes along, and then it will be well and truly fucked.

If one of the paired photons is red, the other will be red. If it is green, for argument's sake, the other will be green. They are correlated. Switch one colour from red to green and the other photon turns instantaneously. How does one photon know what the other's colour is when there is no time to communicate?

You might think that at the moment of separation their colour was determined, but this has been ruled out. The answer lies in relationships.

Angela and I are entangled. All parents share this quantum feature regardless of whether they split apart or annihilate each other. They are entangled through their offspring. Even if they hate each other. Even if their children hate them. Even if one goes to Jakarta and one is abducted by a Kosovan gang, and amidst the bags of cocaine in a container, they eventually end up in Trudeau's garage next to a few caged truckers; even after all the trauma, the family is still entangled, and they have to be grateful that none of them found themselves in Quebec.

"You're not going to ask me how I got on?"

I had taken the day off work. My stripe at the airport had given it to me free gratis under the circumstances but said not to tell the Gaffa. I stopped by Starbucks on Colmore Row in town and had a coffee before catching the train at Snow Hill back to Solihull. I was feeling rather positive about the world for a few moments.

"How did you get on?" said Angela, with the enthusiasm of a Texas death row inmate strapped to a gurney looking at his executioner who is struggling to find a vein. You know he's going to botch it up again. You would think these nut jobs could get an anaesthetist to put their victims to sleep first. We do it every minute of the day before an operation. Amazing how the US can kill gazillions of ethnic groups across the world, but when it comes to their killing their own ethnic minorities, they fuck it up all the time. Unless they are a cop. I know, it's a low hanging fruit; a three-legged antelope by a water hole.

"I called that fella from "*Better Call Saul*. You know the one in the movie *Nobody* who out-did Matt Damon at his own game."

The only problem when you call Saul is everyone thinks you're guilty. Like retaining Johnny Cochrane when he was alive. Remember OJ? Now he was as guilty as Albert Speer, but both escaped proper punishment. We really want revenge. Old Johnny would have run rings around the prosecutors at the Nuremberg Trials. But as the joke went when people hired him: "Yeah, everyone thinks you're guilty, but you get to go home."

"And did he show up?" Angela was on Facebook.

"No. I had to make do with Bobby," I said.

"Sorry to hear...O my god, Andrea's husband has just booked for them to go to New York for Christmas."

Now she really was on the verge of tears. I resisted the urge to say: "Ask Kenny boy. It's the honeymoon period after all. Maybe he'll fork out for the tickets, and you can make a foursome, like at the Belfry, or a quartet playing a symphony by Brahms or Mozart.

"Remember that summer when Hadrian was still a baby, and we went to the Lake District? We had fun, didn't we?" I asked. Attempting to keep the theme of world travel on the table. Maybe I just needed a moment to demonstrate the weird quantum entanglement phenomenon I was just going on about.

"It rained," snapped Angela switching back to reality.

"Not every day. And it's not called the Lake District because of its deserts."

"And you made me walk up hills each day. Again Jack, that was all about you and what you wanted to do. You wanted to do the Wordsworth thing. 'I wandered lonely as a cloud.' I can still remember the poem from school."

She was referring, of course, to Wordsworth's *Daffodils*. Annoyingly, she was right. I had wanted to visit Wordsworth's house where he lived with his sister, as well as visiting John Ruskin's residence. We walked up hills. I carried Hadrian in one of those backpacks. A proud dad at the time. Pre-adolescence and just before the world became truly warped within an orbit of mirrors.

We visited Coleridge's Museum where Hadrian climbed onto a chair despite being told by a young lady that it was part of the original furniture. He fell off and started crying. She smiled as if to say 'Serves you right. Little fucker."

Angela used to like that I could talk about highbrow culture, but also mix it up in the ring: what Churchill called "Yaw

yaw and war war." Churchill was talking about diplomacy and going to war. He had experience in both. Some people can do Yaw but not War. Most can do neither. A few can do both. Remember the scene from *Good Will Hunting*, when the unknown mathematical genius/janitor - like Harvard's version of Hong Kong Fuey - played by Matt Damon who was from the wrong side of the tracks in Boston, confronts the manicured image of an Oxbridge twit. Clark tries the academic equivalent of a cock measuring contest with Will. Size did matter to Minnie Driver who ended up sexually selecting Will. It would be a few years before Minnie succumbed to the phallic extensions of bucks and a Bugatti.

The best bit is when Will whispers in Clark's ear - so as not to embarrass him any further - if he wants to step outside, they can sort it out another way. Clark declines of course. Will gets Minnie. Minnie gets Will. But we all know that Minnie shall one day end up with Mickey. Will is going to end up in a bedsit in Boston's equivalent of Redditch. Drawing equations of string theory on the living room wall, not giving a fuck about losing his security deposit because he is a genius, and one day soon he will find the answer to quantum gravity, and a theory of everything, and Hawking, Feynman, Witten and Weinberg can all kiss his ass.

When all is said and done, and the history books are written - of course by the victors, who else - they will say I got

Angela, and Angela got me. It was never truly in sickness and in health: only in health, sometimes, in the beginning. And as for the “till death do you part” line, Angela let out a laugh. I’m not joking.

Even her dad passed a comment at the reception when he gave his Periclean speech: “I did say to Angela, before the ceremony, that there was still time to run. It wasn’t the first time she failed to listen to me. No doubt some of you heard her laugh after saying the most serious vow! Fortunately, Jonathan, over there, deals with the divorce side of things at the firm.”

Jonathon stood up like he was about to get another bonus. The guests laughed along. Robert even referred to Helen of Troy which was not lost on the classicists in the audience. Talk about not seeing the early signs. We wonder why, when Rolf Harris sang “Two little boys had two little toys…” church bells did not ring out across the land.

Do you find there is something about the dark which inspires actions which you regret in the light of day? Do you ever ask why our fears do not correlate with our environment? Why are we not terrified of birth control and cigarettes? Both impact our reproductive success. Why can't our children give a rat’s ass about speeding traffic when they have their heads buried in their phone, but they are paralysed in fear if they must speak in front of a group. The cost of getting killed once is far higher than overreacting to a thousand false alarms. Our fears are all out of alignment. Another example of *Homo Insanus*.

Here's another. Most people have positive things to say about Scandinavians. Probably because they have never been to these countries. I knew a fella from Sweden years back called Olav, or Olaf or one of those kinds of names. No one cares. Let's face it, who learns Norwegian or Swedish or Danish? You could go through several lifetimes, and never meet anyone who says they are learning how to speak Swedish, unless a crazy ABBA fan who wants to sing along to their songs not realising, they were written in English. Anyway, Olav, Olaf, Ole, had a party trick of smashing a beer bottle on a particular spot on his forehead. Always a nighttime skill which he never repeated during hours of daytime. However, they spend a lot of hours in the dark in Scandinavia, and there is a lot of violence despite the nice teeth and blond hair. Possibly, a remnant of their Viking heritage. Have you noticed every drama they produce is about a serial killer? Saab is literally making a killing these days and it has nothing to do with crap cars.

I had my own beer bottle smashing *Homo Insanus* moment. Add it to my list.

It's night time. I'm awake. In the loft. In my lair. Alone. Thoughts randomly popping in and out of existence like virtual particles in the blackness of space. The worst thing you can do when your wife is sucking the cock of a man called Ken, and when you're facing unemployment, prison, ruin and Redditch, is listen to a romantic mix provided to you by yet another of life's algorithms, this one courtesy of Spotify. That's the moon for you. It ain't called lunacy for no reason.

Bryan Adams starts singing "Everything I do, I do it for you." You know the one. Remember the lines: "Don't tell me it's not worth fighting for, don't tell me it's not worth dying for, you know it's true…" And then there's the one about "Take me as I am..." What the fuck! Why?

But it was night time. That's my only defence. You've done things at night you've regretted in the morning? A text? A social media post? A drunken tirade at a work colleague? A sexual act which definitely needed a condom? I sent Angela that Bryan Adams song. As soon as I touched the screen, I tried to reach into the phone to retrieve it, but Apple designs its products so that not even its own engineers can gain access. Only water can get it.

Next morning, I could hear Angela in the kitchen. She was telling Meme to eat her Weetabix. Meme kept on shouting "Donald's, Donald's, Donald's."

"No McDonald's breakfast this morning. It's Weetabix or famine. There are children around the world without food."

"Donalds, Donalds, Donalds."

I walked into the kitchen with my head down. Like a dog who had just shit in the corner of the living room and suspected he was in for a spot of chastising.

"Morning all. What's this about demands for McDonalds?" I said, kissing Meme on the cheek. She wiped it off straight away. Proof if ever more was needed as to the effect of genetic inheritance.

Angela remained silent. She knew her rights.

So, this question is for people with a cock. They used to be called men. "Have you ever been having sex with someone new and vaginal flatulence escaped? It's an issue of air pressure. Any piston going in and out of a tube causes friction and a pressure differential. It's an odourless gas like Carbon monoxide, but more harmful to a new relationship. You both hear it. It ruins the moment. Nothing is said. Of course, the owner of the piston is less bothered, but it's happened and not even the best problem solvers in history like Archimedes, Newton, Lovelace or Ray Donovan can fix it. I've decided to leave the light on all night from now on.

On The Point, What's The Point?

We all zoom. I'm not referring to meetings of the middle class, middle of the road, middling fragile minds. Perish the thought. I don't like looking at faces too closely unless via a scope. We zoom in and out of our perceived reality. However, this is not reality itself. Reality is granular. Reality is relational. Reality is not objects in motion driven by forces on a stage of space. Our myopia prevents us from seeing it.

Be in no doubt: your entire world depends on this reality. Your very existence only has meaning through relationships whether at the level of particles, atoms, molecules, at the level of chemistry, biology, sociology and psychology. The old certainties of classical physics are an illusion. We live in a universe of probabilities.

Zooming involves the tuning of dials. We live in a middle world where approximations are the heuristic which guide us. Like Charon, the ferryman, who after receiving a soul from Hermes, would guide them across the River Styx to the underworld. Our evolution did not require us to be able to see a gravitational field. It was essential for us to see a wild animal or someone from Merseyside coming toward us. You are a descendent of those who could spot a danger and avoid it. Those who did not, ceased to exist, and so did their genetic line.

If I apply Dirac's equation and try to understand why Angela allows Ken to hold her hand, while she only allows me to hold the shopping, or Maxwell's equations to explain why Billy Jones died after I pushed him - not the day before or the following month - I will be disappointed. The dials must be tuned to the frequency of the problem. If they are tuned to the wrong setting, it results in a conceptual error. Science does not provide us with a hitchhiker's guide to how we should live our lives. It cannot provide a recipe to cook up a meaningful existence. This is where a void has opened with the decline of religion in the western world. It is from this void where *Homo Insanus* feeds off a menu of modern crazy ideas. Don't get me wrong, religion also is a by-product of *Homo Insanus's* search for meaning, and it too has left a trail of travesty in its wake. It's not all Kumbaya and cake sales.

In trying to solve modern life's multitude of troubles, our ancestral survival systems are often tuned incorrectly. We overreact much of the time to the slightest inconvenience. And our feelings - which are simply mechanisms which drive our behaviour - are manipulated by the media and others with their own agendas.

I have mentioned that I became an authorised firearms officer. At every opportunity you may be thinking. Talk about dining out on history. Well, I've got the boots, fleece and coat to show for it, and I kept the holster and a few other bits and pieces. No guns. Here he goes again. Insert whatever genital-like emoji you want. Back in bygone times getting on to “the Unit” was difficult. When I went through the process there was barely any teaching involved. You were shown a procedure once, and if you didn’t get it then you were basically told to fuck off. Few passed. And I would be lying if I said I didn’t feel special at the end of it all. When they welcomed you into the club, and handed you your authorization card, you felt like you had achieved something important. Especially when they gave you a nickname. Mine was *Tenko*. From the 70s television show. One of the trainers said I looked like one of the Japanese guards. It stuck. You were a member of the group.

At any point you could have been booted off for a whole host of reasons. Not being a team player. Not being an individual. Poor decision making. It was all about decision making. If you didn’t pick up all the discharged shell casings on the range, you could be told at the end of the week that you were not what they were looking for. Being able to handle weapons safely and efficiently was a given. Leave the safety off when you shouldn’t - which could result in a negligent discharge - or being cumbersome with all the drills meant you were going to fail. Accuracy was essential. You had to have a success rate of 90% on all targets.

Many were not fit enough. Muscles did not get you through. It was often a case of mind over matter. I saw one fit lad just give up when we were doing a routine of stepping up and down on a bench with a gas mask on, carrying a Heckler and Koch MP5. It wasn't even that tiring. Just a mental thing. He stopped and said "Fuck it." I've had enough," and handed his kit to one of the staff who just took it from him. They never tried to persuade you to stay.

We would go out on containment exercises regardless of the weather. Sat up in bushes or in mud while it was pissing down, waiting for the action to begin, while the training staff were having a brew and food in the shelter and warmth. You trained in different environments ranging from the countryside to urban areas. Countless scenarios with various modes of transport. Stooges, who had been on the team for years, were drafted in to make your life a misery by being awkward bastards, and doing the opposite of what you were telling them to do. It was always about containing and controlling and decision making. Everything was scored and noted down. One fuck up could undo days of good work. Apparently, it's not like that anymore. Maybe for the better.

When we were on the range over at Wednesbury (no fancy Park Lane range and facilities back then), we would step up to the point for a detail. Six officers in a row with a beretta in our holster, and an MP5 as the rifle of choice. An excellent weapon. You could close your eyes and shoot, and still hit the target.

If anyone had difficulty with accuracy it was always with the handgun. Unlike the movies, a handgun at a distance requires a steady aim. Under stressful conditions it can be difficult to hit the target nine times out of ten. You would load your magazine with the number of rounds (don't call them bullets!) as instructed. A member of the training staff would shout: "On the point."

I remember one staff member who would always follow the command up with a derisory: "What's the point!" Then it would be: "Targets are away." Watch and react." The targets would turn and face you, and then hell rained down on them.

"What's the point?" I found this throwaway line amusing even when the occasional burning hot shell casing from the person next to me found its way on to my exposed neck. What is the point? Of anything really? Headstones turn to dust eventually. Shakespeare wrote: "Out, out brief candle! Life's but a walking shadow, a poor player, that struts and frets his hour upon the stage, and then is heard no more." Now if you cannot see how profound those few lines are then there really is no hope.

Despite the popularity of *The Highlander,* who would really want to live forever? Ray Kurzweil does, and some crazy scientists who think they will soon be able to upload their consciousness into a computer. *Homo Insanus*.

Life's value - its very essence - lies in its brevity. How best to grasp those few moments before the Grim Reaper or the in-laws show up? Like when Hadrian and Meme were born. Before Ken came along. Before Billy Jones. But it can't always be about the "befores." Or the far-flung futures. Otherwise, what is the point? The future will always contain its own problems to fret and stress about. I must live in hope.

In Dante's *Divine Comedy* he wrote: "Abandon hope all ye who enter here." Dante defined hell in terms of an absence of hope. The man had a point. He also wrote that you should follow your own path and let people talk. He could have made a fortune in the bumper sticker industry.

Of course, it doesn't mean that one can only find hope through faith in God. By way of salvation. Yet Dante and George Michael had that one thing in common. I can see them now performing a duo of George's song *Faith*. Yes, wearing different outfits. No skintight jeans in the fourteenth century. However, there was bling even back then. And a crucifix was a fashion accessory in the 80s.

Science makes assumptions about the natural world. Even thinking that another person has a mind similar to your own is an act of faith. A belief. It cannot be proven. The external world itself is based on an assumption. All the evidence gathered so far points to it being real, but proving it is not the goal of science. Science *proves* nothing. Mathematics, not science, deals with proofs.

Science assumes the existence of reality and observes and tests hypotheses. The first step is an assumption. This is also true of the foundation of mathematics. This is the famous Incompleteness Theorem of Kurt Godel. I need to have a glimmer of hope. I need to listen to Dante and George. I need to believe in that cringe worthy theme song of New Labour, where Blair and the one-eyed Scottish political powerhouse, Gordon Brown, and that tawdry tale-spinner, Alastair Campbell, sing along to "Things can only get better." Despite the million dead Iraqi civilians. You know the one, right? It's playing in your head right now. Listen. Even if you are a teenager and were not even born when these three amigos held power, simply through the process of epigenetic inheritance, you are now singing along to that song and you have no idea where you learned it. You're like Hamlet driving himself mad, but you cannot get rid of that contagious tune. However, there is a paradox of hope: it brings disappointment. Like the paradox of progress which brings along with it death and destruction. But where would we be without hope? Apparently, it springs eternal. I'm not so sure now.

How To Survive Tragedy

The moment you are born is a ritual. From that second until you're buried, burnt or blown apart by a US drone at a wedding, it is one ritual after another. The more extreme the ritual the stronger the bond between the group. Think what it takes to pass selection to get into the Special Air Service (SAS, another three letter acronym). You've watched those nauseating back slapping "reality" television shows where men in black talk about the "brotherhood" and "never leaving a man behind," when, many can't stand each other.

Consider Tamil Hindus who walk on burning hot coals. Or Albanians taking the perilous journey across the Badlands of Europe at the cost of thousands of pounds to claim asylum in Britain, when they could just jump on a fifty quid flight from Tirana to Heathrow. I mean really. What the fuck! Where's your passport? My nephew went to Albania for a holiday last year. It's hardly Mogadishu in the 90s. Did you watch *Black Hawk Down*? America coming to the rescue of black people. Now that's epic. If only Dr King had lived to see it. They usually arrive to build another military base and check the local geology.

Rituals do not substitute for reality. Throughout history, humans have performed them in every area of their lives. A harvest festival, for example, never resulted in farmers believing the crop would make its own way out of the field while they sat around giving instructions with their feet up like the valuable flowers in higher police ranks. Spiritual practices such as prayer, however, do have a physical effect. Both on an individual and at the group level. We imitate the rituals of our family and group as we grow up. That's how we learn. Non-linear algebra is much harder.

Our semantic memories are laid down through repetitive practice. Picture a green parkland area. If you follow the same path through the grass every day for a year, your footsteps will have created a noticeable trail. That's your semantic memory. However, if you take a tractor and turn over the grass in one go, a dirt road is formed in an instant: that's your episodic memory. Most of your life involves semantic memories which blend into familiar but impressionistic images, like a Monet or Van Gogh painting: you recognise what you're looking at, and yet, there is an abstraction. An episodic memory is laid down like a hammer falling at Sotheby's. This does not mean the episodic variety is all bad. Not at all. Evolution, however, has wired you to pay close attention to the negative. This is why people "rubberneck," and why it is that whenever we hear about a catastrophe of some kind, we are invariably disappointed if there are not a significant number of casualties. It also matters if they are close to your location. Look like you. Talk like you. Remember the song from that great classic which you rarely hear about these days - *Jungle Book*: "I wanna be like you, I wanna walk like you, Talk like you..." Yeah, you're singing along.

We pay attention to those who don't come back. We want to know why. Our very existence may rely on it. Did they take the wrong path or motorway? Did they make a mistake on a hunt, or be enrolled in the wrong US high school? O give over. It's the truth! I know, I know, I seem to be targeting the US a lot but fuck 'em, they target way too many people around the world. They're not going to read this anyway. Too busy preventing women from having abortions, but it's not a problem if an eighteen-year-old wants to lock and load an AR 15 and visit a local gay bar to demonstrate to Richard Dawkins that 'there's more than one way to unweave a rainbow Dick: watch and learn. We "rubberneck" for the same reason: we want to learn. It's not a case of voyeurism. It's true education. It's the best lesson you can ever have. You won't find it in the catalogue of any university, or in any outdated lesson plan on the cause of Covid 19 written by Pfizer and Fauci. Don't get me started. I've already killed one man, apparently. Other people's tragedies are our survival guide. Read that last sentence again. No, I'll type it. I don't trust you. Have you read the bit about my wife sucking Ken's cock? I don't trust anyone anymore:

OTHER PEOPLE'S TRAGEDIES ARE OUR SURVIVAL GUIDE.

"Come in Bobby. Angela is in the kitchen with our little one."

"Thanks Jack. How are you mate?"

"You don't want the truth?" I asked.

"No mate. Not really," said Bobby following me into the kitchen. Angela had just made Meme pasta. Meme was throwing it against the wall to see if it would stick. To make sure it was cooked properly.

I was on a rest day. It was a four on four off shift pattern at the port. Four twelve hour shifts. Seven till seven. It was the only unit in the force still on that pattern. Firearms used to work the same (and traffic but nobody cares about those lot), but they switched to six on three off: two earlies, two lates and two night shifts. When I first started, we had to work seven nights in a row. From ten in the evening, till seven in the morning.

I always struggled to sleep on days. I would run home from Vyse Street. Six miles with a bergen full of kit on my back. Jump into bed. I would be awake at nine. I used an eye mask. No good. I even tried Nytol tablets. Useless. They made me feel groggy. I tried dark curtains to keep the light out. Nothing worked. People I worked with could sleep till six in the evening.

Get up, and eat, and come to work ready for the night ahead. I would be in a semi-comatose state driving to work every evening. When I finished the set on the following Friday morning, I had lost all track of time. A month could have passed. Sleep deprivation for so long and for many years is a route to an early grave.

"Angela, this is Bobby," I said as I removed the new wall decorations.

"Nice to meet you," said Bobby with a big smile. He kept his hands to his side, instinctively knowing they were too valuable to risk.

"Hi," said Angela as she pressed the button on the kettle. "Tea or coffee Bobby?"

"I'll have a coffee please. Four sugars."

"Four?" replied Angela.

"I have a sweet tooth. I got it from my mom's side. All those generations working on sugar plantations."

We all forced a laugh.

"I didn't think Fed reps did home visits?"

Bobby looked at me for help.

"Bobby lives on Stanway Road, so I suggested he pop in for a brew," I said.

"Yeah, I'm just around the corner so it was no bother," offered Bobby as an explanation for his existence in Angela's kitchen.

"Mom and dad are coming around shortly. Dad had the day off to play golf."

"O," I said. I choked on the word "good." It just wouldn't come out. Now the word "fuck" would have dropped out as easily as Dorothy followed the yellow brick road. Meme threw a piece of pasta which landed perfectly on Bobby's bald head. She laughed and seemed very proud of herself. Bobby retrieved the pasta and popped it into his mouth.

"Carbonara sauce?" he said.

"Meme! That's naughty. Sorry Bobby," said Angela handing Bobby a paper towel. "Would you like a bowl? There's some left."

Meme was still eying up Bobby's head. He moved to a better strategic position by the sink. Hadrian joined the party.

"Hadey, Hadey, Hadey," shouted Meme.

"Eat your pasta," said Angela.

"Bobby, this is my son Hadrian," I said.

"Hello," said Bobby.

"Hi," said Hadrian. "Are there any batteries mom?"

The doorbell rang.

"That'll be mom and dad. Can you get it while I look for the batteries?" asked Angela.

"Ok," I said. It was like the Bataan death march. "Hi Robert. Hi Marie. Come in. We're in the kitchen on a battery hunt."

I hear people at work take the piss out of the current ideological notion of safe spaces. University students demand refuge from dangerous ideas. Workers require shelter from harmful pathogens of the mind. Words are now part of the munitions industry. However, have you ever heard the phrase: "Sticks and stones may break my bones, but names will never hurt me." Well, that's true. There are many objects one could add to the list. You can spend a few moments thinking of your very own toolbox of objects for harming another person. Did you consider a knuckle duster? A claw hammer? I'll guess you didn't include an exclamation mark? Or a semicolon? When do you use that thing anyway?

I gave a presentation at a secondary school once upon a time in Highgate. It was an academy school. It was taken over by the private sector because it was so bad. The teachers were throwing pupils out of every classroom window. They couldn't coast downhill anymore like Franz Klammer on an alpine ski run. O be quiet. Who else has half the year off with full pay? A golden pension? As much time off sick as they want fully paid? And they still moan louder than slave labour employed by corporations in China. Okay, all public sector workers for that matter. Spend a few weeks in the private arena and see how the lions start licking their lips when you stop grafting.

Knife crime was the theme of my talk. Males were carrying knives to school. They may forget their schoolbooks, but their iPhone and lock-knife were essentials.

My sergeant at the time at Digbeth Station nominated me to give the chat. The headteacher, Mr Cassidy, had put out an alarm call following an after-school incident where two Somali lads had gone toe to toe with knives in Horton Square. It got quite a few hits on social media. Fortunately, neither of them had managed to puncture the other. I spoke to around a hundred teenagers about the consequences of carrying knives. However, I brought along a few props. Blunt instruments. My goal was not to convert people into being peace loving hippies. It was to persuade them to change their weapon systems. Knives kill. Knuckle dusters, and cascos, rarely do.

The teachers looked horrified. Mr Cassidy took out his phone. I suspected he was going to call 999. The young males sat up. They appeared to be taking notes. Possibly for the first time in their lives. The moral of my talk circled around the idea of preventing the waste of two lives. One in a box. The other in a cell for a few decades. I was not there as a UN representative to talk nonsense. I was not there to preach anti-war sentiments. I was not there to lecture them about the Biblical "Do unto others as you would have them do unto you." Mr Cassidy had requested a police officer to attend his academy to talk about the dangers of knife crime. So, I did. I was not invited back.

Schools in themselves should be one large safe space. Most of us have been to one, and we know that's far from the case. They are a viper's nest of bullying and peer pressure, with a little trigonometry and Tennyson thrown in. Only elderly care homes rival their jungle-like viciousness.

As a child I used to sit in the airing cupboard in my parent's bedroom. It was a place of peace and tranquillity. I would close the door and simply think. No phones back then of course. We didn't even have a house phone. I had to walk to the local shops to use the phone which was often out of use. Local youths would use a screwdriver to try and open the money box. The airing cupboard was my safe space. It doesn't have to be a room. The best location is your brain. Some of us take it with us wherever we go. Many do not. We refer to them as FUCKWITS. They are everywhere. A little like speed cameras. Have you ever seen that dreadful movie "*The Boy in the Plastic Bubble*?" This was John Travolta in his pre-Scientology days. Tod Lubitch is a young man who suffers from a deficient immune system and has to live in a sterile environment to avoid pathogens. I won't spoil the ending for you if you haven't seen it. Sod it, he dies.

Safe spaces do not exist in reality. Nature can be hostile to human habitation. You must build up your mental resilience. We don't have an airing cupboard in our house. It'll be on the top of my list if I have to go flat hunting in Redditch. If we did have one, I would be heading there right now, and leave Bobby to fend for himself.

"This is Bobby. You know Angela, and this is Hadrian."

Meme found it very funny. Or maybe it was just the natural scowl on Robert's face.

"Hello," said Bobby.

"The Fed rep?" asked Robert.

"Yes," confirmed Bobby.

"I didn't think you did home visits? " said Robert, dismissively.

Angela chirped in: "That's what I said."

"We don't usually, but I only live around the corner, and I wanted to chat to Jack."

"He's named after Bobby Sands, the hunger striker, dad," said Angela.

"Is that right," said Robert sitting down on a kitchen stool. "I never approved of the IRA. All those killings. You don't get anywhere using violence. Look what has happened to Mr Jones."

"Well, that was not intentional," said Bobby. "He was told to move, and he didn't. Not really violence. A lawful use of force."

I could have hugged him. I had Freddie singing in the background and just as Bobby finished his sentence, "*We Are the Champions*" had just begun. I suppressed an urge to sing along. A desire to ask Bobby to join me in a duo while we stuck two fingers up to Robert and put our arms on each other's shoulder. It would have been a thing of beauty. I must note, however, that for a long time when I first heard that anthem, I thought Freddie was singing "I've paid my Jews…" like he was trying to separate himself from those who carried out regular pogroms. It was only after months I realised, he was saying "dues."

"How are you Hadrian?" asked Marie.

"Not good Gran. We don't have any batteries," replied Hadrian, sounding dejected.

"O dear," said Marie. "I wish you said Angela, we could have stopped and picked some up. Double or triple A?"

"Double A Gran. Always double A," said Hadrian.

"He's not used to hearing the letter A," I said. It's always been a C or D," I said with a smile. I couldn't help it.

"That's not very nice," said Marie sternly. "Hadrian always did well at school. Didn't he, Angela?"

"Where's daddy going, Meme?" asked Hadrian.

A moment's silence. All eyes fell on the smiling assassin: "Daddy's going to jail. Daddy's going to jail."

She never let him down. Like a set of Goodyear tires. Hadrian left victorious like England's women's football team. The less said about the men the better.

“Daddy’s not going to jail? Am I Bobby?” Talk about being needy. Reassurance, please. Give me something to cling on to. Remember, HOPE? It’s not just a name. It’s the cornerstone of all humanity.

“No, daddy is not going to jail,” said Bobby. He was looking at Robert which was both uncomfortable and amusing. Robert looked disappointed. Marie was looking at Robert. Angela was cleaning Meme’s face.

“When will it be resolved?” asked Robert.

“It’s an IOPC investigation. They have to reach a conclusion soon. If they find criminal wrongdoing, then the case will be referred to the CPS,” said Bobby.

“Well, it’s a binary decision at the end of the day: guilty or not guilty,” said Robert.

“Yes,” said Bobby.

But here’s the thing, it’s not binary. There are shades of grey. And not the kind you’re thinking of. It’s a process. Everything today is dumbed down to a choice between x or y. Proxy wars in Ukraine, Syria, Libya, and Rotherham; culture wars in most western countries. If you probe, and seek a nuanced, well-informed discussion you are targeted as a denier of some kind. A fate worse than death for tribal members who fear being outcast more than anything. An outcast can mean unemployment, an undesirable status at the bottom of the social ladder. Every nation has a caste system and don't forget it.

Billy Jones is dead. I shoved him. It's not a binary thing. You don't think I know he was a little boy once like Hadrian, but with better prospects. That as he got older, he had hopes and dreams. They didn't involve dying alone in hospital after an encounter with state power. Who could imagine that would be how their life would end? Okay, maybe Afro-Caribbeans would say from early years that death at the hand of a cop is a distinct possibility. But who else? Is it simply a binary matter that his life turned out as it did? A yes or no?

Abelard, the Medieval Scholastic philosopher, who I have mentioned already, wrote a book entitled *Sic et Non* - "Yes or No." In it he contrasted arguments to determine the truth of one statement over another. He had his cock cut off by the family of his beloved Heloise. They were not happy with her choice. That fucker Ken should keep Abelard in mind. Angela can't suck what isn't there to be sucked. Now that is an example of a binary phenomenon. See the difference? What happened between Billy Jones and me was the furthest thing from 0 or 1. He had a life history. So did I. We became entangled. Not like Angela and me. More in line with the nurse and Mr VW driver who said "fuck you" to the traffic light. But even here, you can see that this entanglement involved a history of events. Life is not an algorithm.

I think about Billy Jones. I said at the beginning I had regrets. Yes, I regret he had an enlarged heart. Did I not mention the autopsy report? No alcohol. A trace of cannabis, but his wife had said he used it to help with joint pain. Severe liver damage from decades of heavy drinking. Most importantly, he had a diseased heart. Am I glad to hear this? Of course! Am I not human? Do you ever hear people say they have no regrets in life? How self-righteous and narcissistic. Every day you should consider a mistake you have made in order to try and avoid a similar one tomorrow. There's a self-help manual in one sentence. There's a whole industry in a few words. It just involves a few moments of reflection to see what a first class cunt you can be. Try to be less of one tomorrow.

So Robert, it's not a binary matter. It's not a guilty or not guilty verdict. I'm not in court. I'm not a 0 or 1, yet. But I am angry. Isn't everyone? More now than ever. Despite having less reasons. At least in the west. *Homo Insanus* acts out this anger all the time, and in doing so makes bad decisions. I need to turn down the anger dial. It's difficult. When I got married my testosterone levels dropped. Same again when I had children. All men's levels drop. Same with many animals. If you're going to invest in offspring, then better to have lower testosterone levels. Less anger. Less risky behaviour. Less chance of being killed, and the children being left unprotected. Now I may have to go back on the dating market, and my hormone level will increase in order to compete in the sexual arena. But I have blood on my hands, so the competition needs to be aware.

The Renaissance Man Goes on Operation Servator

In October 1517, Martin Luther nailed his 95 propositions to the door of All Saints' church at Wittenberg, condemning the corruption in the Church, especially the papal practice of asking payment - called "indulgences" - for the forgiveness of sins. A revolution had begun.

In the same year, a Dutch humanist scholar called Erasmus, reaching his twilight years, wrote that he wished he was young again as he could see on the horizon a coming golden age. He was referring to what was later called *The Renaissance*: "the rebirth." This is what Inspector Campbell had said to me when he told me I was heading to Birmingham Airport. Not to go on holiday mind you. I was joining the Airport Police Unit. On a temporary basis. Maybe. Like sending a football player out on loan.

Now the real Renaissance began in the 1400s despite Erasmus's futuristic observation. It was a reaction to the real calamity of climate change as Europe got colder. The west had just experienced three centuries of warmer temperatures. The population size had doubled. Then came the mid fourteenth century catastrophic bubonic plague (which many optimistic rationalists, looking at long term statistics, would see as progress), and following along, famines arrived because of poor harvests.

Intellectuals of the time sought to address the undermining of old certainties by turning to the ancient classics for inspiration, and a better model of how to deal with the problems at hand. They were looking for their own self-help books. The payoff was huge. By linking together all the branches of scholarship in the light of antiquity, men (and they were almost all men, and Italians at that!) such as Michelangelo, Leonardo and Leon Baptista Alberti set Europe on a different path to the rest of the known world.

Inspector Campbell must have been hallucinating before he told me about my imminent rebirth. When football players are sent out on loan they always end up in the lower leagues. In the entire history of Nuneaton Town Football Club, no player has ever gone to Liverpool FC on loan. Despite a similar level of crime and incest, and many other interesting symmetries from an anthropological perspective between the two areas, Liverpool has by far the better changing rooms. And unlike the fans of Nuneaton FC, at all home games Liverpool fans offer crime prevention to everyone in the Merseyside area when they sing, “You’ll never walk alone.” It follows, by simple logic, they are telling you to go out in pairs if you visit their lovely city. Now that’s a caring community for you.

I hope you've taken note that I'm not providing you with stories of daring escapades, car chases, gunfights at the Ok Corral, punch ups, gory details of murders with Bonnie Tyler blaring in the background how she will be a hero, or Enrique, Mariah and David Bowie singing their own version of the mythical traveller. There is certainly no attempt to compare myself to Leonidas, Iron Man or Popeye. I hate spinach. I'm giving you the mundane, but all too often unbearable lightness of being anecdotes.

You see, biology has placed a limit on us, on our sense of our own identity. Have you heard of the Ship of Theseus? If you replace every board on this ancient wooden vessel over time, is it the same original ship? Every seven years the cells in your body are recycled so that you are not the same "you" as seven years ago. Memory provides a loose chain of connection. But this chain is not continuous. It is fragmented, and incredibly bad at being accurate. Apparently, evolution did not select a trait for photographic memory. When people say they know someone who has a Kodak ability to recollect the past, it is still an approximation.

I arrived at the airport on a Wednesday morning. My new sergeant Ron Thomas introduced me to the shift. He said I was joining them for a few weeks. It was obvious the four of them had been briefed about me.

"This is Steve. He'll chaperone you for a few days," said Ron.

"Hi," I said.

Steve nodded: "Alright." He was in his mid-fifties with eighteen months left till retirement.

"That's Brian," said Ron, pointing at a fat, bald bloke with a goatee beard. Again, in his mid-fifties, except he had seven months left in the job.

"The short fella there is Matt."

"That's offensive, Sarg. You heard him. Pocket notebook entry," said Matt picking up his pen. Probably for the first time in a while. Matt was the youngest of the group with twenty-five years in the police. Five to go.

"And Linda is the one who does the work."

"Hi," said Linda.

"Hello," I said.

"I've arranged for you to get your photo taken at the ID centre for your airport pass. You'll need it to access the doors, and to go airside. Steve will show you around for the next few days. There's an e-border on my desk Steve, so maybe you and Jack can look at that. There's a Servator deployment at 9 so we'll do a briefing in here around quarter to, and then head over to the terminal. You're in for a treat Jack. Welcome to Operation Servator world."

Seneca, the ancient Roman philosopher, wrote about the shortness of human life. I'm reminded of the slave who used to follow the great Emperor Marcus Aurelius around everywhere he went, whispering in his ear to remind him of his own mortality, his impending death. I've previously mentioned immortalists who believe that science can and will achieve the elixir of never-ending life, whether it be an uploaded version in the virtual world, or a transhuman variety still in the flesh, but augmented in ways barely imaginable today. Seneca wrote that life's meaning is to be found in its shortness. Over the coming days each of my new *temporary* colleagues all spoke at length about their retirement plans which were on the horizon. Each of them, like people in general, suffer from a deferred happiness illusion. Their current reality is a mere prelude to some idyllic future. This idyllic future, however, is often a mirage which fades the closer you get to it. When I retire, I'm going to buy a villa in Mogadishu. When I retire, I'm going to travel the world and preach peace and prosperity and the merits of empire and colonisation.

Carl Jung referred to living a "provisional life." An eternal child-like life with no commitment; not putting all your eggs in one basket. That's what Angela said to me the other evening: she was fed up with living a life with "All her eggs in one place." She meant basket. I said it was a bit late for that type of thinking. Her eggs were in the house. One was on an Xbox shooting the shit out of humanity, and the other was busy gambolling around the living room like she's come into an early inheritance.

"It's not too late for anything", said Angela. "What's wrong with having options in life, Jack?"

"Nothing," I said, struggling to think of a reply. "But you channel surf for an hour. You can't watch a movie from beginning to end. Too much choice is what's wrong with the world. Technology is changing our biology. Evolution didn't stop on the savannah plains."

Talk about keeping it diluted to the point of aromatherapy. I understand about not wanting to commit. Shall I commit to this person? Maybe a better one will come along? Shall I buy this house? Maybe there will be a better deal around the corner. On and on. And we are back to Samuel Beckett where we are always waiting because something better may come along.

Angela had been waiting for years for a better model to come into her life. Fucking Ken? Literally and metaphorically! I mean really. If he was that special, wouldn't she be with him already? The grass may be greener on the other side Angela, but it still needs cutting because we want the lawn a certain way. We always want it green and level, no weeds or leaves, no brown patches, no fungi poking its life affirming head above the canopy. Life is about trade-offs. Have you listened to Thomas

Sowell? And he's a black man in a white man's world. Have you listened to Richard Pryor? Now there's a comic genius who had his fingers on the pulse of living a provisional life.

There is meaning in sacrifice. Making a commitment is a sacrifice, Angela. It means giving up choices. Many of which are a delusion. Most were not even a real possibility. Just fiction. Sacrifice *IS* meaning. You're a Catholic for fuck's sake. Have you heard of Jesus? Life is short. You can't have everything. You cannot do everything. The nuclear family is a dirty term today in many areas. Yet, it is what led to Europe's so-called success story. It is the bedrock of its progress story. It is the cornerstone of all the institutions in the west which have spread like typhoid around the world. Clans and extended families sound cosy, kin selection and inclusive fitness is all well and good, but liberal democracies provide you wealth. Why should you care that it also brings an atomisation of society, loneliness, care homes for the discarded elderly, mental health issues, kids on medication because, apparently, if they can't sit still for hours on end then there is something wrong with them, and they need to be fed drugs by the wheelbarrow load. Where is Monty Python when you need them?

"Two children and almost two decades is a commitment, Jack. I didn't just shag you for a few weeks and tell you thanks, but you never found my g spot, so sorry, it ain't going to work for me. Sling your hook".

"It's a tough period. It'll pass. Maybe you're just rebelling because you know you shouldn't be playing Ken's flute?"

"You know I only play the piano, Jack. Wind instruments were never my thing. With you anyway."

Ouch! That hurt. A low blow, and not the one I would like. Didn't you hear what she said? Apparently, Ken is the only one getting the low blow. I'm just getting fucked in other ways.

"I don't want to live a life of default. I want to live a life by design," said Angela with her hand on her heart. We were in her bedroom. Not by invitation I might add. I was after a pair of jeans from her wardrobe. I stood there in my boxer shorts while she sat up in bed. I was the vulnerable one. It's so pathetically domestic, something only couples can do who have passed the point of sartorial pressure to impress their partner. It's a slippery slope.

"I don't want to be a cork bobbing up and down in the bath, Jack. Do you understand?" Two hands across her chest now as if she was anticipating a quick dive to grab her boobs.

"You're not a cork," I said.

"Is that a dig about my weight again?" Her hands were under the blanket now.

"What are you talking about? When do I ever say anything about your weight?" Though I must admit I was tempted on several occasions.

"When we were in Next a few years back, I tried on a pair of jeans, and you said they looked tight on my arse."

I couldn't remember. She could just as easily have accused me of a war crime.

"I don't recall," I said.

"How convenient! I don't want to settle for a treadmill-existence anymore."

"Well, what is this Ken offering you? What does he do? Does he know about the kids?" I had put on my jeans. I felt like I had clawed back the slightest bit of dignity. Every little helps at this point.

"He's not offering me anything. And yes, he knows about Hadrian and Meme. But you're again missing the point. It's about us, and where we are in life. Our marriage has run its course. It's been over for years. Meme just delayed the inevitable."

Have you ever seen the Christmas classic *It's a Wonderful Life*? You must have. Or I'll call it quits now. George Bailey is played by the great Jimmy Stewart in the days when the American dream felt real, even if it was made just moments after Hiroshima and Nagasaki were destroyed by Fatman and Littleboy and Curtis LeMay. George faces prison for financial irregularities, and decides suicide is the only way out to save his wife and four beautiful children from the shame and destitution he is about to bestow on the family. He is saved by his guardian angel who shows him what life would be like if he had never been born. A wish George makes in a moment of frustration. The movie is about a renaissance: George's re-birth into what is meaningful in life. A journey. Not a hero's odyssey, but an ordinary person's voyage of discovery. If only I believed in guardian angels. George and I have a few things in common.

I do believe, however, that we live much of our lives on automatic. We allow ourselves to be pushed around by so much nonsense. Angela is ahead of me. She knows what she doesn't want for sure. Maybe she has a vivid portrait of the future, of what she wants. I am no longer part of her inner orbit, and therefore, I am not privy to her new purpose.

"You have made yourself too hard, Jack. You're a fighter, I get it, but you have almost made yourself bullet proof like that vest you wear at work. It's not real. I'm fed up with appearing happy to my friends when I'm not happy. I'm the furthest thing from it. And I know already you're going to say that happiness is for fools, and it's fleeting and all that, but I want to be happy Jack, even if it's momentary."

"Ok, I understand."

"You say that but I know you think I'm talking rubbish. I know you're thinking that wanting to live an authentic life is like chasing your own shadow."

I had an energy dump. I suddenly became tired. I crawled into bed. My own. Angela's had claymores around it.

For me anyway. People yearn for a utopia. Thomas Moore wrote a book with the title back in Tudor times. The Soviets thought a utopia would follow the withering away of the state. Lenin's version not Stalin's. Even if they had to kill most of the people to achieve it. Rousseau believed nature was itself utopia. Climate activists today keep this vision alive by believing if humans vanished then utopia would return. For who?

Let me tell you a thing about utopia. Thomas Hobbes was right. You know what happens when you put mice in their equivalent of utopia. Imagine a safe playground where mice can relax and play till their little hearts are content. An abundance of their favourite food and beverages. Love not war. Mice version of hippy heaven. You know what happens to them? It is not a mice version of *The Waltons*. They die. In the absence of adversity and struggle, they decline in wellbeing, and become dysfunctional and unhappy. Their hearts break. This is utopia, Angela. This is what I want to tell Steve, Brian and Matt at the airport when they tell me about the blissful and happy lives they will have in the future: **Utopia is a death trap**.

"Linda, if you'll go over first and establish the baseline. Let us know the state of play, and we'll come over in pairs and form a channel. Steve, if you pair with Jack, and Brian and Matt if you can stick together. We are going to operate around Costa in the arrivals area. Engage with the public. Hand out the leaflets, and let people know what Operation Servator is all about: making the airport a hard target for a potential terrorist attack. We have to be vigilant and at the top of our game. Let the terrorists know they need to go elsewhere. Any questions?" asked Ron.

I looked at the others. Linda had changed into plain clothes for her role. The others were in uniform and wore serious expressions like they were about to embark on a special forces mission behind enemy lines. The enemy of the week would be determined by the Ministry of Information. Whichever fuckers were not complying with the hegemonic narrative. Do they know what we are capable of when we are ignored? Have they seen JR Ewing in *Dallas* when he acts out his anger? That crooked smile under the Stetson hat in the hot sun. It's all about energy capture, remember? Carl Sagan's "pale blue dot" is one great big round glob of potential energy waiting to be exploited. JR instinctively knew this while those around him were busy shagging. This is glorified, global gluttony. Fat cats are getting fatter.

"I'll let you know when to come over Sarg," said Linda.

"Great. Channel 88 for talk through," said Ron.

I changed my radio to 88. I felt sick all of a sudden.

Steve explained what was about to happen: "Linda will sit up in Costa and observe people. Relative numbers. Anyone behaving unusually in the context. That's what it means by 'establishing the baseline.' It's all about the setting. You expect people to be nervous in some contexts. There are some, of course, who exhibit nervous signs when they are waiting to board a flight, or waiting for someone to arrive who they might not have seen for a while. You have to take all these things, and much else besides, into account. We approach and engage a target identified by Linda who she believes is acting strange. One of us will ask some basic questions while the other one observes their behaviour to see if there is any leakage."

"Leakage? Like if they start to sweat or make a run for the exit, then we know something is up?" I couldn't help it. There is only so much I can take. Recall that everyone has a breakpoint!

"Well, maybe a more subtle leakage," replied Steve, obviously not impressed.

"What do we do with these leaflets and cards?" I asked.

I was referring to the information leaflets describing Operation Servator and the role of the Airport Police Unit. Apparently, there was a website, and even YouTube footage, and all sorts of cutting-edge media posts about Servator. I later discovered it is a brand, and where there is a brand there has to be marketing, and where there is marketing, there has to be money involved and exchanged, and where there is money exchanged, there is bound to be corruption somewhere. We were the sales reps. The marketing monkeys. Remember the group and the song: "Hey Hey we're the Monkeys..." That's what was playing in my head as I walked out of Diamond House, the main building at the airport where the police station is located. As Steve and I walked toward the terminal building. Toward Costa. Toward Linda in her plain clothes who was establishing the baseline. Toward the coffee drinkers and members of the public who were minding their own business not knowing that the real terrorists were about to arrive, and that they should all make a run for it while they still could. Have they never been taught about situational awareness? It can save your life. You don't have to be in the Mumbai Hotel. You don't have to be at a pop concert in Manchester or walking along Westminster Bridge. You don't have to be on the fortieth floor of the World Trade Centre. You can just be about to walk across a road at a pedestrian crossing, with the little green genderless figure signalling to you that it is safe to cross. But it is not safe, because that cunt in his VW Golf is out of prison. He is back on the road driving like Mad Max. And if you've been following along you'll know that being a cunt, he doesn't care about stopping at lights regardless of sexless figures (and I AM one of those sexless figures green or no green) and his foot ain't touching the break, because like me, he is a fan of Freddy Mercury, and he has "Don't stop me now, cos I'm having such a good time, I'm having a ball," blaring out. It is intuitively instructing him to floor the fucker. This is where situational awareness comes to save you like the Special Boat Service, like Fireman Sam, like Tom and C Company when they go after Private Ryan - long before Matt got his kickass Jason Bourne skills which could have stopped the Waffen SS, and their bastard offspring the Azov battalions - you'll look up from your phone, because you've been trained, and you'll see Mr Cunt lip synching to "Don't stop me now..." and you will know - the proverbial penny will drop - that he ain't goin' to stop, and that training will save your life. Get it? Got it? Fuck me, it's hard work.

You've spotted it no doubt. You are a little more switched on than what I give you credit for. Maybe. I am being somewhat facetious. I've already said that your brain is a prediction machine. It is establishing a baseline every second of your existence. Whether you are entering a room in your house, or walking into Tesco for bread and milk before the prices go up again, your brain has already predicted the baseline. It is only if something is out of the ordinary that your brain notifies "you" and, hopefully, your limbs will respond appropriately.

To be fair to systems like Servator, they help fine tune our biology to be more aware of things which are not quite right. In extreme environments, this training does make a difference. Where it goes wrong, however, is when it professes to reinvent the wheel, or pretentiously presents itself as being a hard science. And as for handing out leaflets and cards and interrupting people having a coffee to talk about how great you are as a unit, and basically acting like Hari Krishnas at airports (they must have been handed airport banning notices as you never see them anymore), it's embarrassing for all involved.

Supervisors record the number of leaflets you hand out, as if your job on the unit depends on the number of raffle tickets you sell. They are called "encounters." It forms part of your performance assessment. I'm not making this shit up. Seriously. After wasting half an hour or so, you are given the "stand down" command, and you drift off in your pairs with the satisfaction that you may have foiled the next terrorist attack, and head to All Bar One for a well-deserved free coffee.

I only wish I had Servator training a while back. It's possible I would have noticed a baseline change in Angela's behaviour. I could have handed her a leaflet so she would know I was on to her and Ken. I may have noticed leakage, and not the kind you are thinking of. I could have rumbled her Barbie-like behaviour. My predictive brain let me down. But so did Billy Jones's three pound neural device. When his brain saw Cherry Street covered in debris. When his brain saw rioters hurling everything from abuse to broken glass at an advancing police line with shields and weapons. When his brain saw his daily spot for selling the Big Issue on fire. What bit of information failed to tell his prediction machine that the baseline was compromised, and he needed to vacate the scene, pronto? It was not the time to be handing out leaflets, Billy. I mean for fuck sakes mate. It was not the place to be looking for leakage. The whole dam had been blown. It was a cascade. Why didn't you move when I told you to? I did raise my voice. I was the one who was leaking. You appeared as calm as a sniper in Stalingrad. It was a role reversal. If you had only been Servator trained. If only everyone could be Servator trained. Maybe then the wars for profit and power would stop.

The real virulent existential threat we face is the neoCon 19 virus originating in a lab in Washington D.C (you can use the abbreviation neoLibs interchangeably: same wolf). No natural spill over for these *Homo Insanus* extremists. If they were Servator trained then maybe, just maybe, they would stop pushing and realise the threat level. Maybe they would then understand that no underground hotel suite fully furnished with a gym and jacuzzi and heated swimming pool is going to save them. They can have as many retired Navy SEALs and Delta Force on retainer as they want, but if they are so deluded to think they can chill their rich, aromatic beans in a multi-million dollar nirvana safe-haven in a mountain somewhere in the Midwest or New Zealand or Australia, and pop up twelve months after the blow out like a bunch of spring daffodils, then there is no chance for any of us. And they have no idea about the difficulties of making agriculture work, never mind the efficacy of retired special forces. They ain't called mercenaries for no reason.

Yeah, I'm on one, so skip to the end if you don't like it. Things have gotten way out of hand. Where are the Fabulous Four when you need them? Do they think they can stop drone torpedoes armed with 100 megaton warheads with enough bang for the buck to take out a small country? Do they really believe they can water their newly planted wheat and barley gardens while thousands of nuclear missiles pay a visit like unwanted relatives at Christmas? They have been receiving promotions and accolades, bonuses and kickbacks for their messianic power driven Just So Story about the Manifest Destiny of their expansionist narrative. Did you think it was going to stop at Santa Barbara in the 19th Century? Insanity. Do they believe they have natural immunity from Iskander missiles? Have they had vaccines and boosters from Pfizer and Moderna to protect them? Because those fuckers will no doubt come out with some kind of overpriced drug at the taxpayers expense to shield you from ICBMs. Just don't ask for their clinical trial data. "Who the fuck do you think you are anyway? Take it and shut the fuck up or else." There have been no consequences for their endless miscalculations. No, that's not quite right. They receive an Amazon gift card for every death. There is no pushback. No payback. There is no Mel Gibson making a shit revenge movie where they will beg for forgiveness for all the carnage they have caused, pleading for their lives to be spared. There's no Liam Neeson pointing a gun at them while they cower in a lift saying how it was only business Liam, nothing personal. Please, please. Lights out. And you can hear people around the world cheer as the manicured, miserable existence of the neoCons is wiped out for all time. But in the real world in which most of us must live and survive, their fuckwittedness goes unpunished. In fact, it has been rewarded by other fuckwitted people. They belong to the same tribe called the FUCKWITTERS who are as territorial as a starving troop of chimpanzees, or a bunch of lunatic militant transgender cult fanatics parked outside JK Rowling's house shouting for her to be deplatformed and defrocked and defenestrated.

Let the FUCKWITTERS lock and load. Lead the way into battle like Henry V, Richard III or George C Scott. War would end in an instant. FUCKWITTERS could just about manage a frontal assault into Starbucks where they would unleash their aggression if their lattes were not extra, extra hot. Burn that milk or we'll burn your store to the ground. Well, we will have others do it for us, but you get the point. Don't you?

For you and me, there is a strong pressure on us to make decisions that conform with reality even if we are not aware of them all the time. But FUCKWITTERS don't have to adhere to these same pressures. They are not punished for making decisions in their virtual world. This is why societies and empires collapse. At some point FUCKWITTERS take total control and things fall apart.

They are admired and supported in their FUCKWITTEDNESS by the media who accelerate the march into oblivion because they are enslaved to the tribe. The historian Thomas Carlye and the great Frederich Hegel himself referred to FUCKWITTERS as great men of history (and they are nearly always men). They are the furthest thing from great. No one is great. After the age of seven, it's only a matter of trying to minimise how much of a cunt you are going to be. O shut up. It's true. No one cares that you throw a few quid to some cause. Take your sticker and fuck off. I mentioned before how sticks and stones may break your bones. This is true. Ammunition fired through a cylinder does more harm. Nuclear weapons are a game changer for good. We all cease to exist. You would think that would wipe the big Cheshire cat smile off everyone's face. And cats in Cheshire don't smile unless they belong to Premiership footballers. Have you ever been there? It's all bananas. Where is Woody Allen when you need him? He needs to write a script about this neurotic insanity.

I pushed a man with my casco. One man and look at the chain reaction. You really think that any nation with thousands of nuclear weapons can ever lose a real war? FUCKWITTERS think so. Of course, they couldn't lose. Even if their nation is obliterated, if they survive, then it's literally, the last man standing. Or woman, if you listen to Gloria Gaynor, remember? A new global tug of war has formed. Europe is now the serf of an American Lord. It has made its bed, and now it must lie in it, regardless of the cost. It's not about the people in each country. It's about their rulers. Like the interbred aristocrats on the eve of the First World War who drove the masses off the cliff edge, current oligarchs who rule each state, share similar interests. They too will battle it out in the game of who can collect the most resources. It's not like chess which requires real thinking. It's a game of monopoly.

Operation Servator could be a beacon for hope and change. It can show how the baseline of modern human behaviour is irrational. Despite Professor Pinker and Matt Ridley and Hugo Mercier championing our innate rationality, they fail to recognise that reasoning is synonymous with leakage in the current age. It is what happens when the baseline is disturbed, and that's why those of us who have had the course can spot it so easily. The leakage is real, and it drives progress. It fuels science when it is practised correctly which is sadly less and less these days due to how the structure is funded and warped like a Salvador Dali painting. However, when the FUCKWITTERS are alone, they are scared. They suck their thumbs and crawl up into the foetal position and cry themselves to sleep. They surf the net through covert servers for child porn, acts of extreme violence, and to view the Osmond's singing their greatest hits. They fantasise about the second coming and being king or queen of planet earth or having their own spacecraft to visit another world after they have destroyed this one. Not realising that this planet cannot be destroyed by them. The pale blue dot doesn't give a toss about *Homo Insanus*. We are a speck of dust floating in the atmosphere. We harness the low entropy of the sun via plants for a brief period, and soon we will be gone. Sooner of course if the FUCKWITTERS continue their current trajectory. Wake me up after all the stupidity is over. My wife is having sex with a man called Ken. Another three-letter word. We should ban them. Censor them. Why not? Isn't that the way of things? It's the story of us. Recall even the great Copernicus, Galileo and Giodano Bruno were silenced by the church. Their books were censored for 150 years for saying the earth went around the sun. Bruno was burnt at the stake. The state wants to do the same to Ed Snowden and Julian Assange today. That's one for progress.

I'm done. Rant over. I'm stuck at the airport. It's like being signed by Barcelona and being loaned out to Norwich. Please, even Norwich fans are nodding. I have the Beatles on playing *Help* but no one is listening.

I ask you to keep this humble idea in the front of your mind going forward: 50,000 years ago - a mere blink of an eye in the geological record - there were at least six different species of *Homo* alive at the same time on earth. I suspect we killed the others off by territorial expansion, resource capture, and cannibalism. And I've mentioned good ole fashion rape of female captives. There is just us left. There's one skittle left standing. And the neoCons/Libs are literally rolling balls down the lane. Remember Tommy Cooper, the magician, who's stage gag was to always get the trick wrong. With his red Fez cap on his head - which would be classed as cultural appropriation today - he would perform the magic trick and say: "Not like that, like this!" He would always have the same expression which said, 'Surely it can't go wrong again.' It always went wrong. Give it enough time, and it will always go wrong. That's the paradox of development. That's the paradox of violence. That's the paradox of Angela and me.

What If?

I am on a night shift. I thought I had left them behind with my teenage years. Years of fighting and playing ice hockey. Years of trying to fit in, and yet a deep, yearning need to stamp my individuality on the world. Getting along and getting ahead.

Nights cause me anxiety. I know I'm going to be sleep deprived for days. If only there was a God. The phone rang. It was Bobby. God uses angels to communicate, not Three Mobile.

"How are you, Bobby? What gospel do you have for me?"

"That would be good news. Sorry mate, I'm more the serpent in the garden. The IOPC have sent the case to the CPS. We both got emails from DS Bridgeman this morning, but I knew you were on a night shift so I thought I would call and let you know."

"Great! Is that them passing it across so the CPS takes on the responsibility, not them?"

"Yeah, it could be. The CPS could authorise a charge so it's down to the court to decide. That's the problem," said Bobby.

“They have to reach a threshold for a charge. I suppose they could do me for littering. I noticed a Mars wrapper falling out of my pocket on the CCTV,” I said.

“You’re fucked then,” he said laughing. “But you’re right about the threshold. Still, it’s a high-profile job, and they are all protecting themselves. Let’s see what happens next. We’ll know soon enough.”

“Okay,” I said. “It’s all I need on my mind going to work tonight.”

“Sorry, mate. I’ve got to go. The missus wants me to take her to the retail park. I’d rather be at work myself. I call you when you’re off nights or if I hear anything before.”

“Cheers,” I said. Can things get any worse?

I’ve never seriously contemplated suicide. There was a lad at school called Kevin who killed himself. It was in the last year of school. He was sixteen. It was quite shocking. He was an overweight boy. I know he got lots of grief over the years. Other kids would call him “Weeble.” They would sing the catchy tune from the advertisement for these toys: “Weeble’s wobble but they don’t fall down.” Well, this “Weeble” did fall down. He threw himself off the top of a car park in Dale End in the city.

I wonder if any of them regretted the abuse they drowned him in? The harm they caused. Of course, they all constructed a narrative which exonerated themselves from any culpability: Kevin must have been emotionally unstable. Some issues at home that no-one was aware of, maybe. His dad wasn't on the scene was he? A single mom raising a kid all by herself. Tough back in those years. A social stigma. Did he have any brothers and sisters? There were bound to be other reasons. It couldn't possibly be us. Here's the thing fuckers. It was you. Emotional battering over years. He must have been filled with fear coming to school each day. Hoping that he would be left alone. Praying there would be no reference in a physics class to a "large mass" or a reference to a fat character in a book we were reading in an English lesson. Fear every day.

I've been to a number of suicides in my time. As you would expect, young people taking their own lives is one of the worst kinds of incidents a police officer can ever attend. The proverbial "Why" question is always asked. What a waste! If only you had waited a while. Spoke to someone.

Humans are the only species which kill themselves. In fact, I would argue, it is one of the defining characteristics of being human. A bipedal, large, brained primate which kills itself in every nook and cranny of the planet. It is a universal characteristic of all humans. Apart from people with severe learning difficulties and young children. Those who cannot form a coherent sense of a unified self which travels through time with the ability to imagine that self in an array of possible future settings. Everyone else is vulnerable. Not just Kevin. Everyone, including yourself. No matter how high the wave that you're surfing now. Especially teenagers. I suspect it is a by-product of evolution. Another spandrel. When you combine specific substances in a chemical reaction, it can be lethal. Pain and self-awareness, and a knowledge of one's own mortality is one such concoction. All animals react to pain by wanting to escape from it. Nothing special there. No other animal has a unified sense of themselves, and a knowledge of their future death. One can bring that future death into the present to escape protracted pain. That's what Kevin and others do. No matter what you may read these days, the internet is not the ultimate cause. Severe bullying and suicides in the extended family are more accurate predictors. Social media is probably what is termed backward causation.

I have said earlier that we have social brains. We are well adapted to living in groups. In fact, that's why we are clever in the first place. That's one of the main causes of our intelligence. Imagine being born alone on a desert island. You would not develop language or algebra, morality or the idiotic ideas which we are drowning ourselves in today. However, we are not alone. We grow up in a culture which shapes our biology, the plasticity of our brains. Without being able to read the minds of others - with varying degrees of success - we would not last long. When our pain is caused by our group then being taunted and abused, being ostracised and laughed at, triggers real pain, and if that pain is so harsh and prolonged, then one way to escape it is to take our own life. Social media just turns up the dial and brings it into nearly every bedroom on the planet. How sad is that! There is no humour or pithy one liner to be made on this subject. Not when you've ever been the one to pull up the zip of a body bag over a little girl's face who could not take the pain anymore.

Cher and I Sing: If I could Turn Back Time

If Bobby's call wasn't bad enough, a few minutes later Angela's dad called me. This had never happened before so when I saw his name appear on the screen of my phone, I assumed Angela was dead. She had gone out earlier to have her nails done. She had taken Meme along to introduce her to the future ritual. No more picking berries or grinding seeds for these modern women.

I thought I should have taken life insurance out on Angela when she suggested a few years ago that we should have a joint policy. Another regret! I instantly had a panic attack as if I had been given a handover to do at work. And before we move on to any potential funerals, let me say a word or two about "handovers." No police officer ever wants to be given a prisoner to deal with at the start of their shift. They have designated investigation teams these days for the mentally impaired who choose to work on them.

Many moons ago, if you were at the bottom of the police caste system, you had to do everything. It meant, if there was a prisoner(s) in the "traps" the shift had to deal with them. In my early years at Vyse Street, there were always several offenders in the cells at Steelhouse Lane Station waiting to be dealt with, especially on early shifts. The remains from the night before. Usually from all the nightclubs: fights, drunks, drugs, disorders of every kind. Also, more serious jobs resulting from proper crime in the inner-city areas. Only if they were dead, dying, or drug kingpins would CID at Steelhouse Lane take a look. Even then they would say: “We'll be here if you need some advice, now fuck off and leave us in peace to have our cooked breakfast in the canteen.” It meant you had interviews to do, court files to build, and all this on top of being on a response vehicle and trying to manage mountains of other crime reports waiting to be actioned on what was called your “docutrack.” We all cracked on with the work. That was the way it was.

There were also handovers at the airport. No one wanted to be given one. Strange that. It was like a game of pass the parcel, but instead of trying to hold onto the package till the music stopped, people threw it around like it was a vial of Sarin gas. Fights and drunken behaviour on board an aircraft often ended up in Crown Court.

It was a pain trying to obtain statements from people who didn't hang around an airport for too long, including the flight crew. At least I was honest when I said I was only visiting the unit and won't be around long enough to do any long investigations. Also, I don't give a flying jolly roger flag of a fuck so give it to one of the others who always talked like they were officers of the month and year and millennium, but when that stack of papers appeared on the briefing room desk, they had every excuse for not accepting it ranging from, “I have a statement to take at ten” which was arranged when I was in my mother’s womb to, “I have a phobia of custody blocks” (they actually call them “suites” now; another example of how if you control language you control the narrative). If the Sarg handed it to someone else, you felt like you had won the lottery.

It turned out Meme was alive and well. No funeral arrangements were needed for Angela either. Though I did think of whether it would be myself or Robert who would pay. He would want a horse drawn funeral carriage through Knowle with all the trimmings. I would opt for the cheapest coffin, and the disposal ritual at Robin Hood Crematorium. It’s going to get burnt anyway. How much virtue signalling can you do? Have you looked recently at how much it costs to bury someone? You have to remortgage your house to get a headstone. It’s amazing how much information can come to mind in the time it takes to see Robert’s name appear on my phone and think: “What does that fucker want?”

“Hello Robert. Is everything alright?” I asked with a false sense of urgency in my voice.

“Why wouldn’t it be?” he replied sternly, as if I had asked a stupid question and had wasted his £200 an hour time.

“It’s just that I don’t ever recall you having phoned me before, that’s all.”

“We need to have a chat,” he said. “Not at the house. I’ll meet you at Costa in half an hour. The one in Knowle, of course.”

With that he hung up. Cunt.

A half hour later I’m sitting in Costa on Knowle High Street. Ten minutes pass, and I decide to get myself a coffee. No sooner had I reached the counter when Robert appeared.

“I’ll have an Americano with hot milk. In a takeaway cup. Make sure it’s hot milk,” he said as he walked past me, and sat at a table at the very back of the shop.

I had been sitting by the window. Where is a flame thrower when you need one? Or Drogan, the dragon that Daenerys’ herself rides when she swoops down on her enemies, and destroys them all with fire; a little like Bomber Harris.

I bring the drinks to the table. I had the same as Robert. It’s the only thing we had in common. I’m assuming he’s never had sex with his daughter. However, I’ve been wrong about such matters before having policed Birmingham for many years.

The elephant in the corner of Costa was the hidden motives which we all have, but do not present to people. We were two hairless apes sitting across from each other. Robert was wearing an expensive suit. He was showing me who was the boss; who had the higher status. He was demonstrating to me that in the competition between us, I had lost. Yes, there may have been reluctant cooperation in the past because of Angela and his grandchildren, but I should not delude myself that I was needed. Money and modernity have trumped the stone age casco wielding meathead.

"Angela wants a divorce," said Robert. He took a sip of his coffee. "You did ask for hot milk? It tastes a little cooler than when I order my own."

Have you watched *Gossip Girls*? I don't blame you if you haven't, but don't be a cultural snob and say you are too busy reading Cervantes and Pushkin (if the latter hasn't been sanctioned and censored by now). Gossip is what allows us to form coalitions. It permits us to change alliances. It is at the root of all civilisations. Angela has returned to the family fold.

"She told you that?"

"No, I've made it up. My idea of a joke, Jack."

Yeah, I asked for that. I felt like getting up and going into the toilet and punching myself straight in the face. Fortunately, an elderly lady had just gone in to occupy it for an hour.

"What else did she say, Robert?" I felt like I had just moved my king out of check.

"She just said she felt it was the right time for you both to move on. She didn't criticise you. She said nothing negative. She just wants a new life, and she believes the time is right."

The best theory to explain human behaviour is the one which explains the most detail with the minimum fuss. People lie. Often people are unaware of the ultimate causes of their own actions. They focus only on the proximate causes, the most immediate and often superficial explanations of why they do what they do. Many believe there is a subconscious self busily running the whole show. There is no shadow self beneath the surface, at the helm, like a submarine commander. This is another illusion.

I look at Robert taking another sip of his not so hot coffee in his expensive attire, and I realise he is just your run of the mill show off. And yet, people like to associate with show-offs who have something to model even if it's a camouflage or a cheap replica.

I wonder if I should mention Ken or keep that powder dry for a while. A child, after all, can do no wrong in their parents' eyes. I'm struck, as I so often am, by the pettiness of human beings. Including myself. What's good for the goose and all that. We like to believe we are so high minded and principled, but just beneath the swamp is a suppressed tantrum.

"Did she mention Ken?" Fuck it, I told you before I would fail the marshmallow test, miserably. Robert is lucky I haven't strangled him already with his expensive tie which probably cost more than I earn in a month.

"Ken?"

This is where no amount of education and bragging about what university you attended, what bollocks of a degree you got, what your postcode is, how much you earn, what you do for a living, where you live, what kind of house you own, what you read, watch, or listen to, who you know, what you know, what you have, who you think you are, who you actually are is going to help you out. It's all braggadocio and status. Robert, can't you self-examine in the good old Socratic fashion, and understand that you are sitting across from someone, who when they want to, when they choose not to stick their head up their own ass, they can see, smell, and sense bullshit. Robert never had Servator training. He has never been on advanced interview courses. Being a lawyer, he was more used to being a liar. You see, it even sounds like a jingle: being a lawyer, being a liar. That's not just by chance. It's a universal law: mathematical structure out there in the cosmos. Don't misunderstand me, I have already stated that lying is underrated. There's a time and place for many unpalatable traits. And it's always good to know a savvy solicitor.

"Yes Ken. Your daughter, my wife, is having an affair with a bloke called Ken. Didn't she mention that fact?" Check, Robert.

"I didn't call you here to discuss my daughter's personal life. She told me she has asked you to move out. I suggested to her that I make you an offer for your share of the house. That way it's a clean break. Of course, you would pay maintenance for the children. But you can both move on with your lives. So, I thought about a reasonable offer, and came to a figure of £100,000."

He had recovered his composure. He was staring straight at me. It was a good test for my upcoming trial. Words are cheap. Body language is more expensive. This makes sense when you think about it from a purely energy expenditure point of view. I've said several times now that virtue signalling, and simple gestures, have a low cost. Even when corporations spend millions for some pointless signal, that is the equivalent of you and I scratching our genitals in terms of endearment. People who are trained in controlling their body language have already ticked one box on the Servator course without the pain of going through it. This is being aware of behaviour associated with leakage. Actors and lawyers are good at controlling their body movements. However, only when they are in their respective court rooms. In their private lives, as Noel Coward comically depicted in writing, they leak like a burst water main.

"That's interesting," I said. "A fair share? I reckon our house is worth around £500,000 since we did the loft conversion. And I thought you knew, in fact, I'm positive you know, I've paid off the mortgage Robert. I have done that. Because Angela, your daughter, has only worked for about half an hour in her whole life when she was sixteen. In the fish and chip shop down the road. Now I know for certain that you know she was sacked. They didn't even pay her for those thirty minutes. I grant that was out of order, but even if she had saved that one pound for all the years later when we met and married, even if she had invested that one pound, Robert, in Apple or Facebook when they were at their lowest price, that one pound would not pay for the sealant I used yesterday around the skirting board in the dining room. Now I know what you're going to say Robert. You're going to deliver a few words around the themes of motherhood, stay at home wife, homemaker, and I understand how important those themes are. But, and it's a really big but, those themes are not worth £400,000, and a fucking bloke called Ken moving into my house with my kids."

One of the reasons we laugh is to bond with our group. Without laughter we could never have walked on the moon or received a heart transplant. We learn with the aid of laughing. When we play, we can even fight and insult one another with laughter to test loyalty and limits of the relationship. When the laughter stops however, the play stops. The fight or the insult has gone too far. The injured party will wear the insult on their proverbial sleeve.

I got up from the table, and left Robert and his suit slightly more ruffled than when he first strode in. On the way back to my car, I blocked his number. I know, I know, another eye roll emoji.

I'm in my car driving back to MY house, not one fifth of my house, not the garage conversion. I turn on the radio, and

Cher comes on singing: "If I could turn back time, I'd find a way..." You know the one. Cher after she got rid of Sonny. It's difficult to picture those two together. Not like Bucks Fizz or Peters and Lee, or Jay Z and Beyonce, or even Kurt Cobain and Courtney Love, and you must give a throw out to Garth Brooks and Trisha Yearwood. It's more like John Lennon and Yoko Ono. If there was ever a poster couple for the idiotic "war on drugs," it would be John and Yoko. It would be easier to get your head around quantum field theory, or the pathetic Covid modelling by Neil Ferguson and Chris Witless, than understand the mind of a musical genius like Lennon. Cher with her crazy black hair and tight leather pants rocking away. I sing along with the first two lines. Then *Dr Who* comes to mind. The doctor found a way to turn back time. And how appropriate that it was via a police phone box. Fuckers did away with those too. Long before they closed the canteens, bars and police stations. Unbelievable when you stop to think about it. If you said that at any time since the police were founded people would have thought you were insane. And you are, remember? Now it's celebrated in some circles. Until they need the police, of course. Then they find out they either have to go online, or hitch-hike across the bastard galaxy to gain access to the police equivalent of the Horse and Groom.

If I could operate the dials inside the phone box, and turn back time (travel down a wormhole if you prefer) where would I want to come out? Remember Michael J Fox in the classic *Back to the Future* where the character Marty uses a DeLorean car instead of a *Dr Who* phone box to travel back to the moment when his parents first met. How inconvenient that his future mom falls in love with Marty himself. Talk about Sophocles' *Oedipus Rex* where the son marries his own mother, and it all goes terribly wrong. I cannot for the life of me imagine having sex with my own mother, even in her younger years. That's my genes talking out loud. Obviously, they are all deaf in Cardiff.

If I had been raised by a different woman, and met my mom as an adult, then myself and Oedipus could start our own group therapy session. Same applies to siblings. Unless you're a termite or a naked mole rat. It's the familiarity in the early years that counts. Or should, but I'll leave that one alone like a canister full of VX.

If I turned the dials back to 1350, and stepped out of the kiosk door in the aftermath of the Black Death in Coventry, could I imagine that this city, and its surrounding grasslands, would be at the heart of the Industrial Revolution 450 years later? No. I could imagine it being bombed during a war if for no other reasons than it has a shit football team, and an unnavigable inner ring road. What the fuck were the highway planners thinking?

Fifty years later if Tamerlane had not turned his Mongols toward the east after conquering Persia, India and the Ottoman

Empire, Europe may have been overcome, and the modern world might look remarkably different. If I stepped out in Vienna in 1529, I might have seen the Turks batter the Habsburg Empire, and take possession of the city. They didn't. If they had the whole Atlantic economy, which was growing, might have crumbled, and minarets may have stretched from York to Lisbon.

I could have landed my time machine on the top floor of the car park in Dale End in Birmingham city centre when Kevin was standing on the edge. Looking down. I could use all the experience I've gained over years to tell him about the impact his death will have on his loved ones. I would tell him about George Bailey, and the wonderful life he was about to leave behind. Yes, the pain would stop for him but what about his family. The guilt; shame. Yes, shame. Family members often feel shame, embarrassment, even anger at the loved one who chooses death over life. How could they do it to them, the living?

What about parking the box beside St Phillips Cathedral on Colmore Row on the day of the anti-capitalist massacre? I refer to the day Billy Jones died. Everyone is prone to exaggeration sometimes. Everyman confuses an eight with a six. I could come face to face with my doppelganger. I would warn him of the danger lying in wait just over the horizon. Would he listen? Or would he act like Custer and carry on anyway.

Always the glory hunter. I would take his NATO helmet in my hands and tell him his wife - our wife - is blowing the flute of a fella called Ken. “It’s not true mate that she can only play the piano. The bitch has been having lessons from James Galway on YouTube for years.” The Irish are everywhere. The potato blight drove them to the four corners of the world, and when they weren’t building roads, digging canals, laying railways, they were high kicking in lines straighter than the German autobahn, and playing musical instruments with more vigour than Schonberg’s Vienna before the Great War.

I would say to him: “Whatever happens, don’t walk down Cherry Street. Remember the advice your tutor gave you before your first court appearance: ‘If it looks like it’s all going pear-shaped, consider fainting!’”

What if the phone box could only make one stop on its journey through the wormhole? How about landing outside Cleary’s pub the night you met Angela? Stop yourself from going inside. Convince yourself that the future does not only consist of epidemics, bioengineering of every kind imaginable, war and endless pandemic reality tv shows which have nothing to do with reality, because if they did the self-professed stars and producers would be drowned in one big vat of cat piss. Whatever it takes to prevent him from walking through the door, and to his dance with destiny. Literally. Okay, so Hadrian and Meme would never be born. Xbox shares would be worth slightly less, but they scoop up kids like a well-trained human trafficking gang so their profits would continue to soar. Yes, you would miss out on Meme's gambols and cute acts of manipulation but remember you would be saving future men - or possibly women - from untold harm. You would be like Tom Cruise in your very own *Minority Report* saving future victims. Is there any nobler cause I ask you? Meryl Streep only had to sacrifice one of her children to the naughty Nazis. I would be sacrificing both of mine, and there would be no big payday, and certainly no shiny Oscar to be collected at the end of a red carpet. And let me point out to any mothers who may be reading, just in case you find yourself surrounded by a group of ex-Etonians - all now in their forties and running the country - and you are alone with your two young children: a two-year-old and a twelve-year-old. You have wandered into a mysterious hall where a strange ritual is underway which has all the hallmarks of repressed desires which would raise Freud himself from the dead. The old Etonians demand that you hand over one of your children for their sinister ritual otherwise they will seize both. You are distraught. But they insist. They are the ruling elite. You are well and truly fucked, but chances are because you are a woman you yourself are safe. Listen in. This is what you should do. Give them your two-year-old. It's all about an optimal reproduction strategy. You've invested more in the twelve-year-old, and they have proven already that they have overcome some of life's hurdles. Your two-year-old has yet to prove their worth. And they are probably teething and making lots of noise. Make sure you get a receipt from the fuckers before you leave. You might get a tax write off. Maybe.

I pulled up on the drive. Back in the real world. You know what it meant when the Conquistadores burnt their ships on the beach of whatever land they had come to pillage and plunder? It signalled to the cast and crew that there was no turning back. By telling Robert that she wanted to divorce me, Angela had set our boat alight. And to top it all off, I was on a night shift at the airport.

How the Police Let God Down

No sooner had I arrived home with a Caspian pizza for Hadrian (he had sent me a text on my way home whining he hadn't had one for ages) when I received a text from Sergeant Ron. It may just be me, but I believe when others receive a ping or a ring there is an element of pleasant anticipation. My element is uranium. I get anxious. A sense of dread descends. Someone has sent me an implied obligation: reply or pick up. It is unusual to receive a text from your stripe when you're off duty. Especially when you are out on loan to a unit in a land which time forgot. It was not going to be an invitation to pick up an award. Or a thank you text for making up the numbers while half the bastard Airport Unit were off sick.

The text read: "Extinction Rebellion have cut through the perimeter fence, and with their own ladders have managed to climb onto the wing of a Flybe aircraft. Be at work by 6 please."

Hadrian informed me between sniper kills that his mom and little sister had gone out again. In a way I was glad as I knew that she now knew that Robert knew, and her mom probably knew, that her dad had made me a derisory offer to vacate our family home. No doubt she had spoken to him as soon as I left Costa, and decided it may be for the best if she stayed out till I went to work. Good decision.

Don't you hate those movies when the soon to be murdered person is about to enter the house, and they sense there is something amiss - their own spider senses are tingling - and you are telling them not to go in even though you know it's all part of the thin plot (thinner than this gruel) and yet in they go, and you can't believe they are so dumb when they knew themselves that danger lurked within. Yet, there they are treading the boards in fear, and looking around like they are part of Seal Team 6 and someone like Osama Bin Laden is about to jump out at them, AK 47 in hand, shouting how the west has fucked the east, south, and all points on the global map, for way too long now, and it's time to get your ass shot up. Global NATO has expanded faster than the universe, and now there's push back; time for the magnificent G7 to be revised into Huawei 7G via BRICS, SCO and any other acronym the east wants to strike back with like Han Solo and Luke-warm Skywalker; to regain the lead they had over the west for a thousand years since the fall of the Roman Empire till Zenghu had his ships burnt, and China decided to stay home and play in its own backyard.

The world has changed. It's always the declining hegemonic powerhouse who is the last to know and react. How will they throw their teddy bears is **THE ONLY** question? Now that's what you should all really be worried about. Angela would not have a clue how to handle a firearm. I always sneak a peek at the kitchen knife holder to make sure they are all accounted for.

Remember what I said earlier about situational awareness. It can save your life one day. Now it's off to work I go, like one of Snow White's dwarfs. But I won't be singing any jolly "Hi Ho" song. I'll be playing and singing along to possibly the greatest song of all time, by yeah, you've guessed it, Freddy singing *Bohemian Rhapsody*: "Mama, I've just killed a man..." Take it away Fred. And I hope you do know that the night when twenty-four Navy SEALS descended into the compound in May 2011 in Abbottabad, Pakistan was a murder mission. There was no shoot out. No AK47 wielding Osama. Forget *Zero Dark Thirty*! The Pakistanis had him under house arrest there since 2005. Just an execution. Three cheers for justice. One for all, and all for one. Emoji time.

There's heavy traffic. Things are always gloomier at night time when you are going to work. We are afraid of the dark. The real dark. Before streetlights, long before neon and Broadway, we used whale oil to illuminate our inner world. Maybe I should mention this fact to the hijackers. If it wasn't for technology, whales would have gone the way of the dodo.

Our life expectancy has risen from thirty to over seventy in just a hundred years. Nitrogen fertiliser produced by natural gas literally feeds half of the global population. Norman Borlogg, the Nobel prize winning chemist, literally saved a few billion people from starving by genetically engineering wheat. He showed how the Malthusian trap was incorrect. The venerable, but naturally pessimistic, Thomas Malthus stated that food production would provide a ceiling to population growth, and that famine would always follow if the population exceeded the food supply. Paul Ehrlich said the same thing in the 1960s when he wrote *The Population Bomb*. They were both wrong. Despite food shortages in some areas of the world, science and technology has provided engineered solutions.

I too rebel against the idea of extinction. I want to climb onto the wing of the Flybe plane. Much more economical than Ryanair, because they would track you down quicker than the NSA and send you a bill for not booking your hijack online. God forbid any of the protesters brought a piece of luggage onto the wing. MI6 would get involved. Emirates would welcome you aboard with a big, beautiful smile, but it would still take off as scheduled as time is money. It would be like a scene from Kabul Airport when Afghans were falling from the wings of US military planes as they flew away from the twenty years of carnage they had caused. All worth it though according to *Homo Insanus* in DC. Only this time it would be youngsters fleeing from virtual reality and not from abandoned Bradley armoured vehicles left behind by scarpering US troops.

I would point out that each of the four billion human beings in the developing world still have less energy than what these folks use to charge their electronic devices each day. The unprivileged, and truly at-risk billions, often burn dung and cardboard for fuel, and the resulting pollution in such closed spaces causes life shortening diseases. But let's not allow reality to ruin the story.

Energy drives development. The richer countries become the sooner they can apply technology to address the concerns of climate activists. The problems are real, but keeping half the world in poverty is not the solution. It is anti-human. It is saying we have our gluten free existence sorted, but you need to look toward solar panels and windmills and keep burning your shit for fuel. Try building an economy in the modern world on solar energy and you will fail.

If you took a trip in my phone box, and we stopped off in most of the countries in the southern hemisphere, I would invite you to stay over with the locals for a few months and see if the experience would alter your view. Someone should tell Leonardo and company that it's not about *Don't Look Up* from your big house. It's about looking down and around. Real problems require realistic solutions.

Here's the thing. I get it. Everyone wants power. Everyone needs power. It's another lie we tell ourselves that we don't. We are happy with who we are. I don't even know what that means. It's nonsense. Being impotent is not just a male problem. Everyone experiences it. No coloured pills will fix it. The feeling that we cannot control everything. Or anything really. You cannot even control when you need to take a piss. People want to feel like they can make a difference by fighting for a cause. Often, literally. The bigger the cause the better you feel. If the cause is one which threatens our entire existence - a potential catastrophic event like the Permian Extinction or Liz Truss coming back into 10 Downing Street in any capacity other than to deep clean the carpets - then we must take extreme action like gluing ourselves to anything which adheres to skin. Really? Yes! Try it if you don't think it's a major sacrifice. The greater the signalling to the group, and to those outside the fold, the more extreme the action, then the more this demonstrates the catastrophic nature of our cause, and why we must use end of times rhetoric to fight the good fight. It all fits. The story has a beginning, middle and end. It's science based. Okay, not all science, but the science and data we select for our narrative. Anything else is a conspiracy, or simply denial, or politically motivated ignorance. Don't you watch the news? Don't you know anything about anything?

I think people fear their very own insignificance. In the face of the magnitude of time and space. In the brief time we are here (a mere swallow's flight across a Saxon great hall, and then we are no more) we need to feel we have meaning.

Purpose. Victor Frankl's *In Search For Meaning* captures this deep need more than most works of literature. A consequence of surviving Auschwitz. Why does anything matter after gas chambers? The Italian Baroque artist Salvator Rosa painted "The Frailty of Human Life" in 1656 soon after the death of his son, Rosalvo. It is a beautiful and poignant painting. In the scene, the skeleton which represents Death, directs the child to write on a scroll: "*Nadci Pena, Labor Vita, Necesse Mori,*" which when translated reads "Birth is pain, Life is toll, Death a necessity."

Yes, you could say this is grim and gloomy. But it is true. It is the middle sentiment where we insert the need for meaning to make the bookends worth the price. However, this meaning and purpose should never be at the expense of others. No matter what the cause. Science has provided answers to many questions regarding our existence. It has not yet explained how our beating grey lump of neural matter has given rise to a species I call *Homo Insanus* which on its best day can exhibit kindness and care to strangers, and a deep understanding of the universe of which it is a part.

That all said, when I arrive at the airport, I'm going nowhere near that bastard plane. Hijacking an aircraft is an SAS job. You can't count on the West Midlands Firearms Unit, because if the rebels are still on the wings of love after midnight, firearms officers will be asleep somewhere off the beaten track.

This is especially the case for the mandatory pair of gunslingers who have to come to the airport to provide firearms cover. They will be tucked up in some closet or other if the Travel Lodge is fully booked. The airport pays for Butch and Sundance. In fact, the airport reluctantly pays for the whole Airport Police Unit. Millions. It's just another relationship in need of a divorce.

Fast wind. Briefing. Extinction Rebellion are on both wings of an aircraft. Thirty-eight of them. They used bolt cutters to cut a hole in the fence adjacent to the carpark. They entered the airfield. Used their own ladders to climb up onto the wings, and then pulled the ladders up behind them. Some of them have glued their hands to the wings. They have food and water. It's basically a plane spotters' idea of paradise with a picnic thrown in for good measure. The Operation Support Unit (OSU) are on site and have formed a secure perimeter around the plane. They have already submitted their open-ended overtime cards for signing. They too have come with their own picnic. Fuckers are more prepared than the scouts. The Airport Police Unit is at the base of the plane to provide an accessible target for half eaten sandwiches and abuse. There are several force negotiators on the scene all vying for any potential future award. There is even a drone team to provide aerial oversight. No Predator or Reaper drones armed with Hellfire missiles. No involvement from the CIA or MI6 or Mossad that we know of. Just a cheaper version of a drone you could buy in a shop. It's the £150,000 a year in wages of the three officers operating it which should cause the taxpayer to shake their heads. The airport management wants to call in an airstrike. It has lost a shed load of cash from having to close the runway and cancel all flights. What the fuck do they pay the police for if they cannot even prevent a handful of kids with ladders and glue from causing a shut down? What would they do if there were real terrorists in the terminal? Before midnight? And they weren't in the coffee shops. It would be a disaster.

We all kitted up and walked over. I suggested going through the same hole in the fence as it would be much quicker. Instead, we had to go the formal way through the terminal and security. They still insisted on giving us a cursory search. We eventually arrived, and the day shift took off faster than the speed of light. Einstein was wrong after all.

I had whispered to Ron - AGAIN - that I couldn't allow myself to be in direct contact with any demonstrators. There were television crews in the carpark with cameras that could see rock formations on the moon. If I was reported as being present, and the Jones family found out, it could provoke another story in the papers. Ron said I wouldn't be involved in any arrests when the inevitable happened. I could keep a low profile. I had lost the will by this point.

The leader of the gang was a man called Harold. He insisted on being called Harold, not Harry or Has or Harrow where he probably went to school. He had a loudspeaker which was very considerate of him, so we and the world could hear his demands. In essence, stop fossil fuels and save the planet before we all die in the next fifteen years. Everyone who wasn't glued down clapped. The others just cheered along. I was with the airport hoping for an airstrike. With a five minute warning for visitors like me to fuck off at the double. Just watching the scene in real life was another surreal event in a series of twenty-five years of strange happenings.

This group was like all other groups. Bonding together through synchronised behaviour: singing or chanting, praying and reciting the same words and actions; or in the case of the military and the police, marching, obeying commands, and avoiding all forms of friendly fire. The effect of these rituals is an increase in pro-social behaviour. Members trust each other more. They are more willing to sacrifice themselves for each other. They cooperate. And our ability to cooperate evolved through competition. We do unto others as they do unto us: if they share, we share. It's a general heuristic. It's how altruism evolved. We punish cheaters. Within a Hobbesian framework, there's room for charity. It usually begins at home. Our brain's keep a basic tally of who is doing the giving and taking.

What's interesting is how our mirror neurons in our brain activate when we are watching those with whom we are cooperating. We map their movements onto our motor cortex, and we project our own thoughts and intentions associated with these movements and behaviours onto the group. This is how theory of mind works. For some of us anyway.

I look at the non-glued down protesters walking the wings - much easier to do on land than in the air - and I admire them in a way. Yes, they are signalling their virtue, but there is a cost to them. It's not just cheap words. They will be arrested. Okay, so they won't be hanged from a crane despite the cries of the airport overlords, but it's still a criminal record for something they believe in no matter how misguided. There is no room for free riders on those wings. Unlike the police. Where we are similar is how our identity is fused within the group. How our individual identity is merged. Granted, Extinction Rebellion members will not likely lay down their lives for each other, unlike soldiers, and even police officers on occasions. However, they must perform in front of their group to show their loyalty. All members must demonstrate, through action, their right to remain part of the human tapestry. It's a process. The more extreme the rituals of belonging, the stronger the bonds. Special forces and Band Aid are just two examples. These climate activists had planned this operation. Psyched each other up beforehand. They knew they would be sitting in prison cells afterwards for a while. They were a band of brothers and sisters. There is a measurable impact on the wellbeing of the group. A placebo effect. There is a boost to their status in the social circle. Harold is the centre point.

The social circle is important. I've said previously that as societies grew and number, keeping track of social norms and who is doing what, is crucial to social cohesion. Religion expands the moral arc. You need God(s) to enforce morality when tribal members can't see for themselves who is taking the piss. Remember for most of our history there has been no police, no institutions, no human rights. This is where the police have let God down. Nietzsche proclaimed God is dead. A little premature and bombastic. The bloke had a few mental health issues to be fair. There is no doubt, however, that the western world has become more secular in recent decades. More secular in some places than others.

What has filled this void? What has replaced the all-seeing eyes which are omniscient? CrossFit and the internet? Of course, you could argue that secular institutions and religious ones are not mutually exclusive. They can coexist. However, it would be false to think there is a symmetry. There is not. Not between science and religion. Not even in the past when kings fought the religious leaders in words and in battle to decide who had the right to rule in the temporal realm.

The Tory Goddess Theresa May cut the police back to the bone. They have not recovered. Even before this, however, they were disappointing God. The higher power of the security state has come to the rescue once more like Ariel Flyer and Jake Justice. They have restored God's omnipotence and omniscience with the help of social media companies, and *Homo Insanus's* fear instinct being revved up like a new Harley Davidson just purchased by yet another mid-life crisis man who wants to feel the wind in his face instead of a lifetime of treading in other people's shit.

Harold is calling to the Gods to strike plague and famine down upon humans who are destroying everything. Fucking up his creation. What is she/he/it/they going to do about it? He's on a roll walking the wing with speaker in hand, waving to the cameras on the hill like when the Lord appeared on the top of Mount Sinai and spoke to Moses (can you imagine God waving to Moses who is lost amidst the smoke from the burning bush, shouting to him: "I'm over here for fucks sake"), but Harold is no Moses, and those folks on the hill are no Gods. They are simply local reporters. However, they are praying. They are asking the powers that be for an explosion. They are pleading for conflict and chaos. They might even be wearing helmets and Kevlar vests like all the mainstream pseudo foreign "journalists" who are chaperoned from pillar to post to view a bomb site by whichever terrorist group, in whichever country, we have chosen to add to the list of "axis of evil." Then they can fuck off back to your cushy hotel suite and write up the scripted narrative.

The wind has picked up. It feels like days have passed. It's only been three hours. When will it all end?

All the police surrounding this farce are wearing high visibility police jackets. Similar black trousers, black boots, and of course the globally recognised British Police helmet. A symbol of law. Emblematic of classical liberalism. Not the armoured, aggressive, Armageddon type of neoliberalism thrown around the world today via aircraft carrier diplomacy. It was once thought of as a symbol of John Stuart Mill himself. A physical representation to protect the freedom of the individual. The rule of law. The right to free speech unless one feels the need to cry out in a crowded theatre that there is free popcorn in the lobby. Now the police enforce laws which prevent freedom of speech. The thin blue line finds the time to prevent the gathering of any group which threatens "national security." This can even include a single person standing outside a building that the state has designated a place of vulnerability. Like a library. We enforce restrictions on movement. We can use counter-terrorist legislation, and counter-enlightenment laws, to incarcerate people who are deemed to be a threat to whatever is the dish of the day, especially if they have prodded the pride and profits of the Big Boss, the Big Bang, the Big Bad Beowulf across the water. Extradition and eradication await you.

I ask you to think for a moment. The police are just another gang. An armed gang with a monopoly on the legitimate use of violence within our national border. I suppose it's one of the reasons I signed up. Again, it's that sense of belonging. That instinct for connection with others. Like my new friends on the Flybe fortress. Once I got through the process and was accepted into the gang, I strived initially for their approval. This was critical for survival, or you simply would not last. It's yet again an example of acquiring resources. The more I conformed, the more secure my position was.

Obedience is at the heart of everything. It gave me more access to energy. And I gained status outside the job in the process. Despite some people hating us, wanting to defund us, clapping when every police station is closed, wishing we were as scarce as toilet paper at the beginning of lockdown, that emotion is coming from a fear of power. Not an unreasonable basic instinct. Remember what I said earlier: everyone wants power. To have the power of the state behind you means you are part of the strongest group in the land. Like any gang you wear colours and display your membership. It's this recognition of the symbols of authority, and the knowledge that although I don't know you - I don't know any of these officers around this plane - if it all goes horribly wrong, we will all be in this together. Even the least capable, by the force of peer pressure alone, will have to stand and fight.

Being disconnected from a cohort is what causes psychological harm. Whether you're on the wing of the aircraft or on the ground, you are connected to those wearing your colours. Those who are in synchronisation with you. Those who perform the same rituals as you. The group on the ground has a stronger bond due to training, the history of the institution, the energy invested over time, and the power. If you are not part of a gang, you are in trouble. You may delude yourself, but you are vulnerable. This is also true when your relationship breaks down. You can become ill because your connection is fractured. Angela and I are broken. However, she has connected with a man with a flute called Ken. She also has her family clan. Kinship is also a key to survival. Or it used to be for most of human history. No man or woman is an island unto themselves.

I want to go home. I really have had enough of Harold and his prophecies. I've also had enough of the hierarchy around me. The Gaffas who are directing the show, or not as the case maybe, because Harold seems to be conducting the choir. The whole shebang is his stage. I can see the ladders resting against the aircraft's fuselage, and I am on the bottom rung. Yes, I am part of the big armed monolithic gang, but it's not enough just to be a member. Not as time passes. If you remain on the lowest step, then there is a judgement. A constant reminder that you have failed in some way. Take any organisation and those at the bottom will be stressed, sick and diseased, and yes, even die younger than those at the top. This was the theme for much of the 1950s British fiction and films from Alan Sillitoe to Tony Richardson. It's only gotten worse in the 21st century. Now it's in colour 24/7.

On the stroke of midnight as shoes were lost and coaches turned to pumpkins, ladders descended to the ground. I found out later that the lead negotiator's name was Jacob. Seriously, not even fiction can account for it. There was no divine connection between above and below, and the irony was not even lost on the Airport Fire Service who were returning to their luxurious accommodation to do nothing apart from eat and sleep. The rebels had ruined their movie evening.

The protesters were arrested upon disembarking. By the OSU. They had proforma arrest statements at the ready. They performed what I would call a drop and go service. Like Christopher Reeve at the end of the first Superman movie when he drops Lex Luther off (played by everyone's favourite temper tantrum bad guy, Gene Hackman) at a state penitentiary, and the warden looking down like Juliet from a balcony, thanks Superman for being such a patriot, a saviour, and as Superman points his arm up toward the heavens, about to launch off like a Saturn 2 nuclear missile, he tells the warden that they are all part of the same team. A shiver goes up the old spine. That's the OSU for you: drop off, and fuck off, and talk about how it's all about the team.

Before I move on let me say something about horses now that I have brought Superman into this pile of shite.

Fucking horses have caused more death than smallpox. They were tamed over six thousand years ago and have been used in war to devastating effect ever since. Fuck Shergar. Who cares what happened to him. Poor Christopher Reeve fell from a horse. His last role was a real life paraplegic. Twice the number of people in the UK die each year from horse accidents than from taking ecstasy. Run with that wherever you want.

Extinction Rebellion warriors were taken to superblocks where they would be dealt with in the morning by supercops. Their moral superiority intact. A job well done. Both self and group image were enhanced. The story they tell themselves with each of them cast as the hero is an on-going box office success. The same is true for any healthy brain. The story is just a different one with a different cast of characters.

We returned to Diamond House for a break and to watch more Top Gear reruns. The Extinction Rebellion protesters were a thing of the past. It's another fact of life. It does not matter how much noise you make, most people, most of the time, couldn't give a toss what you are going on about. Regardless of your cause or concern, no matter what asteroid or tsunami or iceberg you are frantically pointing at, despite your terrifying pronouncements of Carbon dioxide in the air, compulsory vaccines to prevent an outbreak of any real rationality, or any sign of intelligent life on our own planet, even giving a nano-second of one's time to these and many other issues is to ignore the reality that everyone's brain is simply concerned with staying alive and gene reproduction. Everything else is a comma in a sentence. The Bee Gees nailed it to the mast in the 70s.

"Have you completed your monthly task sheet, Jack?" asked Ron, as he tucked into one of his multi-meats stacked homemade sandwiches courtesy of Mrs Ron.

Ron had informed me multiple times already, how he had been happily married for twenty-seven years. Hierarchy and unfamiliarity prevented me from pointing out that no-one is happily married for twenty-seven years Ron. He is used to all the congratulatory feedback he receives whenever he pronounces such a feat of achievement. More impressive than building the Great Wall of China or the Panama Canal or Will Smith winning an academy award for that shit movie about the Williams' sisters. O please, it was complete shite.

"I haven't Sarg. I thought I won't be here long enough for my performance to matter that much."

Of course, it is easy to ridicule performance figures. Even the American Sniper's kill count was recorded to encourage others to beat his record. Tribes around the world have always kept a mental tally of who is doing the killing and sharing the meat. Who is doing their fair share. Who is cooperating, and who is being a self-serving cunt? Reputation is carried around in the minds of everyone. Men will die to protect their reputation. They kill for it.

"Performance always matters. You could be with us for ages. Fill it in before you go home. The boss needs to know what everyone is doing."

I had finished my tea. Jeremy Clarkson was driving a 911 Porsche over the Himalayas at warp speed with one hand on the wheel and one hand throwing British pennies out of the window to local peasants who had never seen either of the two species before: Clarkson or a Porsche.

"I'm like Greta Garbo: 'I want to be alone.'" said Linda. "There's only so much testosterone I can take, and as I've got older, I'm producing more myself." She laughed.

I had come up to the front office to use a computer.

"Yeah, I get it. I can only take a limited amount of competition myself these days," I said. "Ron wants me to fill out my stats on the unit performance sheet."

"I'll show you," said Linda, logging on to a terminal.

She brought up the sheet. "How many arrests?" she asked.

"None," I said.

"Okay." She typed in two. "How many IMS?"

"None," I said. IMS were intelligence logs. Nearly all of them were a waste of time, and repetitive as the "intelligence" was recorded elsewhere; and what counted as 'intel' was more often than not just information that ended up in a virtual no man's land.

"Okay," she said again. She typed in four. I let out a laugh.

"Seriously, Linda, Ron will know I'm taking the piss." She ignored me and clicked on the heading which said, "Stop and Search."

"Two," I said. I'm a quick learner.

She typed in one. "Now you are taking the piss. You know what it takes to search someone these days?"

Linda had a point. Everything had become more difficult. People wonder why there are more weapons being carried around. It's like having to bring your own plastic bags out when you go shopping. Everyone is more afraid. Fear results in an arms race. Fear triggers the fight or flight response. It causes *Homo Insanus* to make mushroom clouds and mushroom soup. I mean really, what the fuck!

I noticed over the last few weeks that Linda never paired up with anyone. Unless she had a job which required two people. Like an e-border, or a sandwich run to the van parked at the old site. There was a rule which stated you had to patrol the terminal by yourself. If you were seen walking in pairs you had to have a reason. Maybe supervision had a phobia about Noah's Ark. Maybe they feared a flood.

“There are three people who are sick. Useless anyway. Out of sight out of mind,” said Linda. “I can’t stand the bitchiness. Too many women together make us infertile. A tribe of Amazonian women would be fucked from the beginning.”

Linda had a point no matter how you spin it. Men and women are different in some basic ways. Parents never have to tell their sons “Just because she bought you lunch, it doesn’t mean you have to have sex with her.” Or they do not have to warn their teenage lads that young women are only after one thing, and it ain’t the boxer shorts you’ve been wearing for the last five straight days.” That’s a good thing. Almost a compliment to women. For most of our evolutionary history, men had to bond together and go to war against other groups. They also had to cooperate to hunt. However, once the cooperation and the high fives ceased, conflict for status and mating rights began. Aggression was only one hand shake away. Most men today don’t go to war or join the police, and they can get their meat from Tesco. No wonder they play computer games and watch porn. They have been castrated by modernity.

“Why do you think that is?” I asked.

“In general, women don’t want other women to succeed. We want equality. We are more sensitive to competition. More anxious. You know the worst sergeants and Gaffas I’ve ever had are females. It’s a woman thing.”

"I'm a gender-neutral hater when it comes to supervision. Why do you think women are more anxious than men?"

"I have two kids, and most of my life is focused on keeping them safe. If that doesn't cause anxiety! It's an insurance policy having a high-status male around you. Men in general want sex objects, and women want success objects."

"I failed miserably on both counts! Boys, girls?"

"Two girls. Hannah and Holly. Thirteen and eleven. They spend half their life taking sexy selfies. Now that's status seeking among women. Blokes take shots of themselves with cars and watches. Basically, extensions of their reproductive organs."

She held up her phone. Two smiling faces with a water slide in the background. "I bet you're a great mom," I said.

"Well, you would say that seeing as though I've just done your monthly stats for you."

"And look how well I've done this month!" I said. "I don't know how you do these twelve-hour night shifts every week. I've only done them for a few weeks and they're killing me."

"I hate them. But I've been here seven years now, and I couldn't go back out there on the streets. I've had enough. I did twenty years on the F2 dealing with all the crap. I know there's a lot of bullshit to deal with here, but we're left alone for the most part. That's why when people come down here and take the piss, it makes it difficult for all of us. Right, I'm off for a stroll. I'd invite you along, but the fellas are a jealous bunch. See you later."

Linda put her cap on and walked out the front door. One of the perks about being on operations was you didn't need to wear the traditional hats. Baseball caps were the headgear of choice.

I Feel the Need, The Need for Speed

It was two in the morning. Sleep deprivation really kicks in around four. I put my own temporary cap on. I decided to ditch the chaperone. I walked along the front of the terminal. The airport was still busy. Making up for lost time and money. I was asked the normal questions: “Where are the taxis?”

“Right in front of your nose. That whole line of cars which all say taxi.”

“Excuse me. Can you tell me where the car park is?”

“You mean those multi-storey buildings full of cars all over the place?”

I decided to go through security and go airside. How daring of me. I walked outside where I could see the runway. All the planes parked up like sleeping giants. The Wright brothers flew the first aircraft in 1903: the Kitty Hawk. It’s only been fifty odd years since Neil Armstrong stepped on to the surface of the moon with the world watching in complete awe. If you had said at any time in the last fifty thousand years that humans would one day walk upon that shiny disk in the night sky, you would have been laughed at or hit over the head with a stone axe.

Airport workers were driving vehicles to and fro like ants in a colony making sure the structure was kept alive. The stars were out. Pin pricks against the black canvas. It's no wonder the ancients had no real way to conceptualise the sheer hugeness of the universe. Never mind its expansion. The driving dark energy. The ancients were wrong about the nature of the cosmos. It was not a living breathing organism with intentions and desires. It was mechanical. If there was a God, she was a clockmaker.

It was this paradigm shift in thinking about the universe which began the Scientific Revolution in the seventeenth century. If the entire edifice was run by interlocking gears adhering to mathematical laws, then possibly we could understand the whole structure. If we just looked up from the old dusty books and observed and measured the heavens. Hidden secrets were almost immediately revealed. Air was a substance. The heart was a pump. The earth went around the sun. The moon I was staring at - almost completely full - was once upon a time part of the earth before a giant collision caused the separation. And then gravity set to work to form the two bodies which still interact today in a push-pull dance.

How would we tell the kids we were getting a divorce? Even the word "divorce" is a little strange, and yet, it sounds about right. Entropy again at work. So many more ways for things to go wrong than right. It is easy to think Hadrian will be okay due to his age, and his ability to select the most appropriate weapon system for every occasion. Meme is young enough that I can be replaced with a trip to Legoland. What is the ideal time? Parents are selfish fuckers. We say it's all about the children, but that's just another lie. Even separating a new born baby from its parents is an act of cruelty. The baby industry argues it's what the baby needs, and it will inevitably cry itself out of the night-time instinct to be close to its parents. Daddy wants to shag mommy, so baby girl, you're banished till the sun rises. We will leave a light on for you. As if the baby thinks a lamp will be able to save it from predators.

Can you imagine at any time during the previous 300,000 years, a mother saying to the father: "Pack your belongings, your axe, fur coat, those cheap beads you carved and gave to me - only after I reminded you that it was our anniversary - and fuck off. A man named Ken is taking your place."

First, I would know Ken. Second, I would know what kind of hunter he was. I would know his place within our group. I would know if he could kill me. There would also be the matter of kin. His and mine. They would have a big say in what Ken and Angela planned to do. But who would turn the clock back?

In 1957, Britain's prime minister told everyone they have never had it so good. Yes, they may have lost an empire, but now they have lots of shit with which they can fill their little houses and flats. Angela and I were born into a world of televisions, refrigerators, cars, radios, phones, record players, plastic toys, and the Beatles singing "Help, I need somebody

Help...." John Lennon had had enough. In fact, all four of the intrepid tour travellers were signalling a need for change. It's always easier to make changes, however, when you have a stack of cash and a few hit records in the bank. They were ahead of the curve. Always the best place to be.

The twentieth century was a time for everything. "Greed is good," said Michael Douglas as the big city investing crook (Is there any other kind?) Gordon Gecko. Before he made *Falling Down* and came to realise that the Gecko's of this world needed castrating like Abelard. Cheap coal and oil generated cheap electricity for all in the privileged world. Thomas Huxley's predictions of the future world seem prescient.

The American writer John Steinbeck had once upon a time anticipated the dispossessed and the wretched masses rising in revolution in the dark days of the 1930s, as black cotton pickers moved northwards, and the Okies headed to the west. Hooray for big business as they rode in to save the day by using herbicides, chemical fertilisers, electric motors to drain water from fields for planting, and the application of genetically modified plants to generate more food than ever to feed all the new city dwellers.

Where America went, Britain Incorporated followed. Along the way we got bigger, taller, stronger, and fatter. We live longer. We have fewer kids in the western world because they don't usually die before their first birthday. Before their first smartphone.

The human body has changed more in the last one hundred years than in the previous fifty thousand. The upshot of all these modern appliances coupled with birth control, disease control, immigration control, state control and mind control, is that we do indeed live in the best of all possible worlds, and that Pinker bloke may have been right all along. From James Watt and Mathew Boulton laying the groundwork for the Industrial Revolution to Taiwan and the microprocessor transforming the world for both good and ill, we are held hostage in a holiday park with no means of escape. Ironically, the gates of the park are permanently up, and we remain our own hostages.

All is not right in the world of entertainment and entanglement. We have made profound discoveries over four hundred years by tinkering. We have unlocked many of the universe's secrets. We have trampled underfoot thousands of years of foolishness by peering through lenses and applying reason and logic. However, things eventually fall apart. All structures, empires, societies, and book clubs eventually come to pass. Even a lifelong marriage must end when one of the couple dies. I didn't make the rules.

I head back to the station. I'm tired. My pace has slowed. It's an age thing. It's another sign of the times. A British naval commander said on the eve of the First World War that the most important necessity out of all necessities is speed. Two hundred years ago the quickest way to send a message around the world was to put a letter on a boat. A message in a bottle would go nowhere despite the charm and soothing vocal tone of Sting. By 1851, an electrical signal could be sent down an underwater cable, and seven years later Queen Victoria and the American President James Buchanan exchanged pleasantries. The first phone rang out in 1876, followed by wireless telegraphy 1895 and the radio in 1906. You know the rest. It all culminated in the movie Top Gun. Not the Botox sequel which was painful to watch, and yet became a huge box office hit because people are crying out for a return to some kind of standard. Hollywood has sold out to the neon version of *Homo Insanus*, and only produces movies that even a toilet refuses to flush away. It has enough shit to deal with as it is. I know for many of you the original was not a classic. Yet there was that one line where Maverick and Goose, fresh from the cockpit of their F16, a symbol of American world dominance like Dunkin Donuts, when Tom expresses the whole modern world's anxious-driven insatiable addiction: "**I FEEL THE NEED, THE NEED FOR SPEED**." You see them both now high fiving each other. Yeah, you do.

Remember Charlie Chaplin in the 1936 classic *Modern Times*? What about when Captain Kirk is sitting on his throne saying: "Warp speed 5 Mr Chekov." It's a fast fast fast fast world we live in. No wonder we are spinning. We live in a centrifugal global space. Everything is fleeing from the centre. The middle world cannot hold. Like Steve Austin in *The Bionic Man* as his rocket ship is crashing, he calls out: "It's breaking up; it's breaking up." And next thing you hear is a voiceover saying: "Steve Austin, a man barely alive. Gentlemen, we can rebuild him. We can make him better than he was before. Better, stronger, faster." But there is no bionic man. The robotics industry can't even get a robot to climb up a few fucking steps, never mind shag a bionic woman. And who wouldn't copulate with Lindsey Wagner back in the day. Electronic cock or just your plain old evolutionary blood-filled kind. For fucks sake folks. Get with the space program.

Again, and not for the first time, I ask you to listen carefully. I'm almost asleep on my feet now. It's four in the morning. The police station is in sight. Listen. You hear that? It's Mick. Yes, Mick Hucknall. He's singing "**Holding Back the Years**." He's telling you how he's wasted all his tears. How he has wasted all his years. Mick is opening up to you. But he is asking you to open up to yourself. Stop lying. He's holding on. Just. Is that what you are doing? **ARE YOU HOLDING ON? JUST BARELY?** As the centre pulls apart. As Angela and Ken are walking hand in hand along a beach in the Bahamas while I watch Meme do gambols on the kitchen floor and listen to the sound of gunfire from Hadrian's bedroom. Waiting to be sacked.

Waiting for the IOPC, CPS and the KGB to decide my fate. I am just about holding on. There I said out loud. Before I used my airport pass to open the front door. “**THAT’S ALL I HAVE TODAY, IT’S ALL I HAVE TO SAY**.

Avoid People Who Say They Have No Regrets

The secret of the *Homo Insanus* success story is contingency planning. In other words, having a plan B. Chimpanzees have no alternative plan. Ignore what the likes of Frans de Waal may tell you. They don't. Take a simple experiment. Imagine a tube. Drop a grape down it. The grape falls out of the bottom end. I don't have to go on about Newton again, do I? Take a two-year-old child. Ignore for a moment how horrible they are and let them see your simple experiment. Ask them to catch the grape. It can be a chocolate or even a marble if it's your boss's kid, and you think there's a chance he may swallow it. They will put their hand under the tube and catch the item. Maybe they will drop it. It doesn't matter. An adult chimp will do the same if it's an object of food they find tasty. Okay, great. What's my point? Imagine an inverted Y shaped tube. Yes, just turn the Y upside down. Drop the grape down the single point of entry. It can come out of either of the two exit points. Easy. Get your chimp to catch the grape. What will she do? She will use one hand to catch it. Half the time she will miss the grape. Get the two-year-old back on the scene. Straight away the child will realise they can use both hands, one under each exit point to catch the treat. That's contingency planning. It's one of the main reasons we rule the planet.

Understanding that the future may not turn out as anticipated is what underpins the creation of possible strategies to deal with uncertainty. It causes us to take out insurance if something goes wrong. We like to phrase it as giving ourselves options.

The downside is regret. A theme of my current predicament. It is another defining trait of *Homo Insanus*. We have the capacity to imagine alternatives. It's not like observing an animal who gets mad because they see in the here and now a potential source of nutrition being removed from their grasp. I'm talking about a detailed contrafactual imagined fictional vision - an induced account of what could have been. We take our mental time machine and imagine other possibilities. This may be the reason why language itself evolved: to be able to communicate these possibilities to others. If I had only made this decision, and not that one. If I had done this, not that. If I didn't forget my keys, then I would be still here. If we hadn't invaded that country then think of all those smiling faces which would still be intact, and their fictional descendants alive. We are all dunces standing on the accumulated shoulders of everything which has gone before.

Angela said to me a few days ago: "I want to live in the here and now."

“No one lives in the here and now,” I said. “It’s another delusion.”

“You know what I mean Jack. You’re just being a twat as usual.”

Maybe I was being a twat, but I wanted to say before she walked out of the living room slamming the door, that we are always living and daydreaming in the past and future. Swinging back and forth. Not like a pendulum that has a rhythm and a movement which can be predicted. It is random. We live in an imagined world. Even the past is a creation. We don’t have an inbuilt scientific method on tap to measure and cross check and peer review our neurological modelling moment by moment.

There is a man who suffered a brain injury which damaged his hippocampus: an area of the brain associated with memory formation. What researchers found when carrying out experiments on him was that he could not imagine himself in the future. All the ingenious tests they performed showed he was happier not worrying about his future self. He showed no concern about his death. Such a condition would be harmful in a state of nature. The ability to think about all the ways things can go wrong was an evolutionary advantage for our ancestors. It’s just a pain for us in the modern world. Again, it’s a matter of trade-offs. Without this ability we would have no civilization because being able to imagine alternatives helped us to develop tools and technology to address current and future concerns. The problem is, however, that contingency planning causes many people to have a bench.

What do I mean? I'll tell you what I mean by a bench. You are currently on your wife or husband's, partner's - or whatever term you care to use - playing field, pitch, or court. You are playing your game of choice. You have been selected to be on the defined territory. You may even have objects we call "children" playing in the same area. You might have been playing a variety of games over many years. You know the field well, and despite the expensive maintenance fees and general upkeep, you have come to accept that other fields also have similar fees and costs. You are generally content despite the whistle being blown, penalties being incurred from time to time, and the accumulation of injuries; it literally comes with the territory. But then somewhere along the line you become aware of the substitutes bench. It's off to the side. You are almost positive it wasn't there when you first arrived, but as its presence becomes more visible, you can't be entirely sure. There's that memory problem again. Prediction and construction. Then there's that "what the fuck" moment! There is someone sitting on it. In some cases, it's packed like the Supreme Court.

Of course, you are the last one to know when the substitute is warming up. You are not even aware that you are the one who is going to be substituted. Despite the fact that there is no one else who it could be. It was always going to be your number that was held up. Your performance statistics were not only being recorded on the Airport Police Unit's statistics sheet. In my case, Angela had her own hard copy at the ready. Ever the contingency planner. Unlike Ron who asked me to input my figures (which as we know were zero in all categories) Angela took control and recorded my stats herself. Similar to the real and unfalsified performance figures at the airport, Angela had given me zeros in all areas. Where the fuck was Linda when you really needed her fraudulent fingers? Ken had been called on to the pitch. There were now three players. But whereas Angela and Ken knew there were three, I was under the impression there were still only two. Angela was right when she said I was a twat. That would explain quite a lot. And recall, yet again, what I have previously said about the best theory has to explain more not less than the theory it might be about to replace. Think back to your childhood. Did your mom ever get you to sing along to the song: "There were three in the bed, and the little one said, 'roll over, roll over,' and they all rolled over and one fell out." Little did I know my mom was preparing me for life. She was doing her evolutionary due diligence. But like many activities we do as children, we are not aware of the survival skills they are teaching us.

So, I have regrets. I regret not spotting the bench sooner. I regret not seeing my number being held up by Ken himself. I regret the time spent worrying about things which never happened and were never going to happen. I regret not punching Andrew Adams straight in the face when I was twelve, and he tore up my diary and left it in pieces on my desk. I regret pushing Billy Jones most of all. He was minding his own business. What would it have mattered to the events of the day, to the destruction which already occurred, to the state of the planet, to the bigger universal scheme of things, just to let it be? And there you have one of the Beatles' anthems: if only I had listened to those words of wisdom and *Let It Be*, he would still be alive today.

I think back to that kid sitting in the airing cupboard in my parents' bedroom. Was it me? Am I remembering him or making him up? It becomes more difficult as the years pass to be totally sure. I'm almost certain it is all true. It seems so real. I can picture that boy now daydreaming. Imagining what the future would hold. All the possibilities. But along with those hopes and dreams and alternative futures come regrets of what might have been when choices and random acts turn out against us. Anyone who says they have no regrets is lying. Lying to themselves first and foremost. Avoid them. They leave a trail of disaster in their wake.

There's No Happy Ending… Just an Ending

"You're joking, Angela?"

I'm awake. I've slept for less than two hours. I've come downstairs as I can hear my wife singing along with Smokey Robinson: "There's not a man today who could take me away from my guy."

"Sorry, I thought it was on low. I didn't realise it would wake you up," she said. "Alexa, stop." She was mopping the kitchen floor.

"I'm talking about the song. I mean really?"

"What are you going on about? It's just a song."

"It's not *just* a song Angela. "There's nothing you could say to tear me away from my guy."

I was singing, I'm not joking.

"I am not the guy anymore. Ken is the guy, Angela. Your guy. He's the guy who you won't be deceiving. But I'm the fella who you gave your word of honour to Angela. At the altar. Remember?"

"You are being totally irrational Jack. It's impossible to speak to you when you get like this. Reason number one why we can't be together anymore. There's no happy ending. Just an ending." Talk about righteous indignation.

No happy endings? Just an ending? This is not how life feels. Well, not all the time. Don't we all tell ourselves that once we reach the next peak, traverse across the next gorge, that we will reach satisfaction. Despite Mick Jagger telling himself, and the rest of his listeners, that he - and therefore you - can't get no satisfaction. One more push and we will arrive at peace and happiness. Not necessarily the west's interpretation of wellbeing, stitched to the addictive need for adrenaline and its incessant chase for the next hit of euphoria; maybe more in line with an Asian view associated with serenity and tranquillity. Make sure your destination is not an illusion before you drop lots of money on the tickets.

"Relate!"

"What?"

"Counselling," I said. I am totally aware of how pathetic I sound. If I could see myself in the hall mirror, I know I would resemble the figure in Edvard Munch's *The Scream*.

"We are way beyond Relate, Jack," she said, releasing a laugh to reflect the straws I was clutching.

"What if we move house? To Knowle. A fresh start. You always wanted a bigger kitchen. And one of those industrial cookers."

I think I'm having an anxiety attack. Like when I'm being given a handover at work. I am going beyond the basic rules built into my genome. I'm trying to appeal - one might say bribe, but this is not the time to quibble over word choice - to Angela's need for higher status. To join the Rolls and Rolex tribe who we disdain but can't help prostrating ourselves before. We are jealous and resentful. When one's wealth is on display, it breeds inequality like mice in a barn; people become more unfriendly, actively hostile, and exploitation runs riot.

I am well aware that women rate wealth and status higher than men. In fact, they sexually select for it just like men do for youth and beauty in women. We are jointly responsible for mutually assured destruction. I think in our early days Angela saw potential in me. I had confidence, and even a little ambition. She thought I would claw my way up the ranks despite me pointing out that my hands could not grip on to a greasy pole.

"A bigger house isn't going to change anything. And I've been asking for one of those big cookers for years. We need to be grown up about the situation. For the kids' sake. We should go to mediation. That's what Jonathon suggests first of all."

"Jonathon? Your dad's Jonathon? The solicitor Jonathon?" Apparently, if you say a name three times in a row you get a wish. The feeling we refer to as "resentment" evolved because in small groups it helped to keep members humble. Anyone who got too big for their fur lined boots was swiftly put back into their place. If they didn't heed the advice given, then ultimately, the group would beat them to death. Have you been listening to anything I've been saying? Today there is yet another one of those mismatches between the original purpose for our feelings and the modern era. We are surrounded today by people who strut their stuff and display their wares, gained fairly or dishonestly, sparking envy and resentment on stilts. They would be the first to die on the savannah plains.

"I spoke to him on the phone. Just to ask his advice on the best way to proceed. He said it was a good idea to go for mediation. For each of us to state what we want. To listen to each other in front of a disinterested third party and try to reach a resolution."

"You mean which one of us is going to get Ken?" I can't help it. Fuck it.

"You see, Jack. Reason number two why we are getting a divorce. It's a long list. You're like a child when you don't get your way."

She is right of course. I need something to bite down on. I am willing to go into debt to jump castes. Who wants to wait for other lives which aren't coming along no matter what Hinduism, or the many worlds interpretation of quantum mechanics tells you. We could join the Dorridge and Knowle Tribe. It's capitalism's version of eugenics. Forget past lives or genetics determining your fate, it's simple good ole fashion Yankee dollars.

"Okay. I just want to try and make things work. I understand your Ken fling. What does he do again?" I can't help it. It's all about status. If she says he's in the police and he's a superintendent, I will have two kills to put down on that bastard stats form. I would have to get Linda to do it for me, of course. She would need to create a new category.

Silence. She's thinking.

"He's a doctor. A GP," she said, keeping her eyes fixed on the mop. As if it was a fully loaded rifle.

Well, what can I say? I stood there for the first time in my life willing for spontaneous combustion to take me away.

You are told a story when you are young. If you want something bad enough, you can get it. It just takes hard work. Like True Grit, when the one eyed Rooster Cogburn, played by every Republican's favourite, John Wayne, puts the reins of his horse between his teeth and rides toward the baddies, guns blazing, shouting: "Fill your hands you son of a bitch." The truth of the story, however, is what falls out of the arse of Rooster's horse as it is being kicked on into the hail of bullets which is more likely to hit the horse than the old fat lump in the saddle. Your genes and upbringing place limits on the plot. The cast of characters is your peer group. I had more chance of becoming an armed robber when I left school than a doctor. I know two of the former group from my year, and only one of the latter.

"Are you kidding? A doctor?" Deep breaths. Count. One, two, three.

"What does it matter what he does Jack? Yes, he's a doctor. It's not as if I paid his way through medical school." She continued to mop what had already been mopped.

"Well, it matters when you can't get to see them these days. Obviously, that doesn't apply to you. You're getting examined on a regular basis."

"So, it would be okay then if he worked in a shop or a school? Would that make you feel better?" The mop was taking a beating.

"Of course, it would. Right now, it would be like we were on our honeymoon. I think I would even hug you if you said he was unemployed and over 60. How old is he?"

I know, I know. Don't ask a question in these circumstances which you don't already know the answer to. Remember in the OJ Simpson case when the prosecutor told him to try on the glove which he had allegedly worn during the double homicide? He struggled to put it on. A visual victory for the defence. A schoolboy error. Yeah, you're shaking your head as well.

"What does it matter Jack?" said Angela, as she put the mop and bucket back in the utility room.

"It matters to me," I said.

"Jack don't do this to yourself. It's unbecoming, really."

I had no power left. It vacated the house along with my dignity.

"I just want to know."

"He's 45. Happy now. Is that what you want to hear?"

"He's three years younger than you Angela? You're having me on!" I said, resisting the overwhelming urge to start banging my head against the fridge door. It already had a few dents in it as we bought it from a shop in Digbeth which sold ex-displays.

"And eight years younger than you," she said. One-two followed by a left hook. And I'm down on the canvas, and I'm not going to hear the man count ten. Stay down I hear you shout. Like Mickey, Rocky Balboa's trainer, shouting at him with a mixture of love and anger that he has taken enough punishment. Don't get up. I prefer to listen to Taylor Swift, thank you very much, so I shake it off and stand up. And I know that's what you want to see: pain and more punishment.

I think of Ken sitting in the seat of power with his name on the door. Stethoscope ready and waiting for Angela. The scoreboard of life does not lie. Every point is recorded like the Airport Unit's performance sheet. Every success is tallied up throughout your life from school, college, work and your ever changing total is displayed for all to see through your media posts, the clothes you wear, the car you drive, the house you live in, the titles before your name and the initials after it, those who look up at you versus the number who look down: if the top number is lower than the bottom number it's called a fraction and you are less than one, less than human.

"Does Helen know?" I asked.

Helen has been renting a flat just down the road for the past year with her boyfriend Zach.

"She knows I want a divorce."

"And what about Dr Ken?" I might as well double down in the trench like everyone else does these days. This is no time to be different. It's completely irrational, I understand. I have this perfect image of Ken. It is an avatar with gleaming flawless teeth smiling at me, offering me his hand of peace. That look which says: "The best man won Jack. No hard feelings. I'll look after your daughter. I'll make sure she keeps practising her gambols. Especially if you go to prison. I'll leave your son alone to perfect his shooting skills. It's not about toughness and training old-boy. It's not all about uniforms and testosterone. But you know what you said earlier about how things aren't binary Jack? That we should seek out nuance? That all the haters who promote all the "isms" to malign, defame and destroy any group or individual, who even questions their ideologies, should be held to account using evidence-based reason. Well, much of life is now a series of zero sum games. The winner takes it all. You can hear ABBA singing it right now can't you Jack? You can hear them singing, how you Jack - the **LOSER** - has to fall. It is binary. I get Angela. You get the bedsit in Redditch. It doesn't get any more binary than that my friend!

How do we balance novelty versus stability in a relationship? We enter into yet another fictional story at the altar or wherever you make your long-term vows of undying love. Don't we all truly know that, yes, short term sexual exclusivity is achievable? Follow the evidence. But lifelong faithfulness? In the modern world? After total familiarity with every sound, position, moan and groan timed to perfection. The law of diminishing returns applies to the amount of any exchange of bodily fluid except for spittle during increased arguments over trivial whatever-the-fuck-problem-it-is-today. The ultimate race to the bottom. If we just signed five-year sexual contracts and tailored our expectations accordingly. However, our genes would never go for it. No amount of cultural transmission will sedate that truth. Regardless of how skilful you are at performing pointless intellectual somersaults and superhuman feats of Orwellian double-think, common sense truth will eventually slap you upside your head.

A Theory of Everything

It seems like everyone has a theory of everything. Even my own son told me the other day that white elites have established structures ever since time began which have enslaved the masses to hoard all the resources. It is a theory of everything I suppose. It leaves out quantum gravity and dark energy. It ignores why the universe had low entropy at its birth, and why its expansion rate is just right to allow stars and planets and people to form. It doesn't explain the asymmetry between matter and antimatter. It skips nonchalantly over the precise resonant excited state of Carbon-12 allowing for the triple-alpha process to work in the core of stars which allows the Periodic Table - and therefore you - to exist. It ignores the origin of life, consciousness, and whether Ken will buy Hadrian the new FIFA game he wants. One might argue that it ignores 99.9% of all white males in history who also fall into the remit of being slaves, serfs, and generally part of the great group of downtrodden automatons who die younger than their oligarch masters. Why quibble over trivial pebbles when boulders are more obvious to spot. And a theory of everything cannot cover absolutely everything. Another linguistic paradox.

A problem has arisen with the demise of religion. God is the ultimate theory of everything. Without the idea - even a diluted version - there is a void which is filled with a whole host of nonsense, and individuals ready and waiting who profess insane opinions woven into stories for all to read and worship. This partly explains the litany of lunatics who are currently icons of masculinity and femininity, and every extraordinary claim to fame. Rationality is never going to fill the void. It is not a substance to put inside an empty box. Where is Schrodinger's Cat when you need it!

I am meeting Bobby in Costa for a coffee on the High Street. I'm walking up the road. I booked tonight off. I cannot do two nights in a row again. My heart will give out. Have you ever wondered why the heart cannot get cancer? It cannot repair itself. That's why when someone "breaks your heart," it really does hurt. Biology and poetry converge. We stumble through life despite phones and phonies. We really do fake it till we make it, and that's if we make it at all. Our physiology would never be designed by any being capable of creating an organism. Our bodies are a hodgepodge of evolutionary tinkering. And at the level of chemistry, we really are nothing but nuclear ash. Don't buy into the fluffy term which says we are made of stardust. This is where biology and poetry diverge. Remember words are important. They shape the narrative. Control language and you control society.

I ask: what can I control? I need an anchor. Not to drag me down. But to stop me drifting off into the darkness. Angela is set on her course. Like Thatcher back in her heyday, the woman is not for turning. If only it was the unions, I had to contend with then that would be one thing. Remember what the police did to the miners? However, doctors are a different kettle of fish. I can't imagine running lines and baton charges against a group of people in white coats speaking about how they are sick of paying car parking fees; and how does the government expect them to work for the NHS when private health companies are so much more profitable? Then Ken pops to mind, and I can indeed imagine being ordered to take a critical shot as he is a threat to my family. Didn't he take the oath: "Do No Harm?" I think of Angela and the mop, and the revelation of Ken's profession and age. I half expected her to say, "And he drives a 911 Porsche like that cunt Clarkson."

I am a few minutes early so I get the drinks in. A flat white for Bobby and an Americano for myself. I grab a table by the window, and as soon as I sit down Bobby arrives.

"Hi Bobby. How are you?"

"I'm good, mate. How's it going?"

"Drinks are on order. The lady said she would bring them over. No extra cost."

"Cheers. How are you? You look shattered."

"Nights for you."

“That’s right you were on a night. Sorry. I heard on the news about your visitors,” said Bobby laughing.

“So much for making the airport a hard target when a bunch of kids can take it over with a few ladders and some glue. Who needs AKs and explosives!”

Our drinks arrived.

“So, what do you know?” asked Bobby.

“Did I mention I’m getting a divorce?”

“No way. Is it you or your wife?

“Angela is seeing another bloke. A doctor.”

“Ouch,” said Bobby.

“Exactly,” I said. “And then there’s the matter of the house and kids, and my pension. Well, maybe not the kids.”

“Don’t forget prison? I’m joking. I’m sorry. No prison.”

“Mate, there’s always a little humour in the suffering of others. Did you hear about those two bobbies up in Staffs who’ve been done for the death of a bloke they tasered?”

“Yeah, yeah. They had locked him up for a domestic and ended up tasering him several times. Had a heart attack, didn’t he?”

“I think so. They’ve both been charged,” I said.

“I hear they stuck the boot in a few times though, and it’s all on their body-cameras.”

“O right. The truth lies in the details.”

"It won't have any bearing on your incident. I think we'll hear soon enough," said Bobby.

"I hope so," I said.

"Are you going to sell your house?"

"Don't tell me you want to make me a cheeky offer. Even I have my limits."

He laughed. "No mate. I went through a divorce. Seven years ago, now. Three kids. You know what? It worked out okay in the end. Me and the ex get on. Kids are fine. If it was going to happen, better then, than a year after I retire."

I could see his point. Police officers used to die five years after retirement.

"You know what I used to say to myself after it all happened?" asked Bobby.

"Why didn't you get a prenup?"

He laughed. "I had nothing to protect apart from an old Ford Capri. It was a fresh start for me as well. Why tread water when you can swim."

"Did you come up with that all by yourself?"

"That's what a law degree does for you. Have you thought about joining one of those divorced men's clubs? It's like the Masons, but without the looming possibility of a sexual assault."

"Divorced men's clubs? Why am I not surprised!"

“Seriously, blokes sit around like being in an AA meeting. They introduce themselves so really there’s nothing anonymous about it and share their stories.”

“Kill me now and be done with it. Can you imagine? ‘I’m Jack, and I’m divorced. I take it everyone would say hi at that point?”

“Absolutely. You would say how your wife was shagging a doctor, and they would all think that they may be unhappy, but at least they weren’t you.’”

“Ah right. My suffering would be the source of their schadenfreude!”

“Yeah. An ultimate act of altruism,” said Bobby, well into exploiting my circumstances for a few laughs. Fuck it. I get it. Why not!

“I would throw in the whole Billy Jones thing and the bedsit in Redditch.”

“There you go,” said Bobby. “O mate, you’ve got to laugh sometimes, or you’ll get dragged beneath the surface.”

“How come you dropped the criminal solicitor gig?”

“You know what, Jack. You’re going to laugh considering the fact I joined the Old Bill,” he said.

“Go on. I’ve got to hear this.”

“You’ll think I’m an ultra-liberal nut, but when I saw how the entire criminal legal system worked, I thought I can’t spend my life doing what I was doing. You know as well as I do that on the police side of the equation you can come to work and do your thirty years and have little or no real involvement in the prisons and sentencing, and all the bullshit. I'd close most prisons and turn them into apartments. Legalise all drugs, and have the government regulate and dispense them. Imprison the most dangerous people which is a tiny fraction of all offenders. There you have it."

"But you joined the police which puts people into the system. It's still a part of the process," I said.

"I know, but once we put them in the system, the fact that it doesn't work doesn't really matter to us, does it? We enjoy the chase. Victims want an eye for an eye. I understand that. Can you imagine a politician saying they were going to close half the prisons? Prisons are a training ground for criminal activity."

"You're right. But when you and your family have been harmed you want retribution. A home curfew for a few years wouldn't sit well," I said.

"No, it wouldn't. That's where you must make arguments based on evidence. Legalise drugs, and with the money the state would make, they could offer proper drug treatment. We demonise drug dealers as being evil. I represented many who were clever, and most are doing it just to fund their own habit. There's only a smaller number of serious money makers, and they are usually the importers. Remember the cost of drugs is all about the logistics. No matter how many dealers and users you put away, their place is filled within minutes, and their tactics improve. How many kids do we put into young offenders' prison?"

"No, you're right. It's a training ground. And most come from troubled homes."

"From the age of ten. It's nuts mate. Criminalising kids. Those kids become adults. You know what, I could go on. It is what it is as we say. Society is too emotional about it. Revenge is what we want even if it makes everything worse."

"Do you think you could make the same argument at my hearing if I have one? A home curfew only?"

"Mate, you need to be in one of the few prisons I would keep open." He was laughing. I hope he was joking.

I walked home. It was good to have a few laughs. Even if they were at my expense. I appreciated Bobby taking time to meet me outside of work.

I'm thinking about what he said about swimming instead of treading water. I'm suspicious of such metaphors. They sound good. Empowering. It's a prod toward purpose.

If there was an equation which science held up to you and said there you are, there is the theory of everything, what would you say? Maybe it looks like the Dirac equation, or Stephen Hawking's formula for the temperature of a black hole? What if it had just a few symbols yet combined everything there is to know about the universe? How satisfying would it be?

Some scientists would weep at its beauty. Over time I suspect there would be a deep sense of "Is That It?" Your very existence is accounted for in that equation. All the particles of matter of which you are composed. The force particles which determine their movements. The strength and spin and charge of particles are described with precision by the mathematics contained within that single equation which could be printed on a t-shirt. Change anything ever so slightly and nothing would be. Could be.

Everything must include meaning. Right? Living organisms composed of a bunch of Carbon looking at each other; one of them asking for a divorce while the other one would rather read a book and pretend he hadn't heard the request. The demand. Everything must include the brain which produces the emotions, and the uncanny ability to comprehend the deep mathematical nature of it all. You can't tell by just looking at your surroundings that behind the curtain, the natural world is linked by fundamental coded mathematical relationships:

The universe has somehow managed to blindly engineer mindless atoms to bond together, which have then gone on to evolve a conscious awareness, and an incomprehensible ability to comprehend the universe itself.

If that does not blow your mind, then nothing ever will! If you ask the vast majority of cosmologists and physicists, they simply say the universe has no point, and any question posed to address the issue is itself pointless. Observe and measure and predict and theorise. Meaning is for people on the verge of divorce or death, or both.

It is in this meaninglessness, and therefore absurd, universe, where I feel my life. Regardless of other possible universes - possibly an infinite number where Angela and I remain together - I live in this one, and being told I need to follow the Sartrean Road, and bring my own meaning to it all is no consolation. We arrive back at Mick Jagger's mansion where we ain't getting no satisfaction. Someone should have told Mick, however, that he was using a double negative, therefore, all these years, Mick was in fact, getting his fill. You see what an upside-down world we live in.

The Tallest Man in Yemen

"Tea or coffee?" asked Arif.

"Nothing for me," replied Angela.

"Do you have hot chocolate?" I asked. Right then I could see the expression on his face saying, 'No wonder she wants a divorce."

"Sorry, we don't. Just tea or coffee."

Of course, Arif wasn't sorry at all. At least if he was, he didn't show it. Maybe the expressionless face came with years of being a mediator. Years of listening to the same old shit. The same plot with the same inevitable ending. The daily ritual of tilting and turning his head from left to right like he was sitting on centre court at Wimbledon watching the same players groan with every strike of the ball. The occasional nod in affirmation that he was still listening, still in the room but not judging, not taking sides, not spacetime travelling to a place where couples can simply grow the fuck up and stop draining the life out of each other. Turn the tap off. Life is a limited commodity. Like oil, but apparently not as valuable.

We had followed Jonathon's advice and booked mediation. Three hundred and fifty pounds, and no hot chocolate. At least the office was in Solihull, so we parked for free in Tudor Grange car park. Three hours would be enough, I thought. Ten minutes for mediation, and the rest of the time waiting for Angela while she shopped in New Look and Next.

Arif was the spitting image of Abraham Lincoln. A Yemeni version.

I had too: "Has anyone told you you're the image of Lincoln?"

"Jack! I'm sorry Arif," said Angela. She reached out to nudge me, but the chairs were too far apart for contact. A metaphor for the last ten years.

Arif smiled. "That's quite alright. I've been told that all my life. I think I'm the tallest man in Yemen."

He must have been 6'4" but it was the structure of his face which resembled Lincoln. A Lincoln at the end of the Civil War, not at the start. A war weary look which seems to scar all leaders of protracted conflicts.

"So, let's get started," said Arif.

We were sitting in an equilateral triangle.

"It's a positive start that we can share the same space."

Arif went on to explain his role, and the purpose of mediation. He wasn't there as a counsellor or a therapist. He was not a lawyer. This was an opportunity for each of us to take a turn, without being interrupted, to discuss what we wanted. Who gets what in other words. After listening to each other, we could negotiate, and hopefully arrive at a settlement.

"Who would like to go first?" asked Arif.

I put my hand up. Angela rolled her eyes and shook her head.

"Go ahead Jack." I can see Lincoln now with a cup of tea on the table just like Arif (Abe didn't drink alcohol); *primus inter pares* - first among equals - sitting with his war cabinet asking: "What the fuck is McClellan doing? Get me an ass kicking general who is going to sort those slave owning fuckers out!"

"I want us to stay together. I don't want to divorce. I understand you and the doctor are an item at the minute. She's seeing a bloke called Ken, Arif. He's a GP so if you can't get in to see your own doctor because they are working from home, then give Angela a call, and she'll see if Ken is available."

"You see what I have to put up with Arif?" said Angela.

Arif remained silent. He looked at me as if to tell me the ball had just been hit over the net. Are you watching or what?

"I get it. I haven't been paying attention recently."

"Years," said Angela.

Arif looked at her with what could be interpreted as a disappointing glance. It could have been wind. He didn't give much away.

"Sorry, but I thought we were not here to discuss reconciliation," said Angela.

"You see Arif, it's an extension of a punishment ritual. I'm sure you understand. We punish each other over trivial things. All couples do. We lose our sense of perspective over nothing.

Over anything. One test after another. It's all irrational. There may be a kernel of truth in a problem, but then it's blown up out of all proportion. I've been working a lot for years, but that's going to change soon. I killed a man, Arif. It was an accident, and it will all be sorted very soon, but it's brought some additional stress to the family."

Now that did get a reaction from Arif. He shifted in his seat and crossed his legs. "I'm sorry to hear that. I'm sure it has caused a great deal of stress. But to Angela's point, Jack, explain what you want from the divorce."

I think the bit about me not wanting a divorce was lost on him. I want to mention that Ken, or any other future Ken, will not really protect our daughter who is nearly three. Hadrian and Helen are not yet out of the woods. At least Helen is out of the direct line of fire. Is he even capable of protecting them? It's a jungle out there. Okay, so it might be true the police are only a phone call and several hours away, but your brain is not wired for today's conveniences regardless of its plasticity. There's only so far any entity can stretch.

"Why do you think there's fourteen years between Hadrian and Meme?" asked Angela. She was looking straight at Arif. We both wondered for a moment if she expected him to answer the question. Arif coughed.

"Because we only had sex on religious holidays, and so basic statistical probability played a big role," I offered?

"You see Arif? This is one of the reasons Jack and I are sitting here. If I ever raise a serious question, a real problem, he thinks he's funny, and has to come out with a stupid reply. And he thinks that a woman and her children need protecting. Well Jack, it's not all about hunting and killing innocent Big Issue salesmen, it's about kindness and sharing, and yes, physical attraction. Let's be honest, we are not attracted to each other anymore. We are treading water in a smelly, stagnated pond."

Had she been talking to Bobby? This really was not the time and place to bring Billy into the discussion.

"We are shifting off topic a little," said Arif. Jack, tell Angela how you would like your joint assets divided. Also, what access do you want with your children?"

"You didn't want to have a child after Hadrian. You said it yourself. You were withdrawing from me during sex like I was a cashpoint. For years. It was pure chance that I got pregnant. When I told you, you became faint. You had to sit down. You said it was a pleasant shock. But I've only seen a similar reaction from you when you were knocked out during that boxing bout at the Wolverhampton Town Hall."

Okay, a point well made. I was shocked, but by the time she reached her first birthday I had come to terms with it.

"Let us keep to the reason why we are here," said Arif with a slight tone of exasperation in his voice. "Angela? Jack?" There was that tennis thing going on.

Am I resisting failure? It's obvious what is going to happen.

"Why?" I said. I was looking at Arif. He knew the question was not for him. Like Lincoln, he realised that there comes a time when a war needs to end. When Generals Sherman and Grant are required to burn everything to the ground.

"Because it's over Jack. It's as simple as that," said Angela.

I could see she was looking at me. She sounded almost sympathetic. Now that hurts more than anything. Give me a punch over pity!

That's why sometimes you should never ask "Why" questions. Why did a bad thing happen? Fate? Karma? Sin? Someone else's fault? The stars were aligned in a certain way? It's not like asking "Why did the apple fall to the ground?"

"What do you want out of the divorce, Angela?" asked Arif.

"The house. Maintenance each month for Meme till she's eighteen. Hadrian has a part time job and is almost eighteen now, so we can financially ignore him. In return, Jack can keep his pension, and my father has offered him £100,000," said Angela, speaking like she was Jessica Pearson in *Suits*.

Okay, there would be a mass extinction event as she would be accused of ethnic appropriation. The tyranny of the minority in action once again like Chuck Norris leading a team of Delta Force against the enemy horde, against all odds with Phil Collins singing in the background to encourage them on like Henry V, just one more breach dear friends, and victory will be ours. Better Jessica, however, than the character Rachel Lane, otherwise Meghan M, would be having another big sit down with Oprah, and the world would be praying for another asteroid strike.

"And what about access to the children, Angela?" asked Arif.

"If he can get Hadrian out of his bedroom then anytime is fine. He can have Meme every other weekend, and one night during the week." Routine is important for her."

Arif looked at me for a response.

My mind cast itself back to Cleary's pub the first night I met Angela. It was the age of the Celtic tiger. The Irish economy was surging due to foreign investment in the tech industry. Michael Flatley was taking over the world. Ireland was the "in thing." Who would have thought it, over a century before when the Irish spread around the world? More a case of push than pull factors. Famines and political and religious oppression, land evictions, and just your general run of the mill colonial guide to good housekeeping caused people to lay down or throw down. My own parents were part of the more recent diaspora in the 50s and 60s to merry old England. To what was then the shanty city called Birmingham.

If I hadn't danced with her. The one and only time in my life. Pointless mental excursions. Like going to Blackpool or Alice Springs in real life.

"Thanks for your time, Arif," I said. I got up and walked toward the door.

"Jack!" said Angela. "Come back here!"

If only I had left Cleary's a dance virgin. If only my dad had not been drunk at Christmas all those years ago. If only there had been no climate warming 12,000 years ago. If only terrestrial dinosaurs had been more resilient 66 million years ago. If only there had been no way the triple-alpha process could occur 13 billion years ago. If only there had been no inflation, bang or bounce with the right ingredients in the right amounts, then none of this would matter. That *is* the anthropic principle writ large!

Fraud, Freud, and Frank the Fireman

What is a fraudulent relationship? When you met the current love of your life, what promises were made? Was there any bullshit? If you sat across from me in the interview room at the police station would I be filling out a crime report for "obtaining services by deception?" Or "obtaining property by deception?" They form part of the Theft Act 1968. I think. I never paid too much attention at training college. Maybe I should have?

Angela had attempted over the last few days to get an answer to her demands. I decided to let my inner child out for a few days. Freud did say that repression was bad for one's wellbeing. We all have a thumb sucking child inside. Silent and sulky came out to play. Apparently, I had twins, and I didn't even know it.

I was back at work again. Airport control had just asked for an officer to attend the arrivals area. There was a woman there called Alison who was waiting for a plane to arrive from Nigeria. She was meeting her fiancé for the first time. It was Linda's turn to take possession of the airport radio, and to stalk the terminal for the next hour. There had to be someone in the terminal at all times carrying both their own police radio, and one issued specifically for airport jobs.

"You want to come over with me, Jack?" asked Linda.

I was on my phone looking at the Rightmove property site. Seeing what I could buy for £125,000. I was wondering if I could get a mortgage at my age, and if so, for how much? Rousseau was right. He thought deeply about inequality. He wrote that the first person who enclosed a plot of land and said, "This is now mine," is the founder of the modern way of life. Can you imagine the wars, and countless death and destruction and misery and inequality which could have been avoided if someone had taken the opportunity to drown that fucker in the local river. **The idea of owning the landscape is the biggest swindle ever concocted and enforced in all human history by a man with a club.**

"Yeah, let me get my cap," I said.

"You know what this is going to be don't you?" asked Linda. Her attention was diverted as a car had just stopped at the zebra crossing. Not to let someone cross as there was no one waiting, but to unload their passenger and their luggage.

"What are you doing?" said Linda.

The driver was silent. She shouted across to the passenger.

"Put your luggage back in the boot. You're not getting out here."

"But I'm already out," said the bloke.

"I can see that," said Linda. "Now get back in with your suitcase, and you..." she was pointing at the driver who had nowhere to hide. “You put your car in one of the multiple car parks like everyone else and pay the fee”.

The passenger had put his case back in the boot and got back into the car.

“Off you go,” said Linda to the driver with a royal wave of her hand. The driver made good his escape.

“Piss take, Jack. Right in front of us. I know it’s trivial, but it annoys the hell out of me. Anyway, I was saying before we were rudely interrupted, this job is going to be one of those online fraud relationships where she sends the fella money, and after weeks of being softened up with ‘I love you more than anything,’ it moves on to pleas of ‘I need some cash for some kind of emergency.’ Sad. We have quite a few of them down here. Men as well. They are usually waiting for a Russian model half their age to arrive from Moscow via ‘What the fuck planet are you on!”

Linda was right. Alison was standing by the metal railing in the rather small arrivals area. Looking confused. There was a member of airport staff with her wielding a radio. He waved at us when we came through the door adjacent to Costa.

“Hi there,” said Paul, holding his airport ID card up as if the yellow high viz top which said ‘Airport Staff’ didn’t give the game away. “This is Alison. She’s here to meet her fiancé, Akin from Abuja in Nigeria. He was supposed to be flying in on a connecting flight from Vienna at 11.10 this morning, but I’ve told

Alison that there are no flights due this morning from Vienna. We have one scheduled for 17.40 hours this afternoon."

Paul scrunched up his face like an empty crisp bag. "Sorry folks, can I leave this with you?" he asked, already walking off toward Spar. That's years of experience for you.

Alison was in her early sixties. She was wearing a tight black dress with high heeled black shoes, and even with the additional height, she was still quite petite. She had dyed her hair dark brown, and she had it brushed down the side of each cheek.

"Hello, I'm Linda, and this is my colleague, Jack," said Linda.

"Hello," replied Alison. "I don't think he's coming."

We took her back to Diamond House. I made her a cup of tea.

"How silly you must think I am?" she said.

"No," said Linda.

Alison went on to tell us how her husband Pat had died from pancreatic cancer three years ago. How she had been lonely. Her friends were supportive, but over time she had become more reclusive, not wanting to go out apart from food shopping. Gradually she had become depressed. She went online, she said, to find hope. Akin provided her with that. They began chatting for weeks. He was kind and attentive. He listened to her talk about her life with Pat, and how their marriage was deteriorating before he got diagnosed. She hadn't even told her friends that her relationship was in trouble. Yes, she knew the stereotype about younger men from Nigeria exploiting older women for financial gain, but Akin was different. He loved her. She loved him. He asked her to marry him. He got down on one knee - on zoom of course - and held up a ring for her to see. Three real diamonds. He would give it to her when he came to visit. Soon. But first he had a problem. Maybe she could help him? It was perfectly understandable if she didn't want to. It wouldn't change their love for each other. His nephew needed a medical procedure. He showed her a picture of Musa. Such a beautiful boy. It ended up being three payments totalling £7,000. All of Alison's savings. Linda told her that there are other fish in the sea, and that she will find a man who is trustworthy, and who will become her companion. Of course, she was just trying to be nice.

I kept my mouth shut. I wanted to say that dating sites and nightclubs and Nigerian conmen on the internet are a recent phenomenon. For most of our evolutionary history we lived in small groups, so the pool of potential partners was extremely limited. Even when you take children out of the equation, it may have paid to stay with your chosen one. This may explain - to a degree at least - why people stay in abusive relationships, and why a person may continue to send money overseas to a man they have never met in person.

We got Ron's permission to drop Alison home. She lived in Sheldon which was only a few miles away down the Coventry Road. She invited us into her maisonette for tea, but we politely declined. A sponge can only hold so much fluid. There was nothing else we could do for her. US special forces have a tough time tracking down Boko Haram in Nigeria, there's no way a couple of airport officers are going to find Akin, and have him extradited to the UK to face the music, to stand before Lemar, and hear him sing: "That there's not much justice in the world, No no no."

When Linda and I got back to the nick, I had a cuppa and a few digestive biscuits. I decided to go for a walk around Car Park One directly behind Diamond House. By myself. Good exercise walking around each of the six levels.

Linda had been called to the search area where all the travellers passed through before going airside. A member of staff had reported she had just been racially abused by a man who said she couldn't search him. Linda had asked if there was any racist language used as women security staff were not allowed to search males. It seemed like a misunderstanding. There was nothing else. The staff member stated that it was an "unconscious racist bias" and she wanted proactive action taken by the police. Linda asked if anyone wanted to go over with her, but the rest of the team scurried for cover like mice being discovered in a pantry. They recognised a potential pandemic from training courses, and no face mask or hand gel would help them out when this type of job goes wrong. Linda, thoughtfully, knew better than to ask me to come along for this one.

I admire these airport officers. I don't know how they do it. Ron sent me over by myself to the Champagne Bar last set to take a report of a stolen cushion (I know, I've put myself in for a quality achiever's award). The bar is located airside in the main lounge.

"You want to report a theft," I asked the manager.

"O yeah," he said. "Thanks for coming over. I'm Phillipe."

He managed to pronounce the 'e.' "Someone stole a pillow?"

"A cushion," he quickly corrected me. "Two of them. They have our logo on them. I have them on CCTV."

"Them?"

"Yes, they were two old women. I think they took them to use as head rests on board whatever flight they were taking. They are small."

"The old women?"

He looked confused. "No, the cushions. The cushions are small. They were left out there in our designated seating area in the communal area," he said, pointing out of the bar into a seating area a few metres away.

"So, they weren't even in here?" I asked.

"No. We were closed. It was a late flight." He was staring at me with a look of fright on his face. Afraid of what I might ask. He looked in his mid-twenties, but already had grey, thin hair. The world is one big stress ball. Everyone is an alienated consumer. I am trying to hold on, but I feel the need to lie down and put my head on one of his cushions and take a nap. I am dizzy and disoriented. It's as if I am in a hall of mirrors where appearance is warped, and reality has no relevance. Only the spectacle matters. Memes all the way down. Illusions stacked up like pancakes. A hypnotised, commodified globetrotting tribe twisted this way and that by screens and the powers behind them.

"Hello. Are you okay?" asked PhillipE?"

"Not really, I'm having a bad few years." Not the answer he was expecting but I don't care about Phil or his pillows. "You mentioned CCTV?"

"Yes, we have them walking off with the cushions toward the gates. You'll be able to track them and find out who they are. I suppose they left the cushions on the plane, so we won't get them back. But we can claim compensation from them, can't we?"

I suddenly thought about how I walked out of mediation with Angela calling me back. How I felt a brief moment of freedom. Then David Soul came to mind. Do you remember him? Hutch from the 1970s classic cop show *Starsky and*

Hutch. Friday evenings at 9.25. Do you recall him singing, “Don’t give up on us baby, it’s still worth one, more try…” He’s singing and I’m cringing. It was terrible then, never mind now. This is what divorce does to you. This is what life does to you.

I look at Phillipe. I know he’s aware that I have not taken out my pen. I want to put my hand on his shoulder, and tell him about Billy Jones, all about Angela and Dr Ken, about my daughter who I might see every other weekend, and my white privileged son and his weapons of choice. I want to tell him about the price of property in Redditch, and how we have evolved from apes without pockets to neoCons with nukes and Nandos. I cannot help him with his stolen cushions. I am completely unable to look at his CCTV with the offenders fleeing the scene of the crime. An officer who gives even one iota of a fuck will have to come to his assistance at some future point.

“Where are you going?” asked Phillipe. “What about the CCTV?”

I am in Car Park One. Hiding and walking at the same time. I am thinking about how power corrupts. How over time people with power diminish their ability to blush. In other words, they can become shameless. Blushing is a facial display which enables the group to keep track of who can be trusted. Power over time can cause this natural blushing response to vanish, and consequently, it allows leaders everywhere to behave in any manner they want. We call it corruption. They become detached from the people they govern. Those they rule become unworthy, and they develop a resentment that such underlings can remove them from office.

I've previously said how a uniform is a symbol of power. Police officers don't blush either in the public sphere. Try arguing with the law and you'll be singing how "I fought the law and the law won." On a side note, why is it we could get on stage at the O2 Arena, and sing songs from decades ago, off by heart, not even remembering how we learned the lyrics, and yet try recalling a few lines from Shakespeare or Shelley, and you will be stuttering and scratching your head while the audience gives you a slow hand clap before telling you to piss off.

When will I hear from the IOPC? I wanted to call them up, but Bobby said there's no point. It will be sorted when it's sorted. I wanted to tell them, anyone really who would listen, that I didn't join the police to take someone's life. When you hear young men talk about violence and killing and what they would do in certain circumstances, I want to tell them they are talking rubbish. Most soldiers in war don't even aim at the enemy when they pull the trigger. Bombs and artillery do most of the killing. We haven't evolved to be murder machines. Our hands are fragile. We are not very strong. We get injured easily. Fight a baboon and see who wins. Maybe I should call that DS Bridgeman to see if he knows anything. Anything at all.

As I walked up the ramp to the top level and a bright blue sky, I saw Frank the fireman on the far side. There were no cars up here, so I had an unobstructed view of him. He was sitting on the narrow wall. The problem was his legs were dangling over the side, and he was looking down at the ground six storeys below.

"9998 control. I've got a male on top of Car Park One at Birmingham Airport who looks like he's thinking about jumping off. He's sitting on the ledge with his legs hanging over. If you can let airport supervision know."

"9998, That's well received. Airport supervision, are you on the air?"

I could hear the controller speaking to Ron. An ambulance was being called for, and the airport fire service was being notified. Other airport officers were shouting up on the radio to say they were heading over to my location.

Frank looked over his shoulder and saw me. He waved at me to come over to him. I didn't even know his name yet, but I had his namesake, ole blue eyes himself, singing "It had to be you, wonderful you, it had to be you," playing out as I took slow steps toward him, praying in between the lines, that he would understand that I was only at the airport temporarily, and that my tolerance and patience for other people's suffering was paper-thin at the moment; that I had walked out of mediation, and walked away from cushion-gate at the Champagne Bar recently, and he had really drawn the short straw if he needed empathy and encouragement to remain in these games of life. Why the fuck didn't I go with Linda to dredge up all the unconscious biases destroying the planet?

"You alright officer?" said Frank. He had positioned his body now, so his torso was slightly twisted in my direction. I stood about ten feet away from him. Frank was an Afro-Caribbean man. He looked like he was around fifty years of age. He reminded me of an older Arnold, played by Gary Coleman, from the American show in the 80s *Different Strokes*. He had a big smile on his face.

"I'm okay, thanks. Well, I was till I saw you sitting on that wall. How about coming off it and we can have a chat?"

"Sorry, I don't want to do that."

"I'm Jack. I work here. For now, anyway," I said.

"My name's Frank. Nice to meet you." He looked over the edge.

"Hey Frank, what brings you here today?"

"Life ain't good at the minute, you know. I just retired from the fire service. After thirty years." He shook his head.

"Difficult time adjusting?"

"9998 are you receiving?" It was the controller.

"Yes, yes. I'm just talking to Frank now. Stand by please."

"Yes received, just to let you know ambo and fire are on route to you, and other officers will be with you very shortly," she said.

"Received, thank you. Sorry about that Frank but you know how the procedures work after thirty years in the fire. Should I ask you how many smoke alarms you fitted during your service, or this isn't the right time?"

He let out a big laugh. "That's funny. Too many!"

"So, what's going on in your life to cause this then?" I asked.

A deep sigh. Another shake of his head. He was wearing a black jacket which he unzipped. "Gambling. I've lost all my commutation money from my pension. Our savings. I took out a big loan against the house which I'm going to lose. Credit card debts. Loan shark debts. I owe my brothers money which I lied to get in the first place. And my wife doesn't know. I promised her I wouldn't start it all up again. But here we are. Here I am."

He took a deep breath. Let out a sigh. Looked up at the blue canopy above. And with that he jumped. Or to be more precise, he slid off and let gravity do its job.

Who Wants to Live Forever?

Freddie Mercury asked one of the most profound questions: Who wants to live forever? Many people do. Rich people especially. Silicon Valley types. Despite most of them being in therapy, and de-stressing, de-toxifying and de-generating in "retreats" in various luxury pseudo minimalistic settings, trying to isolate their true self and get in touch with who they truly are, who they really want to be, an attempt to reattach to their own indigenous spiritual core. When all is said and done, we all originated from the same place regardless of the amount of melanin in our skin cells. It's really like Peer Gynt's onion. Don't tell me you haven't read Ibsen? Strindberg? For fucks sake! Keep peeling away the layers of social sediment laid down since the time of your birth, and you will eventually find there's nothing there. There is no core. There is no magnetic centre swirling around in time. Waste as much money as you want amidst the trees, the sound of flowing water, the smell of incense, and Simon and Garfunkel singing the "Sound of silence," but what you're looking for does not exist.

I come back to the nature of relationships. Because that's really what defines existence itself. Whether at the level of particles popping in and out of the void, or husbands and wives popping in and out of other people's beds and surgeries, relationships are all we have. They define everything. The very idea of "you" as a single isolated entity with some intrinsic meaning which you need to "get in touch with" is a fiction.

I can say with a high degree of probability that my brief relationship with Billy Jones resulted in his death. But what about Frank? Would he have jumped if I had not turned up? Or would he have thought a little longer about his life? His two kids? Yes, two children: a boy and a girl, both in their twenties. His wife? I am almost certain he still would have slipped into history that afternoon. You get to know the real deal after a while. I remember the first time I went to the coroner's court to give evidence regarding a retired police officer who had killed himself in a city centre hotel. He too left behind a wife and two children. Again, due to financial problems resulting from gambling. I met the family in the canteen at Steelhouse Lane Police Station before we went to court. They were distraught. Beyond reason and comprehension. In a universe where suffering has meaning.

Remember what I said at the beginning of all this that if you want happiness or the algebra of wellbeing then you are in the wrong place. That is unless you are a little savvier than the average bear in the woods. If you are, then you may be able to see light between the trees. I've been telling you that real meaning is, often, defined by the absence of things, not by the presence of something. Frank has never meant more to his family than he does now. I see you shaking your head. When you are in pain you would give almost anything for it to stop. When and if it eventually does pass, you soon forget the suffering, until another node of negativity crosses your threshold, and the process will start all over again. You will tell yourself: 'If only the pain, whatever its form, would cease then life can begin.' Whenever a material good or personal achievement is obtained, even before the proverbial ink is dry, you are on to your next purchase or episode or thing to be obtained. This is a life of accumulation. It is defined and measured and assessed by what is present. It leaves you feeling hollow and unsatisfied like eating junk all day, yet still feeling hungry. That is why if anyone says you should be grateful for what you have because that is what brings meaning and purpose to your life, you should never say cheers for the words of wisdom. **THE TRUTH IS YOU SHOULD ALWAYS BE THANKFUL FOR WHAT YOU DON'T HAVE BECAUSE IT IS IN THAT VERY ABSENCE WHERE MEANING BEGINS**.

It's a Long Way Down from The Bottom

"Thanks for calling me back," I said, although I wanted to add how it had been two days since I left a message. Even Virgin Media doesn't keep you waiting that long on the phone.

"Sorry Jack. I've been busy. No end to the jobs," said DS Bridgeman.

"Yeah, I bet," I replied. Like my heart bleeds for you. But it's painful down here under the wheels of the bus. All that metal gets heavy after a while. Especially if it's a double decker which mine just so happens to be. It's also full of people cheering along hoping for a hanging. Fuckers don't even have tickets. And it would be almost bearable, despite the weight, if they were chanting "Justice for Jack." Kind of catchy. Try it. Chant along for a bit to see what I mean. I'll wait. I'll even start you off:

Justice for Jack
Justice for Jack
Justice for Jack

How hard was that? Instead, the chorus is singing: "Gallows for Garner." Let us bypass that one like a rattlesnake curled up on a walking trail.

“I bet you’re anxious to hear the news?” he asked.

Now there’s a question for you. First, it implies there is news to be heard. The second obvious point is the news itself is your news, not the BBC or CNN or CBeebies.

“Yeah, you could say that Sarg,” I said with the faintest of false laughs.

“Well, I have the IOPC investigation on my desk,” he said.

Then there was silence. My heart was racing. I wondered if there was a defibrillation kit in the station. I had never seen one. I know they have them in the terminal because during my second day down here, a passenger collapsed and went into cardiac arrest. A call came over the airport radio for any staff to attend an emergency in the baggage hall. Steve and I were close by, so we went along. When we got there two airport staff were using a defibrillator on a male who was on the ground surrounded by people with their luggage. A few of them, of course, had their phones out recording the incident. Social media never sleeps. They saved his life. Paramedics arrived and took over.

“I bet you want to know what it says?” he asked.

Is he taking the piss? I thought. I don’t like to see an opportunity for a laugh go to waste. No more than the next person. I was sweating.

"That depends! I think I should," I said. I had come out to the foyer area for privacy when I saw the withheld number. Companies trying to sell you stuff use mobile numbers these days.

"The conclusion they reached is that the force you used was deemed reasonable under the circumstances. That's the bottom line. There is not going to be criminal prosecution. However, they do point out you didn't follow procedure by completing a use of force form before you went off duty as you are required to do. That can be dealt with on a local level. The family have been notified with all the details and reasons behind the conclusion. That's it mate. All done and dusted. There's obviously a huge amount of material in the report, but I'll send you an email with all the details, and cc your Fed rep into it," he said.

"Thanks," I said. One word. It was all over with six letters. Isn't that true with many things in life? An end with a whimper not a bang. A marriage. A career. The earth far into the future at the behest of the sun.

I called Bobby straight away.

"That's brilliant," he said. "You would think they would call you as soon as they knew."

"I know. But at least it's over now. They'll probably sack me for not putting the use of force form in," I said, only half joking.

He laughed. “Yeah, how funny would that be. I’ll send you my bill,” said Bobby.

“I’ll gladly pay it! Let’s have coffee soon. I can only deal with one break up at a time.”

“Absolutely, Jack. There will still be a few loose ends no doubt over the coming days. Emails et cetera. Nothing to worry about. I’ll be in touch.”

“Thanks for all your help,” I said. And I meant it.

I looked at my phone. I became aware that the first person I called was Bobby, not Angela. I decided to send her a text telling her the news. I hesitated but I put a kiss at the end.

Seconds later came a reply: “Good.” No x.

My Endless Love

Our wedding dance. Lionel and Diana look into each other's eyes and tell each other: “There’s only you in my life, the only thing that’s right.” They sing how forever they will hold each other, and there will be no other, and no one can deny it, not Judas Iscariot, not any three-letter acronym agency using the ‘plausible deniability’ excuse. But here’s the thing. Ready? It’s a load of bollocks. Lionel does not really love Diana. Not in that way. Not how the song serenades the listener’s lovesick pangs of desire. Angela did not love me. Not really. Not in the way she should have. Remember the laugh at the altar. A bit of a giveaway. Apparently, not in the way she does Ken, according to an insider, my own son, who I suspect takes more than a degree of pleasure in telling me how excited his mom becomes before Ken arrives. I only experienced that response when I was going out.

Our “endless love” was yet another fiction. And no record sales and incoming dollars could justify the narrative.

I agreed to Angela’s terms and conditions. Like I was taking out a loan. They were not unreasonable at the end of the day. Part of me derived satisfaction from the idea that Robert had to give me a hundred grand. It is true that a fool and his money can be parted. Tight fucker even resented having to buy a coffee, and he always asked for the receipt. Always business, never pleasure.

The kids will hardly notice I've left. I took pleasure in telling Meme that I was not going to prison so she could stop doing her gambols now and make something of her life. She just laughed and sang "Daddy's still going to prison, daddy's still going to prison" followed by the habitual tumble. Maybe she knows something I don't. Maybe she's like the Oracle at Delphi, or the three eyed raven. Time will tell.

The divorce itself was a paper exercise. A few signatures. Again, just a matter of time. One thing is for certain: I am not going to rent a bedsit in Redditch. Fuck that!

Why We Are All Alone and I Did Warn You

The closest the human species ever came to extinction before the loonies took over the asylum was around 10,800 years BCE, when a vast icy lake in North America drained into the Atlantic Ocean and lowered its temperature enough to switch off the Gulf Stream. There followed a twelve-hundred-year ice age now known as the Younger Dryas. It put an end to the early agricultural revolution which was underway in Mesopotamia and beyond. If such an event happened today it would cause the deaths of untold billions and displace much of the world's population causing state failure, and wars which no doubt go nuclear. It is the cold which really kills.

If a two mile wide asteroid struck the planet it would be the equivalent of setting off two trillion tons of TNT. Everyone would perish. The good news, however, is that no imbeciles in charge of real geopolitics can engineer either of the above scenarios. Up until recently, there was nothing any leader could do to cause the end of us all. No matter how genocidal they were, regardless of their ideology, there was only so much carnage they could commit. Now it is different. You should be worried.

Most people are totally unconcerned. The few who think about such a possibility often conclude there is nothing they as an individual can do to stop it, so what's the point of dwelling on the negative. We heavily discount the future. To the point that I would suggest there is an inverse square law in action. Just like Newton's. Our worries decrease via an inverse square rule with each passing year. Meaning we are four times less concerned about things two years into the future compared to twice after one year. Are you with me? It isn't calculus for fucks sake! This same law can be applied to location. The further away a problem is in space, the less we are bothered.

What's my point? Stick with me, we are almost there. We just cannot generate a great deal of interest, and therefore action, to ward off future potential catastrophic, yet preventable events. This is why there is no advanced technological civilization anywhere in the universe. If it ever existed, it inevitably destroyed itself. Game Theory will not save you. Mutually Assured Destruction will not be your messiah.

Remember the title? ***Homo Insanus***. You and me, and everyone. Yes, we can be rational as the term is defined using rationality itself. We are, however, all too often insane human beings in so many of our behaviours in the modern world. The democratisation of nuclear weapons, in the hands of *Homo Insanus,* driven by crazy ideologies and advocated by fools of the same species, is a recipe for disaster. We have been lucky so far. That good fortune cannot last. And don't think Elon and friends will whisk you away to Mars. Even if they did, that would just be a case of kicking the can across the solar system. We are alone.

Or should I say, "You are alone." It is why things are often not quite right. You cannot put your finger on why. Maybe you are just bored, you tell yourself? Maybe you are having a crisis as everything is a crisis these days? There is a permanent state of emergency about all things. One fictional story after another. Maybe a holiday will sort you out? For sure. What about a phone upgrade? A friend recommended a new tv show which will be right up your street. You can binge watch all six series. The neighbours have got a new car, and although you only took out a three year lease last year on the one you currently have, there's no harm in shopping around for one which will stand out on your driveway. A friend has got a promotion. Fucker. Nothing worse than seeing a friend doing well despite the smiles and congratulations. As Gore Vidal said it perfectly: part of you dies. And there are only so many pieces of you which can slowly rot. Apart from Schrodinger's imaginary version, even a cat only has nine lives. Maybe you should get that PhD you always wanted? Forget that the market is saturated with these certificates, you can introduce yourself as Dr Dumbwit even though you are not fit to rub cream into a rash on your own arse. Maybe a child or a dog will sort the ennui out? A place in the sun? Of course, money, money, money would fill the void. If ABBA says it is so, then you have to hear them out. The Swedes are not just about arms sales. It'll be fine once you have retired and have the time to do everything you haven't been able to do: exercise, travel, and "pack up your troubles in your old kit bag and smile, smile, smile." Relax and watch the sun setting. Simply observe the world going by. Maybe it's the pace of the modern age? You need to slow down, get in touch with the real you. Maybe you are just smothered by those around you? Those you love the most? You have lost your identity over the years? Your roots? How can you be you and still remain part of the tribe? A tribe which requires the individual to sacrifice to the collective. Maybe you want to be slimmer? Taller? Younger? You want to redraw your own borders and make up your own classification because the hundreds which already exist do not quite fit who you are, who you want to be. But maybe after much soul searching through all the religions and philosophies, this is just the way things are meant to be? Everything will be dandy when I get to Heaven or Valhalla, when I return to a higher caste or a friendlier species, one which if you were forced to trade places with anyone on the planet, it would be okay. Maybe that's it. You are the star in your very own production of Waiting for Godot. But remember how that ends. Or maybe you just need to accept what you can't control. Like Buddha taught. Like it says in the *Desiderata*.

Maybe you'll see the void itself evaporate away like a black hole. Maybe you sense your own radiation drifting away from your body until you are no more than a sprinkle of energy in what is effectively nothingness? Repeat to yourself: "I am content." Hum a tune if it makes it easier.

I am sitting by myself. In my two bedroom flat in Hall Green. I am just renting for the moment. It is only a mile up the road from the house I grew up in. A short walk from the airing cupboard in my parent's bedroom. Nearly half a century separates who I was then from who I am now. The past really is a foreign country. This story has been about relationships. Entanglements. There is nothing new under the sun. It has been three months since I moved out. It took me less than an hour. I have the kids over whenever they want to visit. Angela is more flexible since she and Ken started doing hot yoga together at a local gym. She said Ken would like to meet me. Just so I'm comfortable with him being around the children. I'm not quite ready for that. I couldn't help replying that if I was not okay with him being around Meme then he would know about it. She told me to grow up. Of course, she was right.

I secretly hoped he was like Dr Shipman who killed 250 of his patients just so I could say: 'See, I wasn't that bad after all. I only killed one man, and he wasn't even my patient. He was just an innocent Big Issue seller minding his own business till the state - ME - told him he had no right to stand where he was standing.' I suspect, however, that Ken is more like Dr Ross out of ER (I'll save you the search: George Clooney) than Harold out of Hyde.

I took a few weeks off work. I am still out on loan at the airport. I have put in a transfer request. Sixteen pay checks left till I can retire. Let's see which one arrives first.

There is no mention of Billy Jones in the press these past months. I occasionally check. No interviews with his family. Why would there be? I am mindful about using him as a psychological crutch. I have no right to do that. It would be easy when I am having a biochemical slump to think about him and assign some causality between what I did on that day and why I might be feeling a little low. I can choose a different story instead. There are a handful available. As there is for everyone. We must always be aware of the stories we tell ourselves.

****

Printed in Great Britain
by Amazon

22344776R00192